HAYNER PLD/ALTON SQUARE
OVERDUES .10 PER DAY. MAXIMUM
FINE COST OF ITEM. LOST OR
DAMAGED ITEM ADDITIONAL $5.00
SERVICE CHARGE

Praise for *The Grace Kelly Dress*

"A charming, heartfelt novel.... Fast paced and entertaining from beginning to end."

—**Kristin Hannah, #1 *New York Times* bestselling author of *The Nightingale***

"Exactly the type of book I love: charming, smart, and brimming with heart."

—**Emily Giffin, #1 *New York Times* bestselling author of *All We Ever Wanted***

"A poignant and delicious novel about how a dress can define a family, and how family can lovingly reinvent itself."

—**Laura Dave, #1 *New York Times* bestselling author of *The Last Thing He Told Me***

"Brenda Janowitz's gift is understanding and revealing the nuances of complicated families.... A seamless intergenerational modern-day fairy tale."

—**Mary Kay Andrews, *New York Times* bestselling author of *The Newcomer***

"Just like the multi-generational wedding dress of the title: elegant, layered, and utterly original."

—**Fiona Davis, *New York Times* bestselling author of *The Lions of Fifth Avenue***

"This beautiful and poignant novel makes us ponder what invisible threads unite us and what textures will always be our own. A truly wonderful read!"

—**Alyson Richman, internationally bestselling author of *The Lost Wife***

"Brenda Janowitz seams together a delicate and beautiful story of family, love, fate, and, yes, fashion. I loved it!"

—**Jamie Brenner, bestselling author of *Blush***

Also by Brenda Janowitz

The Grace Kelly Dress
The Dinner Party
Recipe for a Happy Life
The Lonely Hearts Club
Jack with a Twist
Scot on the Rocks

The LIZ TAYLOR RING

A NOVEL

BRENDA JANOWITZ

GRAYDON
HOUSE

GRAYDON
HOUSE®

Recycling programs
for this product may
not exist in your area.

ISBN-13: 978-1-525-89987-4

The Liz Taylor Ring

This edition published by arrangement with Harlequin Books S.A.

Graydon House
22 Adelaide St. West, 41st Floor
Toronto, Ontario M5H 4E3, Canada
www.GraydonHouseBooks.com
www.BookClubbish.com

Printed in U.S.A.

To Doug, Ben, and Davey, my dazzling diamonds

The
LIZ
TAYLOR
RING

"It's not the having, it's the getting."

-Elizabeth Taylor

PART ONE:
COLOR

1

The ring

The ring was back in play.

No one had given the ring a thought for over ten years. To each of the Schneider siblings, it was gone, baby, gone. Like a dream you could barely remember upon waking.

Addy was sure it had been stolen, back in 2008. She was positive. She would swear on her children's lives, even, if she did that sort of thing. (Which she did not.) But she was sure.

Nathan was convinced that Lizzie, her Alzheimer's rapidly progressing, placed it in Ritchie's casket when he died in 2015. And he was always right about everything. Just ask his husband.

And Courtney? She knew for a fact the ring had been gambled away in the fall of 2006. Not like she had a gambling problem. Why, what did you hear?

The ring: a D-color, eleven-carat Asscher-cut diamond. Perfectly colorless, internally flawless. Gifted by Ritchie to Lizzie in 1992, after a nine-month separation Courtney does not remember at all, but that Addy and Nathan remember as if it were yesterday. Lizzie and Ritchie's friends thought it was so romantic, that he'd given her a huge engagement ring even though they were technically only separated, still married, for a short spell. But it was symbolic, this giving of the ring. And Lizzie thought it was funny that Ritchie had gifted her with such an enormous diamond, much like their Hollywood namesakes Elizabeth Taylor and Richard Burton, who also were married, then not married, then married again. Lizzie gave the ring a name: the Liz Taylor Ring.

Addy, the pragmatist, thought her father bought her mother the ring for security, as a sort of insurance policy. If things ever got bad financially, they could always sell it.

Nathan, the romantic, thought his father bought his mother the ring out of love, as a symbol that they would never separate again. After all, a diamond was forever.

Courtney, the lost soul, thought her father—who she still mourned with the same ferocity as the day he died, even though he'd been gone for seven years—won it at a poker game. He was unbeatable when he was on a streak, once upon a time.

None of these stories are true. All of these stories are true. More than one thing can be true at once.

2

Lizzie, 1969

Sixteen-year-old Lizzie Morgan was obsessed with Elizabeth Taylor. There was just something about her. It was the eyes, Lizzie thought. Like so many others before her, she'd been drawn in by those gorgeous eyes that glowed violet, rimmed with two sets of lashes, a genetic mutation that only made her more stunning, more extraordinary. Lizzie loved her for her beauty and talent, she loved her for the behind-the-scenes drama. Lizzie read everything she could about Elizabeth Taylor in the gossip magazines she collected.

Lizzie's mother, Katharine, hated Elizabeth Taylor. Hated what she represented. Called her a harlot, having broken up the marriages of Eddie Fisher and Richard Burton alike. Found her over-the-top nomadic lifestyle to be tacky and gauche, especially once Richard Burton gifted Elizabeth Taylor the Krupp Diamond, a 33.19 carat Asscher-cut stone, D-color, perfectly colorless, internally flawless.

"How vulgar," Katharine said, wrinkling her nose in disgust. But Lizzie had other opinions.

Lizzie thought that Elizabeth Taylor was adventurous and

glamorous. All the travel, to places she'd never go—Puerto Vallarta, Gstaad, the Seychelles—all the excess, the things she'd never have—diamonds the size of boulders, hundred-foot yachts, elegant, utterly marvelous parties. And breasts. Enormous breasts. Where Lizzie's body was flat and straight, Elizabeth Taylor had curves, a figure that Lizzie only prayed she'd attain one day. Simply put, Elizabeth Taylor smoldered.

Lizzie did not smolder. With her pale blond hair, shoulder-length and limp as wet spaghetti, and blue eyes that didn't glow violet, plain and bordered by barely-there lashes, she could not compete. It was her sister, Maggie, who smoldered. But that didn't stop Lizzie from envisioning herself as Elizabeth Taylor. She even tried to get people to start calling her *Elizabeth*, or at the very least *Liz*, instead of the childish *Lizzie*. Of course, Elizabeth Taylor, herself, hated how the press called her and Richard Burton *Liz and Dick*. She hated being called *Liz*. But anything was better than *Lizzie*, wasn't it?

Lizzie went to sleep at night, dreaming about finding a great love, one like Elizabeth Taylor and Richard Burton had. When she met Ritchie Schneider, she immediately knew that he was the one. Even though she was only sixteen. Even though he was secretly dating her sister.

From the moment Lizzie met Ritchie, she fell completely and madly in love. Now, her dreams were filled only with him: he would realize he was with the wrong sister, and they'd have a whirlwind romance. They would be like Liz and Dick, and with Ritchie, she would live a life of love and excess and adventure, just like their Hollywood counterparts.

Lizzie imagined their love story as a sweet fairy tale, but she had misunderstood. (Blinded by the gorgeous Krupp Diamond, no doubt.) She was too young to know what *tumultuous* really meant, too naive to interpret what the gossip columns were intimating about the Elizabeth Taylor–Richard Burton relationship, behind the scenes. The jealousy, the fighting, the immense sacrifices they made to be together.

But she would learn.

3

Addy

Addy looked at herself in the mirror. Surely every woman looked like a wet dog after getting their hair washed at the hairdresser, didn't they?

She examined the lines of her face, the rings under her eyes. She looked tired. She looked old. She didn't look like herself anymore.

"Just to lighten you up a bit," Roberto said, running his hands through her hair. He'd been styling her hair since she was nineteen—just over twenty years—and his pleas to color it had gotten more insistent as of late.

But she would not be one of those women who colored her hair. She simply would not. After all, she had daughters to raise, twin girls who were sixteen years old. She had to set a good example.

"You know how I feel about coloring my hair."

"Remind me again."

"It's antifeminist."

"Coloring your hair does not have to be a political statement," he said, self-consciously examining his own hairline, receding ever so slightly, in the mirror. "Forty is the new thirty, you know."

"I'm forty-one." Addy pressed her fingers to the lines that led from the edge of her lip, up to the side of her nose. Marionette lines, they called them. As if women were just wooden dolls, controlled by a master. Most women her age had already started Botox and fillers. They threw Botox parties at each other's houses, getting shot up by people who weren't even doctors. Still, they looked good. Better than she did.

"Oh, well, forty-one's the new sixty." They both laughed.

"Just a trim."

"I could easily make you look the way you looked when we first met. It would only take an hour."

When Roberto referenced *when we first met,* he meant the summer she turned nineteen. When she let her blond hair lighten in the sun, when it flowed in wavy bursts down her back. She could let her hair dry naturally and it would still look like it had been professionally done. She walked into the salon carefree, unencumbered by kids' schedules, what to make for dinner that night, and college funds. She walked into the salon with a smile on her face, open to the possibilities of life in a way she could no longer fathom now. That's how he saw her. That's how he remembered that summer.

That's not what Addy remembered. It was the summer after freshman year of college, and she'd come home to work with her dad, to learn how to run a retail store. Her father was still learning the retail game himself. Recently sworn off gambling and desperate for a job (a real job, not one of those get-rich-quick schemes he'd been chasing since the day he met her mother), he'd gotten the place for a steal from a friend of the family. It was a small store in the center of their Long Island town, filled with fast fashion. The sort of clothes that were ridiculously trendy and would go out of style in a season. (Which was good, because the quality only lasted a season, too.)

He called the store "Lizzie and Ritchie's" in a romantic gesture, and new to the retail game, he did all the books by hand. Addy was dying to put her digital marketing class to use, and when she told her father that one of her classmates had started a website and then quit school because the company took off, he wanted in. She got him onto QuickBooks, created a website, modeled all the clothing herself, and turned Lizzie and Ritchie's into a dot-com. Ritchie barely understood what his daughter was doing, but he humored her because he loved her so much. He humored her because he was a doting father who hated to say no to his daughter. (Also, she was the smart one.)

Within a month, he understood. They could barely keep up with the online demand, and Addy brokered a deal with a classmate from Texas, whose family owned a manufacturing plant, to start making the clothing themselves. Within six months, Addy was back at school, and Ritchie had expanded his operation to a team of four. Within a year, the store was a half a million dollar a year business. Within three years, he expanded his team to ten. Within five years, his company—one brick-and-mortar shop and an online store—was a multimillion dollar enterprise.

And it was all because of Addy.

"We don't even have to go to your old color," Roberto said, pulling up a picture of a model on his phone. "We could make you a buttery dirty blond."

"Showing my girls that I'm ashamed to get older is not the example I want to set," Addy said, even though the sound of butter and dirt was intriguing.

"Your girls are all over Instagram giving Gigi and Bella a run for their money."

"The modeling thing is just for fun," Addy explained, as she'd explained to countless other people countless other times. "Gary really started having them do it to build their confidence." (And because Addy was now too old to model the clothes herself, but better to leave that part unsaid.)

"I'd say they're confident enough. Have you seen this?" He turned his phone toward Addy, and she immediately recognized it as the Lizzie and Ritchie's Instagram page. A picture of her girls filled the screen: the clothes were beside the point (but they *were* wearing clothes, weren't they?) as they stood, legs wide apart, mouths open, thumbs tugging on their bottom lips. The image was bold. It was strong. It was undeniably sexual. Addy was horrified.

"Of course I've seen that." She had not. "At least they're not coloring their hair."

"Are they eating?" Roberto closed the photo and began scrolling through their individual feeds.

"Of course they eat." When she was sixteen, Addy still had baby fat. Her girls had cheekbones like razor blades, bellies flat and taut. When she'd ask, Emma would laugh and explain how easy it was to manipulate the way you looked with makeup, camera angles, and filters. But Addy wasn't so sure. "Lemme see that."

As Roberto handed over his phone, Addy's own phone rang out, the sound of an old-fashioned telephone filling the air.

"Do you need to get that?" he asked, holding up her purse with the ringing phone inside.

"No," she said, transfixed by the store's Instagram account. And then, instantly remembering herself: "I mean yes." Addy swapped phones with Roberto. "It could be the girls or their school." Addy looked at the screen. It was a number she didn't recognize. The exchange looked international, a jumble of extra numbers. "I can let this go to voice mail."

It would be hours before she remembered to check her messages. Long after her girls came home from school. After her husband came home from work. After she cooked dinner and served it. After she fell into bed at ten, too tired to stay up to watch TV with Gary. It wasn't until the next morning, after breakfast, that she remembered to check her voice mail.

And after that, nothing would be the same.

4

Nathan

Nathan picked at a stray cuticle on his thumb. He needed to moisturize more. Get manicures more. Take better care of himself.

He put the lawyer's business card back into his desk, hidden underneath some papers, and tried to get back to work.

Nathan bit at his thumb again, but the cuticle was too hard to peel off. He picked and picked until it came loose. He pulled at it—it had no give—and when it finally tore from his skin, it bled.

He was sucking his thumb when his brother-in-law walked into his office.

"Bad day? Should I get you your blankie?"

"I just cut myself," Nathan said, showing his brother-in-law his thumb. He rummaged through his desk drawer for a Band-Aid.

Gary opened the top drawer of the filing cabinet and produced a first aid kit. He chucked it across the room to Nathan.

"Thanks. This is why you're a good business partner."

"That's all it takes?"

"Depends on the day," Nathan said, laughter in his voice, as he dabbed bacitracin on his thumb and then covered it with a Band-Aid.

Nathan and Gary *were* a good match as far as business partners went. Gary was the friendly salesman-type, good-looking, and good with the customers and vendors, a natural at negotiating with a smile. It was a thing they said in the family: *Everyone loves Gary.* And it was true. Nathan was more cerebral, and enjoyed handling the nitty-gritty, the day-to-day of running a business. The financials, the endless amounts of paperwork that a retail business generated, and all the behind-the-scenes tasks that enabled him to sit in his office alone, without being bothered. Gary loved going out to lunches and dinners with vendors and buyers, and Nathan loved staying late in his office, long after the store had closed for the night, making sure every last *t* was crossed, every *i* dotted. Loved making a good to-do list, and then the feeling of accomplishment that rushed over him each time he could cross an item off. Nathan found that a beautifully executed Excel spreadsheet brought him a calm that rivaled even the best Caribbean beach retreat.

"The lawyer can meet with us next week," Gary said.

"What lawyer?" Nathan asked quickly. Without thinking, his hand went down to his desk drawer, to where he'd hidden the divorce lawyer's business card.

"About that trademark infringement claim," Gary said. "We just have to sign a few papers. And stop manufacturing that belt."

"Right, that. Even though Gucci doesn't own gold bumblebees. You can't trademark an insect."

"Would you like to go to court to find out?"

"No, I would not." Nathan held his hand over his desk drawer. He wasn't ready for anyone to know that he had a divorce lawyer's card in his possession. And he certainly wasn't ready to call.

Divorce seemed so final, didn't it? And surely after waiting years for gay marriage to be legal, he couldn't possibly do it. Getting divorced just seemed like a defeat. Like giving up.

Nathan never thought he'd get married. From the moment he'd realized that he was gay, he just didn't think marriage would ever be an option for him. But he so desperately wanted what his parents had, what his mother told him about in whispers late at night: a great love story, epic in scope. The kind they wrote movies about. Grand, sweeping musicals. Messy, sure, but a story in which the love was always there. He would listen with awe as his mother told him, over and over again, the story of how she met his father and fell madly, desperately in love. Nathan could never hear it enough times. He would beg Lizzie to tell it again, on late nights when he couldn't sleep, on school days when he was home sick, during bad times when he needed cheering up.

When he was younger, Nathan kept a hatbox filled with love letters that his father had written to his mother, reading them endlessly until the paper was soft as silk. He read them on days he was happy; he read them on days he was sad. On important days, he'd fold one up and carry it in his pocket, like a good luck charm. Fortified with concrete proof of his parents' love, where he came from, he was invincible. Theirs seemed like a love story for the ages, and Nathan wanted that. It was more than just love; it was *fate*. He might not have been legally allowed to marry, but he would have that one great love.

And now he did. Was he really thinking about divorce?

Gary sat down on the old leather couch. Since Nathan had taken the less desirable office, the one at the back of the building with no light, Gary told Nathan it was only fair that he get Ritchie's old couch. (Nathan had secretly wanted the back office, anyway.) Now that Ritchie was gone, the things that had once belonged to him took on a deeper meaning. How many times would Nathan have to listen to Gary tell the story of Ritchie sitting on that very couch when he asked for permission to marry Addy? Nathan could recite the punch line in his sleep: Ritchie looked Gary dead in the eye and said, "Whaddya asking my permission for? Seems to me, the only permission you need is hers." (Though Nathan's story was better: he sat his father down on the couch to tell him he was gay, and his father said, "I know. I was just waiting for you to know.")

Gary lay back on the couch and pulled his phone out of his pocket to look at social media. "Addy's swinging by with coffees in a little bit to touch base about the girls and their modeling schedules."

"What's that supposed to mean?"

"Something about yesterday's Instagram post and their thumbs being in their mouths? Must be a family thing, inherited on the Schneider side."

"Funny," Nathan said. He looked down at his thumb, now covered by the Band-Aid. The bandage was bright red. Was his finger still bleeding? "We've got a busy morning. Let's see if she can do it another day."

Gary responded with a look.

"Can you ever say no to my sister?"

"Where the business is concerned, no," Gary said. "After all, Addy did invent the internet."

Nathan laughed. It was their little in-joke about Addy, since she always harped on about how she was responsible for making the family business profitable one summer back when she was nineteen years old. Nathan always thought she had simply been in the right place at the right time—working for their father's small business at the apex of the internet boom—but Addy acted like she was owed something. Like Nathan and Gary had taken the business—her business—away from her.

"Is she at least bringing the good coffee from that place we like?"

"She always brings the good coffee from the place we like. Fresh blueberry muffins, too."

But when Addy got there, she seemed to have forgotten about her girls and their modeling. All she wanted to talk about was the voice mail she'd heard that morning. The call from the Caymans that would divide their lives into before and after.

5

Courtney

"Hit," the old man said.

Stick, Courtney thought in her head. You should always assume the dealer has a ten concealed in his blackjack hand, but she wasn't being paid to give Sy gambling advice.

Sy Pierce: octogenarian, master of the universe, billionaire, founder and CEO of Pierce Industries, a conglomerate of companies with concerns ranging from clean energy to airplane parts to spandex. And Courtney's date for the evening.

Courtney smiled at Sy, remembering to let the smile meet her eyes—*Convince him that you like him*, Lindsay had cautioned her—and as he swiveled to face her, his knee brushed across her bare leg. She jumped back, her whole body an exposed nerve. Courtney took a sip of her drink—whiskey neat—to settle herself.

"Blackjack," the dealer called, and Sy groaned as his chips disappeared.

Courtney adjusted her dress. She knew she should never have worn a dress from her family's store. The quality was crap, and it probably wouldn't last the night. But when she was at Addy's for Christmas the year before last, she just couldn't resist the lure of free clothing. The stuff from the store was the perfect metaphor for her relationship with her family: looks pretty on the outside, but in reality, it's about three seconds from breaking apart.

"Taking a break to visit the men's room," Sy told the dealer. "Courtney is going to sit in for me for a round." The dealer looked back to the game runner for confirmation. He nodded and let Courtney sit in Sy's spot. Courtney was pretty sure that this was against protocol—after all, only Sy had been vetted for this underground casino—but just like her daddy taught her (real dad, not a sugar daddy like Sy), it always paid big dividends to be nice to everyone, treat each person equally. And she'd been smiling at everyone here, making them feel special, feel seen, the whole damn night.

The hotel suite was gorgeous—it was hard to believe that an illegal casino had been set up in it. She wished she could take a nice, long soak in the tub with those expensive bath soaps she'd seen in the bathroom. She wished she could sleep on the one thousand thread count sheets, instead of her friend's lumpy sofa. (Not that she was complaining. Chrissy's lumpy sofa was better than having nowhere to stay at all.) She wished she could forget all about what brought her here, why she was so desperate for money, but she could not. She got her head into the game.

Courtney downed the rest of her whiskey in one gulp. She ran her hands over the chips parked in front of her. Ten thousand dollars in hundred dollar chips. And a couple of five hundred dollar chips thrown in for luck.

"Ready, miss?"

"Born ready."

Courtney melted into the plush chair. She liked fancy hotels like this. It reminded her of her childhood, when her parents had money, when they went to expensive places like this—just the three of them—all the time. Only twenty-nine years old with both of her parents long gone, memories were all she had left. The fun times. The good times. The best days of her life. Decadent dinners in Atlantic City of escargot and caviar, comped by the pit bosses, a hotel suite in Vegas so big it had its own private pool, and languorous two-week trips down to Puerto Rico, where she would sneak into the casino at night, pretending to be her mother's sister, fooling everyone. Would her life ever be like that again? Safe, easy, secure.

The dealer set two cards down in front of her: six of hearts and three of clubs. That one was easy. She tapped her forefinger on the table, the signal to the dealer. *Hit me.* Their eyes met as he dealt the next card. His eyes were ice blue, his brown hair so dark it looked black. If she didn't need the money so badly, he'd be the type she'd be going out with. Not one of these sugar daddy "dates." But there was no easier money, Lindsay had said, as she set up a profile for her on sweetdaddy.com. They paid you cash just to go out with them, to be seen at dinner or a club or, as it turned out, an illegal casino. Fast money, Lindsay had promised her. And, no, Lindsay assured her, you did not have to sleep with them.

Courtney knew Lindsay from the audition circuit. Both five-seven with dirty blond hair, blue eyes, and pale complexions, they often found themselves going out for the same roles. Neither of them booked anything, but at an audition for the Will Smith movie last week, Courtney noticed Lindsay carrying the new Chloé cross-body bag. And wearing Valentino strappy sandals. The next day, Lindsay was showing Courtney how to set up a profile on a sugar daddy website. That was four days ago.

The dealer gave her a ten. Then, the dealer flipped his own cards over and showed twelve. He'd have to hit until he got to seventeen, and she figured he'd probably bust before hitting twenty-one. He took his first card. Ten.

"Dealer busts," he said. He paid Courtney the chips she was owed, and she smiled at him. And then, the smile faded the tiniest bit: Would Sy let her keep the money?

The cards were dealt once again, and the game started over.

Courtney had a pair of aces. She tried to play it cool, but she couldn't hide the edges of her mouth from betraying her.

"Split, please," Courtney said.

"Are you sure you want to do that?" Sy asked, sidling back to the table.

Courtney got up to give him back his seat. "Split is the way to go," she said. "You need to play the odds. You play with your head, not your heart."

"Is that what you do?" he asked her. "Play with your head, not your heart?"

"Always."

"The lady says split," Sy said to the dealer.

The dealer looked Courtney in the eye as he dealt out the hand. The old man ended up with two beautiful blackjacks, side by side.

"Blackjack, my friend," the dealer said to Sy.

Two thousand dollar bets. Two fifteen-hundred dollar wins.

"Well, aren't you just my good luck charm?" Sy asked Courtney, as he passed her a thousand dollar chip.

"Thank you," she whispered. "Would you excuse me?"

"Come back quick."

Courtney rushed over to the game runner, careful not to look too desperate. "May I please cash this out?"

"Sy's feeling pretty generous tonight," he said as he unlocked the cash box.

"He says I'm his good luck charm."

"I bet you are." She didn't like the way he looked at her. *I'm just an actress*, she wanted to tell him. *A very unemployed one.* He handed over a stack of bills. One large. A dime. Courtney tucked the cash into her bra. She couldn't trust leaving it in her clutch. On their text chain, he'd said that he'd pay her a grand to go out with him for the night. They'd had dinner and then ended up here. Was this her payment for the date? This seemed like a separate transaction. She'd earned that money. Wasn't she entitled to it? She texted Lindsay.

COURTNEY: at underground casino w sy. won him 3k at black-jack-he gave me 1k. is that payment 4 date?

LINDSAY: new phone, who dis?

COURTNEY: haha. srsly, tho. help!

LINDSAY: depends on guy, but he'll prob pay u end of nite 2.

COURTNEY: k. ty.

She walked back to the table. She really wanted to know if he'd be paying her again at the end of the night or if this was it. But it's not like she could ask. This was her first date from sweetdaddy.com, and she was still learning the ropes. And anyway, it wasn't like she had anywhere else to go.

"I have an early morning," Sy said. "Shall I have Edgar pull the car around?"

"Sure," Courtney said, glancing back at the blackjack table, wondering how much more she could have won if Sy had let her play. She *would* have won more, she thought, ignoring one very simple fact of life: the house always wins. After all, isn't that how she got there?

"I've had a lovely evening," Sy said as they entered the elevator. "May I take you on another date sometime soon?"

"Sure," Courtney said again, unsure of the protocol. It wasn't a regular date, not really. "I'd like that."

The car was waiting as they exited the lobby. Sy held the door open for her as Courtney slid across the soft leather seats of his Bentley.

"For you," Sy said, passing a thin envelope to Courtney.

She discreetly put it into her clutch. Counting it, she thought, would be tacky. But Lindsay had been right: Sy paid her for the date, even though he'd given her the thousand dollar chip at the game. She'd made two grand in just under four hours.

Sy gave her a chaste kiss on the check as they pulled up to Chrissy's apartment building, and Courtney rushed upstairs. Chrissy's dog Scout was sleeping in her spot on the couch, so Courtney kicked off her shoes and sat down at the kitchen table. She swiped open her phone and began to scroll.

She opened Instagram and posted a selfie: *#partyallthetime #lovemylife #positivevibes*. Then, she continued scrolling, stopping on the Lizzie and Ritchie's account. She double tapped a photograph of Olivia and Emma. Since they lived on opposite coasts, this was as close as she could get to quality time. (Especially since her bitch sister hadn't even invited her to Christmas this past year.) Her nieces looked back at her, looking more like sugar babies than she ever would. Fingers dangling from the lower lip. Courtney would have to incorporate that move in her next audition. (Or, more realistically, on her next date with Sy.)

She fell asleep on the couch with Scout an hour later, forgetting to plug in her phone. She would miss the text from her brother the following morning. Only after being woken up by Scout, plugging in her phone, and trying in vain to do a little yoga in the tiny living room, would she realize that he'd texted. And the second she got it, everything would change.

6

Addy

"But Dad was never in the Cayman Islands," Addy said, setting down the coffees and box of muffins. "That's what's so weird."

"That's the part you think is weird?" Gary asked. He sat up on the couch in Nathan's office.

"If there's a casino, Dad would've been there," Nathan said, leaning back in his chair and throwing his feet onto his desk. Addy sat down next to Gary, nodding her head in agreement as they continued to discuss the call.

The phone call: from a banker in the Cayman Islands. After Hurricane Amelia, the vaults had been flooded. All safe-deposit boxes needed to be claimed or moved to another bank. They discovered that the safe-deposit box belonging to a Mr. Richard Schneider needed action. The owner was deceased. (Addy: "I'm aware.") Since the box was registered to only Mr. Schneider himself, it was a bit of a challenge to track down next of kin. First, through a Google search, they determined that he was married to an Elizabeth Schneider, but they soon discovered that she, too, was deceased. (Addy: "Again, I'm aware.") The next hit on Google was his retail store, www.lizzieandritchies.com, and a search of the ICANN WHOIS database gave them Addy's cell phone number as the owner of the website, miraculously unchanged since the summer of 2000.

"He said that we need to go to the Caymans to collect the contents of the box," Addy said.

"Can't they just mail it?" Gary asked. "We can give them our FedEx account information."

"Once they discovered that Dad was gone, the government sealed its contents. We have to go in person," Addy said.

"Did he say what was in the box?" Nathan asked.

"It was sealed, by law. They don't know what's inside, or what did or did not survive the flood."

"What could possibly be in some forgotten safe-deposit box down in the Caymans?" Nathan asked. "I'd bet you a hundred bucks that it's just a bunch of junk."

"I don't gamble," Addy said.

Nathan rolled his eyes in response.

"Don't you find it odd that our mother's name wasn't on the account?" Addy asked. She looked from her brother to her husband. Neither man responded. "I don't like secrets."

"All marriages have secrets," Nathan said. "Don't they?"

"That's not true. Ours doesn't," Gary said, squeezing Addy's hand.

"What would he be hiding so far away?" Addy wondered aloud. "Hiding money from creditors? A secret will? Maybe he had a secret life?"

"Our father did not have a secret life," Nathan said.

"Maybe he was having an affair or something."

"He was not having an affair," Nathan said, forcefully. "He would never do that to Mom."

"Right," Addy said.

"Most likely is that Mom and Dad went to the Caymans for a vacation," Nathan said. "Dad won some money in the casino,

Mom bought some jewelry, and they put it in the safe-deposit box and then forgot about it."

"But wouldn't you like to know for sure?" Addy asked.

"So, we're going?"

"Let's go online and see how much tickets cost," Addy said. She had no idea why she was considering this. She had survived this long without knowing what was in some random safe-deposit box in the Caymans. She should tell the banker that they would not be claiming the contents and that he should just get rid of it. But Addy couldn't do that. She had to know what was inside.

"What about Courtney?" Nathan asked.

"Courtney."

"Courtney."

They each said her name differently. In Addy's mouth, it was a curse word, a thing that was forbidden to discuss. Anger, disappointment, resentment. On Nathan's tongue, it was altogether different. It was a sad song, a remembrance. Sorrow, resignation, regret.

But it wasn't Addy's fault. She barely knew her baby sister. And she and Nathan were practically twins, born only eleven months apart. They'd had years to bond before Courtney came along. She'd never stood a chance.

After their parents' nine-month separation in 1992, all Addy wanted was for her family to be whole again, for things to go back to the way they'd been before. Addy had never asked for a sister. She had everything she needed or wanted in her brother Nathan. A best friend, a confidant, a partner in crime. How was she to know that the joy of her parents reconciling after their separation would be short-lived? That her family coming back together would bring a new family member into the fold?

Addy was already twelve years old when Courtney was born. She resented her from the moment she came home from the hospital. The baby took all of Lizzie and Ritchie's time and attention. Time and attention that should have been spent on Addy and Nathan, especially considering all they'd been through. A storm weathered entirely on their own. Courtney was an endless void of need—a colicky baby who couldn't be soothed. And then, an annoying toddler who wanted too much of her attention. (Read: *any* of her attention.) And now she was, of course, an actress in LA. A perfect profession for a needy, insecure girl. Addy didn't have the time for it.

Addy struggled to recall the last time she'd seen Courtney. She hadn't come back to New York for Christmas last year, had she? She definitely had not. And she certainly never came for Easter, but Addy didn't make as big of a thing out of Easter as she did Christmas. Easter was just church and then a family brunch. But Christmas? Christmas was special. Addy held a gigantic Christmas Eve party at the house, the way her mother used to, with a guest list as long as Santa's Naughty or Nice List. (Which is to say, very long.) And then Christmas was an all-day affair. Nathan and Diego always slept over on Christmas Eve, just to wake up to the spectacle of the massive tree, presents overflowing underneath, and the breakfast Gary was famous for cooking: pancakes cooked to order (Nathan loved chocolate chip, but Diego preferred blueberry, like his nieces), bacon made crispy on the griddle, and eggs three different ways (scrambled, fried, and hard-boiled). Friends would come over, and the house just oozed warmth.

It was the year before last that Courtney had come for Christmas. She had insisted on making mimosas and then got drunk before noon and vomited behind the tree. Addy winced as she recalled why she hadn't pushed for Courtney to come out last Christmas.

"Let's not tell Courtney for now," Addy said. "If we find anything interesting or important, we can call her then."

Nathan looked up from his iPhone and turned to Addy. "I just texted her."

7

Nathan

"I love the Caymans! I know just what to pack!" And with that, Diego spun around and rushed into their enormous walk-in closet. Nathan followed him in tentatively.

Nathan had said it wrong. He'd said it all wrong. He'd meant to be firm, to explain to Diego that he'd be going to the Caymans without him, but it hadn't come out that way. Diego assumed it was an invitation. Diego assumed *everything* was an invitation.

"Addy was thinking that maybe it would be just a sibling thing?" Nathan said, fully aware that he was doing that annoying thing where he ended the sentence like a question by raising his voice at the end. He didn't know why he'd done that. Actually he did: he hated confrontation. He'd spent his life avoiding confrontation. That's what he had Addy for. She was not afraid of confrontation. She handled most of his confrontations for him—from April Moore in the second grade, who teased him mercilessly at recess every day (calling him *fag*), to the brothers of Theta Alpha Nu at Georgetown (same thing).

"Oh,that'ssilly,"Diegosaid,alreadypullingswimsuitsoutofadrawer.

Nathan took a deep breath. "I meant to say, it's just Addy, Courtney, and me going."

"Oh, did Addy remember that you guys have a baby sister?"

Nathan laughed nervously and picked at the stray cuticle on his thumb, which seemed to have grown back with a vengeance.

It was hard to explain Addy and Courtney to his husband. Diego was an only child. He couldn't possibly understand. What it felt like to have your life upended when you were eleven years old. What it felt like to have your entire family dynamic change. First with the separation, and then with the reconciliation, accompanied by a new sibling.

Addy always resented Courtney simply for being born, and Nathan was always the one in the middle, trying to make the peace. Trying to make Addy hate Courtney just the tiniest bit less. Which was hard, because he had his own feelings to contend with. But there was no time for his feelings, because Addy's feelings washed over everything else, like a tsunami.

Addy. His big sister. His best friend. From the minute Courtney was born, Addy made it clear that she was public enemy number one. He had to choose: it was her or the baby. Who was he to say otherwise?

Nathan didn't hate Courtney quite as much as his sister did. He felt badly for how he and Addy had treated Courtney her whole life. Like an afterthought. Like she didn't matter. Like a mistake. But by the time he figured that out, Courtney had already left for college.

Diego looked up from the bathing suits. "I can't believe Courtney ranks higher than me. I thought Addy hated her?"

"I know," Nathan said. And then almost immediately: "Addy doesn't hate Courtney. Courtney's our little sister."

Diego responded with a look.

Nathan nervously continued talking: "It's not even a vacation. It's a trip. We're going in and out, Friday night to Sunday morning. Just to claim the contents of the box and then go. You deserve a real trip. An actual vacation. How about I scout out hotels for us to go to next New Year's?"

"What do you think is in the safe-deposit box?"

Nathan regarded him. He didn't answer. He didn't know what to say. Why had he said the thing about a New Year's trip? Would they even still be married, come New Year's?

When Nathan met Diego, he knew that he was the one. Immediately, instantaneously. Without question. After meeting cute one night, Nathan and Diego became inseparable, their lives and fates intertwining within weeks, and once gay marriage became legal, it was a foregone conclusion that they would tie the knot.

But his husband was no longer the man he married. Some days, he looked at him and couldn't recall exactly why they'd been together since right after college, married over ten years.

"He knew you before you had money," his brother-in-law would always tell him. Wasn't that something celebrities and uber-rich people always said about their spouses? It was true. Diego had been with him since the days he was waiting tables in Manhattan, before he was anybody, before he was working in his father's business, before he had money. But the more money Nathan made, the more Diego wanted. There was barely a day that went by when packages weren't delivered to their building. When there wasn't a massive charge on their credit card.

Diego didn't choose him for his money. (Diego's family was the one with money, lots of it, not Nathan's.) But now that Nathan had it, Diego certainly had no problem in spending it. One day it was high-end kitchen appliances. The next day it was shoes with those pretty red soles. And lately, exercise equipment. First, a simple row machine. Next, one of those indoor bicycles that required a monthly membership.

And now, the fortieth birthday bash he was planning. Nathan wanted a party, of course he did, but it was getting out of control. What Diego was planning would be a party that was bigger than their wedding. (A charming backyard affair at Addy's house; close friends and family only.) Diego had settled on a *Guys and Dolls* theme, because Nathan and his sister, Adelaide, were named after the main characters of the show. (This was back when their mother, Lizzie, thought that Ritchie's gambling was still cute, and not a full-blown addiction.) Guests would be asked to dress in costume, their 1920s best, and a full casino would be set up so they could gamble the night away, just like Nathan Detroit and Sky Masterson.

Nathan had tried to explain that the theme wasn't in good taste (read the room, Diego), that the theme wasn't something he wanted (read the room, Diego), but deposits had been put down. Plans had been made. Anyway, Diego wasn't really listening.

Did he listen to anything Nathan said anymore? Nathan tried to recall when they'd last had a real discussion. Their nights were mostly spent side by side, transfixed by their phones, not each other.

Diego was having an affair. Nathan was sure of it. Wasn't that the first sign of an affair? Your partner stops listening. Your partner starts dressing better, getting into great shape. Why the sudden update to his wardrobe, when jeans and a T-shirt used to be all he needed? Why this sudden zest for working out, when in years past, long walks and a few simple free weights were all it took? Everyone knew that when your spouse got a renewed interest in looking good, the marriage was over. And the party was just a total overcompensation. A way of announcing to the world that he was definitely, certainly, and in no way having an affair. Like those vow renewal ceremonies—anytime Nathan and Diego got an invitation to one of those, they'd take bets on how long the couple would last before getting a divorce. Usually the over/under was around eighteen months.

Also, the receipt. Two days ago, Nathan had worn Diego's leather jacket to work and found a receipt for an off-Broadway theater, paid in cash. Nathan had worked late all week, so he figured that Diego had caught a show with a friend. But when he'd asked him how the show was, Diego had said that he was at the gym that night.

He knew he needed to confront Diego. But what to say? Nathan didn't know how to talk to him about it. That was the problem with their marriage. Or was that *his* problem, in general? (Better not to think of that.)

Nathan remembered a time when he and Diego couldn't bear to be away from each other. When even an eight-hour shift at work felt like an eternity, waiting to get home to recount every last minute, moment, of their days to each other. When they would be sitting at the theater, unable to bear not touching for three hours, legs turned toward each other so that their knees could bump as they held hands. He recalled one summer when Diego went with his father on a trip to Spain, how Nathan missed him so much, he'd felt it as an ache in his bones. A physical, visceral thing. When did that feeling go away?

In the early days of their relationship, Nathan could always sense Diego looking at him, before he saw it. They could be at a three hundred person wedding with a fourteen-piece band blaring out big band music, and Nathan would feel it: his love's eyes on him. He would search the room, and he would see Diego, staring at him slyly as he talked up the bride's mother.

When they were at big parties, or nights at the bar with friends, they had a secret gesture they'd send each other—Diego told Nathan that a pointer finger, tapped gently against the lips twice meant that he was sending a kiss to him, across the room. He could practically feel Diego's lips on his every time he gave that signal. And he would send one back in Diego's direction, always.

Nathan couldn't recall the last time his husband had sent him a kiss telepathically. (Or in real life, either, for that matter.)

"Earth to Nathan," Diego said, waving his hands around, as if he were trying to get cell phone service. "You could just call your father's old insurance agent. I'm sure whatever he had in that box was insured."

"Right," Nathan said. After his father died, Nathan had been the one to go through all the insurance policies. If there had been a policy for items kept down in the Caymans, Nathan would have retrieved them then.

Unless it was cash. After all, his father was a gambler. Gamblers hid cash. He loved his father, of course he did, but he always saw him clearly, and for who he was, unlike Addy, who had this completely different image, a much gentler image, of the person he was. When their parents separated because of his father's gambling addiction, it was Addy who had made excuses. Nathan stepped up to be the man of the home, taking care of his sister and mother in equal measure. He reminded Addy about taking her vitamins in the morning, and he got the mail each afternoon, setting out the bills on his mother's desk in the kitchen.

Nathan wasn't sure he even cared what was in the safe-deposit box. If it was cash, would it be enough money to break even on the cost of flying three people down to the Caymans in the first place? Two nights in a hotel? And if not cash, then it was probably just a box of junk. Nathan needed to start standing up to his sister.

Diego put the bathing suits back into his drawer. "Guess I won't be needing these after all." Diego made an exaggerated frowny face, and then brushed by Nathan to get out of the closet. "Love you," Diego called out, as he made his way down the hallway.

Nathan didn't respond.

8

Courtney

SY: I had a lovely time last night. Dinner again this Saturday?

COURTNEY: i had fun, too! next week is better. need to fly to ny this weekend.

SY: Do you need a ride? I keep a plane at Van Nuys.

Courtney looked at her phone. Was it really this easy? Maybe Lindsay was right—acting was for suckers, and this sugar baby thing was the way to go. Courtney hadn't booked an acting job in three years, and she'd made two grand in one night. And she didn't even have to do anything with Sy. Didn't remove one item of clothing.

Courtney hated going back to New York. Going home was a defeat. She'd promised herself when she moved out to LA that she wouldn't return until she had an Academy Award or, at the very least, a recurring role on a prestige network drama. She hadn't made it yet. She'd made so many mistakes along the way instead. She didn't even have an apartment anymore.

The apartment her parents had bought for her. She'd lost that six months ago. But things would change. She just knew they would. Whenever her father was losing his shirt in a casino, he'd tell her, "In an instant, your luck can change. If you have ten dollars left in your pocket, you can still win big on just one bet."

Courtney did not have ten dollars left in her pocket. After throwing some of the two grand from Sy to Chrissy for rent and the rest to her bookie, Lefty, she was back where she started. Broke.

Still. Today could be the day her agent called with a big audition. One that she wouldn't fuck up. One that would lead to a callback. And then another. She'd get one role, and that would lead to another. Before she knew it, she'd be on the A-list.

Seemingly on cue, her cell phone rang. Courtney looked down to see if it was her agent calling—she spent half the day looking down at her phone to see if her agent was calling—but it was a blocked number. Tempted as she was to let it go to voice mail, she picked up. Maybe it was her agent calling from another line? Or maybe it was the casting director from that Will Smith movie. She'd had a good feeling about her line reads that day.

Courtney picked up, but didn't speak for a beat. You could generally weed out spam phone calls by not speaking when you answered the phone.

"Miss Taylor?" a voice asked. "Is this you? Sy Pierce gave me your number. This is his assistant, Samantha."

"Oh, hi," Courtney said, sitting up a little straighter on Chrissy's couch. "This is Courtney."

"I'm readying the jet for you as we speak. Where is your destination today?"

Wow, Courtney thought. So, it really *was* that easy. "I'm heading to New York."

"Teterboro," the woman said under her breath. "And when is your return?"

"Oh, I'm not sure," Courtney said. "I'm going with my brother and sister to the Caymans from there."

"Oh, Sy didn't mention an additional trip," she said. "Hold on."

"No," Courtney protested, as she heard Samantha typing furiously. "I just need him to get me to New York. I wasn't asking to take the jet twice."

"Mr. Pierce gave me specific instructions to make sure you are taken care of. And he will be in LA for the next two weeks for meetings, so that means the jet is at your disposal. Could you please spell the names of the passengers on the Cayman flight?"

"Oh, you need our names?"

"Yes."

"Okay, well, first things first, my name is Courtney, C-O-U-R-T-N-E-Y, Schneider, S-C-H-N-E-I-D-E-R."

"I see."

"I'm sorry." Courtney winced as she thought about the fact that she hadn't even given Sy her real name. And here he was, acting perfectly gentlemanly.

"Mr. Pierce would also like to send over a little spending money for your trip to New York. Do you have a checking account?"

"Spending money?" Just as Courtney was puzzling over how she would tell her brother and sister how she'd procured a private jet for their jaunt down to the Caymans, a plan began to take form.

9

Ritchie's notebook, 1978

My love,
Seeing you again has ~~turned~~ lit my world on fire.

My every thought, every waking hour, is ~~filled~~ consumed with thoughts of you. Your ~~soft~~ silky hair, your full lips, the soft skin at the small of your back.

Each day, I count the minutes until we can see each other again. I long to taste the sweetness of your mouth, feel the touch of your fingertips, ~~touch~~ graze the insides of your soft thighs.

MAKE MORE ROMANTIC, STUPID!

10

Lizzie, 1978

When she saw him again, there was no turning back. It was as if her sixteen-year-old self's dream had come true, this man appearing in her life once more. Like her Hollywood namesake, Elizabeth Taylor, Lizzie was meeting her Richard Burton for a second time, nine years after they'd first met.

Their eyes locked across a crowded Long Island house party. She recognized him immediately. Recalled every detail. But she could see it in his eyes: Ritchie did not recognize her. She supposed it was fair. After all, the last time he'd seen her, she was a girl. Nine years later, age twenty-five, she was certainly a woman. Her face had filled out, her body had, too, and her hair was shorter, grazing the lines of her jaw, unlike every other woman at the party, whose hair was long, reaching down to their waists.

"I know you," he said. He searched her face for a clue.

"Of course you do." Lizzie couldn't contain her smile. After all these years, Ritchie was even better looking than when she'd first laid eyes on him.

Years later, when she'd tell the story to her children (mostly to Nathan), she'd explain that it was so much more than the simple fact that he was handsome (so, so handsome). Lizzie couldn't be sure if it was because she recognized something familiar in him (and he, she), or if it was the lure of the forbidden. Her parents thought he was a degenerate, unworthy of dating one of their girls.

And he had secretly dated her sister, nine years prior.

Lizzie and Ritchie would not date secretly. They would date openly, brazenly, to the disgust of her parents and the not-so-hidden anger of her sister, Maggie. But Lizzie was drawn to him. Like a delicate paper clip, no match for a powerful magnet. She would tell friends that she simply couldn't help it. They were meant to be. It was more than just love: it was *fate*.

"Remind me?" Ritchie said.

Ritchie couldn't remember Lizzie, but Lizzie knew all about him from the stories her sister had told. Ritchie Schneider: lovable scoundrel from Brooklyn. Never met a job he could hold down. Never met a bet he wouldn't take. Never met a woman he couldn't get to fall in love with him inside of five minutes.

He would help old ladies carry their groceries three blocks to their house. He was kind to children, even the one who lobbed a baseball through the front window of his car. He was a hopeless romantic in the body of a hustler.

"Well, if you can't remember who I am, then I suppose you don't deserve to know." Ritchie was the sort of man who liked a challenge. Lizzie planned to give him one.

"I think I deserve it." Ritchie put his hand on the wall behind her. She could smell his cologne, and she breathed it in: grapefruit, vanilla, coffee. "Tell me your name."

"Tell you my name," Lizzie purred. It was working. She was reeling him in, she could feel it. "Where would the fun be in that?"

"How am I supposed to ask you on a date if I don't even know your name?"

"How can I accept a date when we already met and you don't know who I am?"

"If we'd met, I can assure you I would remember your name."

Lizzie liked the effect she was having on him. She shrugged her shoulders, as if to say: *Well, we did.* She pursed her lips as she turned away from Ritchie, back to her group of friends.

"Give me a second chance?" he asked, tapping her lightly on the shoulder.

She contained her smile before spinning back around. "I suppose. I mean, if you're going to beg."

"I'm begging."

"All right, then," Lizzie said, fumbling in her purse for a pen to write down her telephone number.

"No, I mean now."

"Excuse me?"

"Now," Ritchie repeated. "Let's get out of here. If we met before, and I let you slip from my fingers that time, do you really think I'm going to let that happen again?"

Lizzie bit her lip, considering it. She should make him wait. A man like Ritchie liked the chase, not the actual prize, so if she wanted to keep him interested, she'd have to let him chase her.

"I don't think so."

"Please?" Ritchie asked, his fingers grazing her hand. She felt the electricity go from her hand to her heart to her head, making her dizzy. Lizzie took a deep breath, steadied herself. But it was no use. She told her friends that she didn't need a ride home, after all.

11

Lizzie, 1978

"So, who are you?"

Lizzie bit her lip. Moments after leaving the party with him, she sat nestled in Ritchie's muscle car, deep in the leather seats, which tilted back in a way that made it feel like a warm hug. She looked out the window and watched the world go by, taking in the fresh nighttime air. She loved these Long Island house parties that were so close to the water—you could smell the ocean with every breath.

"You still don't know who I am?" Lizzie could hear her voice going up an octave as she spoke. She wanted so badly to sound like the sort of woman who Ritchie would want to date. A woman who knew what she wanted, not some little girl who, at age twenty-five, still worked for her father at his dry-cleaning business.

Ritchie regarded her as he stopped at a red light. "You left the party with me, you're in my car, and you won't tell me your name?"

"Maybe I should make you sweat."

"Is that what you want to do with me?"

Lizzie felt her breath catch as she realized the double meaning of what Ritchie was saying. "I beg your pardon," she said
primly, but with what she hoped was a bit of flirtation. She didn't
want to seem too easy. She knew a man like Ritchie wanted
something difficult.

"Wanna go to the beach?" Ritchie asked.

"The beaches are closed at night."

"Not if you know the right place to park."

Lizzie considered this. The thought of going to the beach at
night when she knew it was against the law made her a bit jit-
tery. What if they were caught? "And you know the right place?"
she asked Ritchie.

"Yeah, I know all the right places," he said with a half smile
on his lips. "Ask anyone."

"Your friend Ace?"

"You know Ace?" Of course she knew who Ace was. Ace
Wheeler: Ritchie's best friend. His ride or die. His only true
friend, maybe. They'd been calling him Ace since they were
kids, because he always carried a deck of cards in his back pocket.
Lizzie had memorized every detail she could about Ritchie when
she was sixteen years old.

"He was with you the first night we met. And I think I saw
him there tonight."

"Yeah, I was his ride home. He's gonna kill me. Okay, so,
clue number one—the first time we met, I was with Ace. Were
we on Long Island or in Brooklyn?"

"Long Island."

"Silly question. I hear Long Island in your voice."

"And I hear Brooklyn in yours."

"That an insult?"

"Merely an observation." Lizzie let her hand dangle out of the
window as Ritchie drove, enjoying the sensation of the nighttime air hitting her skin. She felt drunk on the moment—alone
in a car with this man she barely knew, a man she had fantasized

about for years. A man who didn't know who she was. A man who had secretly dated her older sister. It felt illicit, sexy. She didn't want the moment to end—could she live in it forever?

"We're here," Ritchie said, pulling into a parking lot.

"I thought you said beach?"

"You don't seem like a jump the fence kind of girl."

"You have no idea what kind of girl I am," Lizzie said, sounding flirty, she hoped, as Ritchie got out of the car and walked over to her side to open the door for her. He held out his hand, and Lizzie took it—she felt his touch from the tips of her fingers, up to her head, down to the very depths of her belly.

"Shall we?" Lizzie held Ritchie's hand as they walked inside.

The place looked like nothing from the outside, like a little shack. But once they were through the door, it opened up, got bigger. From the entry, you could see clear out to the deck out back.

"But the beach is that way?" Lizzie pointed across her shoulder. She didn't know where she was exactly, but a girl from the South Shore of Long Island knew in which direction the beach was.

"We're on the bay," Ritchie said, and led Lizzie to a table in the back, outside on the expansive deck, overlooking the water. The place was kind of a dive, with plastic tables and chairs. And not nice ones, either. They were cheap, and as you sat down, they bent ever so slightly, as if at any moment they might break. The tables were barely clean, stained with salt water and baked by the sun, and the menus had seen better days. Still, Lizzie couldn't think of anywhere else she'd rather be.

"Drinks?" A waitress set down paper placemats and utensils wrapped inside paper napkins.

"I'll take a beer, please," Ritchie said. "And my date will take a—"

"White wine spritzer, please."

"Great. I'll be right back," the waitress said.

"You hungry?" Ritchie eyed the menu as he waited for Lizzie to respond.

"I could eat."

Ritchie ordered a bucket of steamers when the waitress returned with their drinks. Just then, a band started to play.

"Dance?" Ritchie held out his hand. He led her to the dance floor as if they'd done it all the time. There was something so self-assured about him, like he knew who he was.

Ritchie put his arm around Lizzie's waist, as they gently danced along to the music. A cover of Fleetwood Mac's "Dreams." The singer wasn't half bad. Ritchie pulled her closer, and Lizzie didn't try to stop him. She could feel his entire body against hers, the heat, and she took a deep breath to steady herself on her feet.

"So, you going to tell me your name or what?"

Lizzie shook her head. If she told him who she was, the date would be over. What man wanted to date his ex-girlfriend's little sister? Lizzie wasn't ready for the night to be over. From the moment she'd met Ritchie, she'd dreamed of him. He would be the Richard Burton to her Elizabeth Taylor, and they'd have an epic love affair for the ages, just like their Hollywood namesakes. If she told him who she was now, all that would be over. And it hadn't even started yet. She had wanted the night to last longer, to have one of those nights where you stayed out until dawn. The ones like her older sister and friends were always telling her about.

"I'm going to keep you guessing," Lizzie said, and Ritchie drew her closer.

He brought his lips to her ears. "Tell me your name."

"No."

"Shouldn't I know the name of the girl I'm about to kiss?"

"You seem like the sort of guy who kisses women he doesn't know all the time."

Ritchie laughed. "I have no idea what that's supposed to mean, but I'm pretty sure that this time, it was an insult."

"Oh, no," Lizzie said, righting herself. "I was trying to sound flirty."

"Is that so?"

"Did it work?"

"Do you want me to kiss you?"

"Yes."

Ritchie pressed his lips to hers. Tentatively at first, testing the waters. Then, when Lizzie kissed him back, the kiss went deeper. His lips were so soft, softer than Lizzie thought they would be, given his rough hands, and their mouths seemed to fit perfectly together. As if they'd been made for each other.

Lizzie hadn't had much experience, but she was pretty sure that it was the best kiss of her life.

"What's your name?" Ritchie murmured into her ear, his warm breath lingering on her neck.

Without thinking: "Elizabeth." The second she said it, she realized her mistake. She'd revealed her cards too soon, and now the game would be over. One small consolation: at least she had the kiss to remember it by.

Ritchie pulled away to look Lizzie in the face. "That's why you're so familiar. You're Lizzie Morgan, aren't you?"

"I go by *Elizabeth* now," Lizzie said.

"Do you?" Ritchie said. "I always loved the name *Lizzie*. It suits you."

"You remember me?" Lizzie felt like her cheeks were on fire.

"Now I do."

"Is the night over?"

Ritchie looked her straight in the eye. "No, it's not over. Not even close. In fact, the night has just begun."

12

Addy

Addy fingered the delicate diamond studs. Gifted to her by her parents when she turned twenty-one, they were the thing she reached for whenever she wanted to feel strong. Ready for battle.

Addy kneeled in front of the wall safe in her family room. "Hidden in plain sight," the real estate agent had said when they bought the place, showing Addy the safe tucked inside one of the base cabinets. She and Gary didn't have much of a need for a safe, but eventually found a way to fill it: their wills, the kids' birth certificates and social security cards, and their passports. Addy also kept the few pieces of jewelry from her parents in it, since she didn't wear them on a regular basis. She felt like she was at church when she went to retrieve them. Genuflecting at the altar of diamonds.

Wearing diamonds always had a way of making Addy feel like she was in control. And Addy needed to feel in control. The news of the safe-deposit box in the Caymans had sent her reeling, had made her feel unmoored and unsure of everything she knew. Addy had a sneaking suspicion that the reason she didn't know about the box was because, even in death, her father had kept one more secret from her.

Growing up with a father with a gambling addiction made Addy wary of secrets. She tried to live a life that was completely transparent; she wouldn't stand for anything less than full honesty. Not from her husband. Not from her girls. Not from anyone.

"Why are you going if you don't know what's inside?" Emma asked, appearing as if from thin air.

"You startled me," Addy said, self-consciously laughing at herself. "I am going precisely *because* I want to know what's inside."

"But it could be a humongous waste of time."

"It could be anything." Addy smiled at Emma.

Emma smiled back. "I'm intrigued by this idea of *anything*." It was times like these that Addy was reminded how different her girls were from each other.

Olivia: driven, ambitious, fierce.

Emma: relaxed, congenial, amiable.

Olivia, older than her twin by just five minutes, was pure Addy. That made Emma, she supposed, more like Gary. Addy recognized her own type-A spirit in Olivia, and she saw Gary's lazy belief that everything would always work out in Emma.

Addy had the sudden thought that she shouldn't go. How could she leave her girls? Sixteen was such a confusing time—one day, they were happy, the next, the world was ending. What if something happened while she was gone?

"Maybe I should stay," Addy said.

"No, you should go," Emma said. "Like you said, it could be *anything* inside that box. Just promise if there's something good, you'll give it to me."

Addy smiled. "I'll let you know if I find anything good."

"Can I try on those earrings?"

"Of course," Addy said, handing them over. "You know, I always think of this diamond jewelry as armor."

"Armor?" Emma crinkled her brow as she put the earrings on. "Is armor usually this sparkly?"

"Wearing these earrings makes me feel invincible," Addy said. "They make me think of my parents, for one, as if they're still with me, still by my side. And they make me feel like I can handle anything that comes my way."

"Because diamonds are so strong they could cut glass?" She leaned over to the window and pretended to cut the glass with her ear.

Addy couldn't help but laugh.

Emma looked at her mother. "These tiny little things make you feel stronger?"

"First of all, as far as diamond studs go, these are huge," Addy said, opening her hand so that her daughter would give them back. "And yes. They do."

That was the power of jewelry, wasn't it? Just putting it on could change your mood, the way you felt about yourself, how you went about your day. Jewelry could make you feel beautiful; it could make you feel powerful. The right jewelry could serve as armor. It could make you feel loved. It could make you feel like you were walking hand in hand with the person who gave it to you.

Emma walked over to the mantel and picked up a framed photograph of her grandparents. "Now, *that's* huge."

Addy turned to see Emma pointing at her mother's favorite piece of jewelry, a diamond ring Lizzie had nicknamed the Liz Taylor Ring. "That thing was eleven carats. Grandpa Ritchie gave it to Grandma Lizzie—"

"After their nine-month separation in 1992," Emma said, filling in the details. "I've heard the story a million times. I wish you had it."

"It was stolen the night of my parents' thirtieth anniversary."

"Right. I've heard that story, too," Emma said. "I bet it would've looked great on me."

"Yes, it would have," Addy said. "That thing was a stunner. And so are you."

Emma smiled and then turned her attention to her iPhone. She tilted her face to one side, and then the other. She pouted, and moved her face up and down, trying to find the perfect angle. Emma snapped a selfie. "Can I take a pic with your earrings on?"

"That's not a good idea," Addy said.

"You're right," Emma said. "I'll just wait to see what you come back with from the Caymans and take a picture with that."

Addy smiled and thought about the vault. What, exactly, was she hoping to find there? Why was there this inexplicable pull to whatever was hidden there? Was she still trying to prove that her father was a good guy, after all this time? He'd been gone for seven years—seven long years. Why was Addy still defending his honor?

Addy knew her father had had a gambling problem. But she was able to separate it from who he was as a person, what a wonderful father he was. She was always able to reconcile these two thoughts at once: her father had a gambling problem; her father was an excellent husband and father. Two things could be true at the same time. But an affair? If that were true, it would mean she had spent her entire life worshipping at the altar of a false god.

"How baller is it that Aunt Courtney is now doing well enough to charter a private jet?" Emma said.

The diamond studs weren't enough. Addy reached into the safe until she found what she was looking for. A diamond solitaire. A gift from her father to her mother on the day that Addy was born, she treasured the necklace.

Emma's eyes widened as Addy took the piece out of its box. Addy motioned for her to turn around, and she put the necklace on her daughter's neck.

"How do I look?" Emma asked.

"Like you could cut glass," Addy said with a smile.

"Okay, you're right," Emma said. "There's something about this necklace. I do feel different."

Addy smiled at her daughter, who reluctantly took the necklace off and gave it to her mother to wear.

"When I get back, I'd like to talk about social media with you girls."

Emma narrowed her eyes at her mother. "You're on social media?"

"As a matter of fact, I am. And I don't like seeing sexually suggestive photographs of my children."

"Sexually suggestive?"

"That picture of you and your sister with your thumbs in your mouths."

"That was just fashion."

"It was borderline pornographic."

Under her breath: "Well, then, if you don't like that, you're definitely not going to like what we're planning to do next."

13

Nathan

Diego was artfully arranging a very involved cheese plate on the kitchen island. (A *cheese platter* Diego would correct.) Once the brie was placed perfectly so, right next to the jar of fig jam, he drizzled honey into a ramekin and draped almonds around its base.

Nathan walked into their massive chef's kitchen quietly. When Diego's parents bought them the loft in Soho as a wedding present back in 2012, Nathan had suggested they didn't need a big kitchen. Neither of them cooked. But Diego's parents insisted on paying for the renovation, too, so Diego got what he wanted: a professional kitchen that was as beautiful as it was large, with top-of-the-line appliances and marble imported from Italy.

Nathan took a bottle of pinot noir from the wine fridge and set about opening it. He poured two glasses and then watched his husband. The way his long fingers carefully placed each item on the cheese plate. The way he hinged over at the waist, making his back look long and lean. The way he used his forearm to brush his long black hair away from his eyes while he worked.

At one time, he would have grabbed Diego and whisked him off to the bedroom before the company arrived. At yet another, he would've just dragged him down to the kitchen floor.

When had all of that changed?

"You still love him," Addy said, when Nathan had tried to broach the subject of divorce two nights ago.

"What if I'm not *in love* with him anymore? People fall out of love."

"That's just a stupid thing people say to justify getting divorced when nothing is actually wrong. Relationships are hard. Marriage is harder. Things wax and wane. You may be having a rough patch now, but you should just work through it."

But it wasn't a rough patch. Addy had talked over him—talk, talk, talk—and hadn't let Nathan say the part that he wanted to say. The thing he needed to say. The only thing that mattered: Diego was having an affair. And he had the ticket receipt to prove it. Nathan narrowed his eyes as he looked at his husband's back.

Diego spun around toward Nathan and threw his arms out, as if to say *Ta-da!* "It came out great, right?" His accent was always more pronounced when he was trying to be cute. He was originally from Mexico, but had lived in New York since his twenties.

"That is a very nice cheese plate," Nathan said. And he had to admit, it really was.

"*Platter.* And it's the honey," Diego said, nodding his head. "The honey makes it special. Here, try this."

Diego dipped a piece of parmesan into the honey and held it out for Nathan to taste. There was something so intimate about the gesture—Diego offering to feed his husband. Nathan almost couldn't accept it. Diego beckoned him closer, raising his eyebrows in a gesture that, for Nathan, was always a reminder of the night they first met.

It was 2005, and Nathan had just graduated college. New

to New York City and new to the auditioning scene, he made friends with a group of aspiring actors who worked at a restaurant on Theatre Row, carrying on the grand tradition of hope that proximity to the Broadway stage would somehow get them onto it sooner. They auditioned all day, served tourists crappy pasta all evening, and then barhopped downtown all night, before collapsing into bed in their tiny apartments after last call at four in the morning, ready to do the whole thing over again the next day.

At a downtown dive bar one night, all of a sudden, the energy in the room shifted. You could feel it, this magic in the air. Someone had walked in, and a flurry of whispers went through the crowd, from the door to the back, where Nathan stood with a few friends.

"Pedro Garcia Flores is here," a guy standing next to Nathan said. He grabbed Nathan's arm for emphasis and pointed to the front door.

"No way," Nathan said. "My mother used to play his records on repeat when I was a kid." The guy smiled in recognition. (Everyone's mothers played his records on repeat when they were kids.)

"Did you hear who's here?" Nathan's friend, Paul, yelled at him, over the steadily escalating din.

Nathan nodded and then got up on tippy-toes to try to catch a glimpse over the crowd.

Pedro Garcia Flores was a star. A huge star. Born a poor kid in a tiny town in Mexico, he got seriously injured in a factory accident when he was twelve. Doctors didn't think he'd ever regain movement in his right hand. Convalescing in the hospital, a nurse gave him her son's old guitar, as a form of physical therapy. His hand healed as he taught himself to play, and by age fourteen, he was playing at local hotels each night, singing a mix of covers and original songs. An agent discovered him at age fifteen, and by age twenty, he had become one of the most famous singer-songwriters in the world. He'd sold more than two hundred million records worldwide in eleven different languages. He wrote the theme songs to two separate James Bond movies. He performed at the Super Bowl halftime show. He won a Grammy, an Oscar, and an Emmy. A star on the Hollywood Walk of Fame. Either based on his looks, his velvety voice, or his brilliant lyrics, you would fall in love with Pedro Garcia Flores. Just like your mother did.

"You beautiful woman, get out of my head," Nathan and Paul sang out in unison, one of Pedro's biggest hits from the '80s.

"Think he'll get up to sing?" Paul asked the bartender.

"He won't," a man replied from out of nowhere, as he raised his hand to get the bartender's attention.

Nathan's breath caught in his chest at the sight of him—enormous brown eyes with flecks of yellow, eyelashes that were so black it looked like he wore mascara, and thick black hair that flopped into his gorgeous face. In that first glimpse, he could see their entire life together: lazy Sundays spent doing the Sunday *New York Times* crossword in Central Park; big, elaborate dinner parties with tons of friends in a tiny New York City apartment; bringing him home to meet his sister, Addy, who would, of course, fall head over heels in love with him, too.

Nathan looked at this handsome stranger next to him and lost himself. "I love you," Nathan said. He'd meant to say *hello*, truly he did, but somehow the proclamation of love came out instead. Luckily, Nathan's words could not be heard over the loud buzz of the bar. He closed his eyes and thanked the gods above for the noise.

"How do you know he won't sing?" Paul asked the man playfully. He did a little faux punch to his arm and let his hand linger for a beat too long. This was Paul flirting. "Maybe he will."

"He just played a sold-out show at the Garden," the handsome stranger said. "He played three encores, and he really just wants a drink with his wife and his son. He thought that if he came here, no one would recognize him."

"I'd say people are recognizing him," Nathan said, motioning toward the door. Pedro was surrounded by fans, clamoring for autographs and handshakes.

"He's going to kill me," the stranger said, closing his eyes for a beat.

"How could anyone want to kill *you*?" Nathan asked. He resisted the urge to put his arms around him to comfort him. He resisted the urge to rub his back in tiny circles to make it all better. He resisted the urge to kiss him full on, right on the mouth. (That would come much, much later in the evening, in addition to a number of other very comforting activities.)

"Because I told him that if we came here, no one would recognize him."

"Are you his assistant?"

He raised his eyebrows. "Something like that."

It would be three months until Diego would tell Nathan the truth, that his father was Pedro Garcia Flores. It was Diego's biggest secret, as he did the audition circuit in New York, hoping to make it on Broadway on his own. It was a secret he'd kept for five years, living in New York by himself, auditioning relentlessly. His covert plan: he would earn the Tony that his father never could, and he would do it without using the family name. He went by his mother's maiden name, de la Cueva. Diego didn't want his father's help or influence to get him a job. He would only be satisfied, he told Nathan, once he'd made it completely on his own.

He didn't make it on his own. Diego's voice was no match for his father's, which took him out of contention for the Broadway roles he so craved. Nathan suggested he try for TV. There were soap operas still filming in New York, and with his devastating good looks, Diego was a shoo-in. But those weren't the sorts of roles that Diego wanted. He refused to rely on his looks, going out for character roles, meatier roles, roles in which his appearance wouldn't be a factor. Roles that he wasn't a match for. He never landed a job. (Neither did Nathan, but he didn't have nearly as much to prove as Diego.)

Eight years after they met, seven years after they started living together, and one year after officially getting married, Diego landed a part. It was a low-budget film, but that didn't matter. What mattered was that Diego was finally being noticed, and Nathan was happier for him than if he'd been cast himself. This was it. This was the moment when everything would finally change.

The first day on set, the director asked Diego if his father would be willing to write an original song for the movie. Diego walked off, walked home, and never attended another audition again.

Diego raised his eyebrows again, returning Nathan to the present. Nathan took a bite of the parmesan that his husband held out for him.

"That *is* good," Nathan said as he tasted the combination of sharp cheese and honey.

Diego licked the leftover honey off his fingers. "You sound surprised."

"Not surprised."

Their eyes met. Diego raised his eyebrows again at Nathan, and Nathan couldn't help but smile. Was this what being *in love* was? Remembering who they were when you first met because of a crease in the forehead? Was being *in love* with someone just lust? Something physical? Or was it the sum of your experience together? Remembering how tongue-tied you were on the first night you met. The way he comforted you when your father died. And then your mother. The way he woke up early each morning to make you coffee, even though he didn't drink the stuff himself?

The buzzer rang, breaking the spell. "Courtney," the men said in unison, as if they'd only just then remembered.

Courtney blew in like a hurricane, seemingly before they even had a chance to fully open the front door, in a blur of bear hugs, expensive perfume, and endless chatter about the flight over (apparently it was fabulous yet lonely to fly private by yourself).

"Now that you have access to a plane," Diego said, taking her bags, "you'll be able to come to Nathan's birthday party! I'll be sending out save-the-dates this week. It's June 4th."

"You're still having the party?"

"Of course we're having the party. Why would you ask such a thing?"

Turning to Nathan, Courtney said: "Yesterday you said you didn't even want the party."

"Did I say that? You must have misunderstood," Nathan said, his words falling out in a nervous jumble.

"You don't want the party I'm planning?" Diego said.

"No, of course I do!" Nathan said, his voice rising an octave. "Of course I do!"

"Oh, I thought—" Courtney began, but then realized. "Sorry! I don't even know what I'm saying. Jet lag."

Nathan looked to Diego apologetically, but Diego refused to meet his eye.

14

Courtney

"But it's worth it."

Her siblings looked back at her and smiled politely. They sat quietly, side by side in a row, at Teterboro, waiting to board the private plane to the Caymans.

"We're very proud of your success," Addy said, with a smile that didn't quite reach her eyes.

Courtney could tell that she didn't really mean it. Addy wasn't proud of her. Anyway, it was such a condescending thing to say, "We're very proud," as if Courtney were still a child. As if Addy was still twenty-one years old and Courtney was still nine. The age difference barely meant a thing at this point. What was a twelve-year age gap once you were almost thirty?

Nathan didn't say a word. Why had she had so much champagne on the plane ride to New York yesterday? Just because it was free didn't mean she had to have so much of it. But once the flight attendant had opened the first bottle for the takeoff toast, Courtney felt it would be rude to leave her with a mostly full bottle. You couldn't put a cork back into a bottle of champagne the way you could with a nice bottle of pinot grigio. (Not like she ever let one of those go to waste, either.) The least she could do was have another glass. And then another. If she hadn't been tipsy when she got to Nathan and Diego's loft, she never would have spilled the beans about Nathan not wanting the fortieth birthday party. Nathan was usually her ally. And now he was mad at her. How could she be so stupid? Stupid. Stupid. Stupid.

"We're so glad you were able to make the time for us," Nathan said, a tight smile plastered on his face.

"I always make time for you," Courtney said, and reached out to touch Nathan's arm. But Nathan brushed it away. He stood up and walked toward the window.

"So, have you picked up any Japanese?" Addy asked.

"You don't need to speak Japanese to be in a Japanese commercial." Courtney didn't mean to sound defensive. She smiled at her sister and vowed to speak less. After all, who was Addy to say that she *wasn't* acting in Japanese commercials and that the jet *wasn't* chartered with her own money?

"I think it's great you've been able to find a niche for yourself," Addy said. "I know from Nathan and Diego's experience how difficult auditions can be. How demoralizing. But this is great. Just be careful to build your savings and not spend it all, you know?"

Leave it to Addy to ruin even her fake good fortune. How could her daughters stand her?

"I hope you're giving the girls the same advice," Courtney said.

"They're only sixteen."

"Yes, but all of the modeling they're doing for the store. They should be careful with that money. One day they'll need full portfolios and head shots, and all that stuff is expensive."

"Oh, they're not going to go into modeling," Addy said, making a face. Courtney immediately grabbed onto the subtext. Her daughters were too good for modeling. For acting. For every goddamned thing she'd dedicated her life to.

"Oh."

"And anyway, it's not like we pay them to take pictures for Instagram." Addy laughed, as if such an idea were ridiculous. As if the idea of being paid to model was ridiculous.

"May I please have a vodka rocks?" Courtney said to a passing waitress.

"It's eleven in the morning," Addy said.

"Splash of OJ."

"I'm not a waitress," the young woman said. "I was coming to tell you that your plane is ready. I'll make sure your flight crew knows to get you a drink before takeoff."

"Nathan, let's go," Addy said to her brother, who was still over by the window.

Addy followed the woman out to the plane, with Nathan following closely in her wake. Courtney fell behind, and couldn't help but think that this was how it had been in their family. Addy charging forward, Nathan her faithful second-in-command, leaving Courtney behind, always.

15

Courtney

The following morning, Courtney woke up early and carefully dressed, as she would for an audition. It wasn't to impress her siblings—she would never admit that to them or to herself—rather, today she would again be playing the role of the fabulous younger sister who was a success in LA. She took a selfie in front of the window, palm trees in the background. *#partyallthetime #lovemylife #positivevibes*

The plan was to get there at ten, right when the bank opened, but Nathan had overslept, so they'd pushed it back to eleven.

As she made her way to the elevator, she saw Addy.

"Morning." Courtney smiled brightly at her sister.

Addy barely looked up. "Morning. How did you sleep?"

"Good," Courtney said, and then a beat later, corrected herself: "Well."

"Good."

Courtney couldn't tell if Addy was making fun of her. She'd learned on an audition for a nighttime soap that rich people always responded with the grammatically correct *well* when people asked how they were. It was never appropriate to say *good*. Did

Addy know this? Did Addy think badly of her because of the way she spoke? But then, Courtney remembered: Addy never really thought of her at all.

Courtney looked at her sister from the tip of her head to the bottom of her toes. Who was Addy to judge? Would it kill her sister to get her hair colored, cover up some of the gray? Her dirty blond hair was more dirty than blond these days, making the gray hairs even more prominent. Addy seemed to be playing the role of dowdy housewife.

Even her shoes were all wrong. Courtney wore delicate strappy sandals with a two-inch heel to complement her cotton shift dress. Addy was wearing a very plain pair of flats. Couldn't she get a pair of cute ballerinas with a bow on top? Courtney wouldn't be caught dead in shoes that were so basic. Or a pair of flats, for that matter. While Courtney had dressed to impress, Addy had not. The straps on Courtney's sandals suddenly felt a bit tight.

As they walked into the lobby, she saw her brother sitting on one of the couches, looking rested and ready to go. Nathan stood up, ready to greet his sisters, and Courtney noticed that the old man sitting across from him on the other couch stood as well.

What happened next Courtney could only describe as the world swimming in slow motion. One minute, she was walking out of the elevator with her older sister, thinking horrible thoughts about her shoes. The next, the clawing realization that one of these things was not like the other. There was someone there who did not belong.

She couldn't place him at first, which made sense, of course, since she'd only met him once. But he had paid her quite handsomely for that first pleasure, and she was presently in possession of his private jet.

Sy Pierce. In the Caymans. In the lobby of her hotel, which both of her siblings could see, clear as day.

"Surprise!"

16

Lizzie, 1978

"Well, isn't this a surprise," Katharine Morgan said, standing at the front door to her house. Lizzie heard her mother's voice from the top of the stairs—her tone made it clear that she was not pleased.

"A good one, I hope," Ritchie said. Lizzie could hear his voice, too: hopeful, eager, bright.

"Maggie," Katharine called over her shoulder, "someone's here for you."

Lizzie flew down the staircase, ready for her second date with Ritchie Schneider. She had planned to be waiting downstairs by the door when he arrived. But a fight with a set of curlers had made her late.

Her mother regarded her as she got to the bottom of the steps.

"You look beautiful," Ritchie said, holding his hand out for Lizzie.

"Thank you," Lizzie said, placing her hand in his. She tried to ignore her mother's glare, which burned her skin. Lizzie kept her gaze focused on Ritchie, refusing to look back to the top of the steps, where she knew her older sister, Maggie, would be standing, stunned.

Later that evening, there'd be hell to pay. Maggie would accuse her of "stealing" him, even though they hadn't dated in nine years. (And she'd married and divorced someone else in that time, but better to leave that part unsaid.) Her mother would call Ritchie a "degenerate," unworthy of dating her daughter, even though Lizzie's grandfather had made his fortune in bootlegging, and not the dry-cleaning business they currently owned.

But that was the problem with living at home. No privacy. Too many opinions. Lizzie certainly hadn't planned on living at home for quite so long, but her father didn't pay her enough at the dry-cleaning store to get her own apartment, and her English lit degree hadn't set her up for any sort of job that would pay well.

Maggie was only back in the house because her marriage had blown up. Married to the son of a prominent family, Maggie had inspired the envy of all her friends. And Lizzie. Everything in the Morgan house was a competition, and Maggie had scored the grand prize: William McMurphy, heir to a real estate fortune. He was rich. He was handsome. He had all the right connections. But after a few months of marriage, things changed. First, the broken arm. Then, a dislocated shoulder. Lizzie expressed concern for her sister, but there was always an excuse. First, it was that Maggie had fallen off her horse during practice. Then, it was that she'd slipped while getting out of the bathtub. By the time she ended up in the hospital with a concussion, the police called the Morgans, and they immediately moved her back home.

Lizzie and Maggie, both back in their childhood house, the Morgan girls together again under one roof. They slid into their old family roles easily, smoothly, like they'd never left: Maggie was the pretty one, but Lizzie was smarter. Lizzie was funnier, but Maggie was the one that people gravitated to. Maggie had lots of friends and boyfriends, and Lizzie mostly kept to herself. Their parents encouraged what they called *healthy competition* between the sisters, which was anything but, making the girls adversaries more than siblings. Whether it was a *friendly race* at the club's swimming pool or a *little contest* to see whose artwork would be good enough to be displayed at the local bank, there was always an opportunity to pit the girls against each other. Even now, at the dry cleaners, their father had begun an "Employee of the Month" program, and the sisters tried to outdo each other with the customers for the honor of having their photograph tacked to the wall.

Was this why her parents insisted that they both still live at home? To keep them firmly under their control? Surely the Morgans could afford to pay Lizzie and Maggie more at work so that they could move out. But they were as stingy with their money as they were with their love.

Lizzie quickly pushed Ritchie out the door of her parents' house, without saying goodbye to her mother. Without looking back to see her sister Maggie's reaction. She would worry about that later, when she got home after her date.

A half hour later, Lizzie and Ritchie pulled up to the hottest nightclub on Long Island. Lizzie had heard about it, but hadn't dared try to get in with her friends. The line to get in snaked around the block, and Ritchie pulled the car around back to park. He opened her door, and Lizzie considered whether she should have asked him to let her off in the front. The thin straps of her high-heeled sandals dug into her feet as they touched the pavement, and she didn't know how long she'd be able to stand in that long line.

But Ritchie didn't lead her around front. He walked them directly to the back door, where he shook a man's hand and they walked right in.

"How did you do that?" Lizzie said, clutching Ritchie's arm as they made their way through the kitchen.

"I know a guy," Ritchie said, flashing Lizzie a smile.

Her eyes took a second to adjust as Ritchie opened the kitchen door, and they were enveloped in the darkness of the club. Music blared out from every direction, so loud Lizzie could feel it in her body, pulsing. Three huge disco balls let off beams of light, and they reflected off the mirrored walls, which gave it the feeling that it stretched on forever, filled with endless people packed in closely, dancing and drinking and laughing.

Ritchie led Lizzie to the dance floor, and they began to move in time to the sound of the Bee Gees. Drinks magically materialized from a passing waitress, and Ritchie put the glass against the back of his neck. They'd only been in the club for a few minutes, but it was hot on the dance floor, hotter when they moved together. Lizzie drank hers down—a white wine spritzer, her favorite. When they were done with the drinks, another waitress appeared to whisk the glasses away.

Lizzie wanted to memorize every moment of the night. Remember every sensation: the music, pounding in her ears; the lights, dazzling from above; the man, summoned from her dreams, now here. Lizzie twirled, the fabric of her gold halter dress floating out around her, as Ritchie held her hand. She felt light and carefree as she spun on the dance floor, and could feel the constant soundtrack that played in her mind—*You're not good enough, you're not pretty enough, no man will ever want you*—replaced by the one that the DJ supplied: "Take a Chance on Me," "Kiss You All Over," "Got to Give It Up."

Lizzie crashed into Ritchie, laughing, just as the DJ changed the song. The opening beats of "Three Times a Lady" by the Commodores rang out. Ritchie pulled Lizzie close. She felt the heat coming off his body, pressed up against hers, barely covered in the thin material of her halter dress. He leaned down and sang the lyrics gently into her ear.

She turned in to him, and they kissed.

"I'm sorry if I got you into trouble at home," Ritchie whispered into her ear. His breath was warm, and Lizzie felt it go up her spine.

"I have a feeling you're going to get me into a lot of trouble."

17

Lizzie, 1978

After a date, Lizzie often received flowers from a suitor. Roses, peonies, and one time, a small fern. Sometimes she got chocolates. But Ritchie didn't send Lizzie flowers or chocolates. Ritchie did something that no man had ever done for her before.

Ritchie wrote Lizzie a love letter. Handwritten on ivory linen paper, Lizzie read the letter so many times, she committed it to memory. Any time her mother or sister gave her an angry glare, she would go back to the letter, and read it again. Her family may have been mad at her for dating Ritchie (her mother, angry that she was dating someone who wasn't *good enough* for her, her sister, furious that she'd *stolen* him), but Lizzie didn't care. Ritchie was worth it.

Lizzie had spent the week lost in Ritchie's words. She had folded the letter up and carried it with her wherever she went. But today, Lizzie would have to leave it at home. There was no place for a love letter where she was going that afternoon. Ritchie was taking her to a pool party.

Lizzie folded the letter carefully and placed it on her bedside table before packing her bag.

"Are you seeing him again?" Maggie asked, walking into Lizzie's room without knocking.

Lizzie stopped packing the bag. She regarded her sister. "He's taking me to a pool party. Not that it's any of your business."

"I don't want to see you get hurt."

Lizzie laughed. "The only thing that hurts are my feet, from dancing so much the other night."

"I'm just looking out for you," Maggie said, adjusting her face to feign concern.

Lizzie couldn't help but hold back a laugh. "No, you're not."

"I know how immature you are."

Lizzie looked at her sister. "You have no idea what I am."

"You're not right for him," Maggie said. "That much I know."

"And you are?"

"I was," Maggie said, turning to face Lizzie. Her eyes burned hot. "And I could be again. If I wanted to."

Lizzie froze. Maggie always took what she wanted. Would she try to take Ritchie? She took a deep breath and remembered that she was the one seeing him today. "Then why am I the one packing a bag?"

Maggie sat down on her sister's bed and looked at the bedside table. "What is this?" Maggie asked, unfolding the paper. She laughed. "A love letter?"

"It's mine, is what it is," Lizzie said. "And private. Please put it back."

Maggie turned the letter over in her hands. "I've never gotten one of these before." Then, instead of putting it back where she found it like Lizzie had asked, she read it. This was why they had no relationship. Friends, boyfriends, their parents' love— they were always forced to fight over crumbs.

"Keep the letter," Lizzie said, without really meaning it. "I've got the guy."

Lizzie brushed by her sister to wait for Ritchie by the door.

This time, Lizzie would be prepared. She was waiting downstairs when Ritchie arrived.

"I wanted to say hello to your mother," Ritchie said, as Lizzie kissed him hello.

"Oh, that's not necessary," Lizzie said, picking up her bag and readying herself to leave.

"I don't want to be disrespectful," Ritchie said, poking his head into the foyer. He called out: "Mrs. Morgan, I wanted to say hello before Lizzie and I left the house."

"Hello," Katharine's voice called out from the kitchen. Icy cold. Ritchie waited for her to come to the door to greet him, but after a few moments, it became clear that Lizzie's mother would not be coming out. Lizzie saw Ritchie's face fall, as he realized the truth: while he was careful not to disrespect Mrs. Morgan, Mrs. Morgan did not seem to have any problem in disrespecting him.

Even the gorgeous pool party couldn't cheer Ritchie up. He walked in, sullen. But Lizzie's eyes widened as they walked through the gate. The party was in full swing, with a bar set up at either end of the enormous pool, and beautiful people lounging, everywhere you looked. The sun shone brightly, not a cloud in the sky. Bright yellow umbrellas dotted the patio, with matching yellow floats in the pool. A small band played next to one of the bars, with a crowd in front, dancing. Lizzie couldn't help moving her hips as they walked into the party.

Ritchie pointed to Ace and his date, who had set up court on two chaise lounges, right in the middle of it all. They'd already helped themselves to the buffet, so plates filled with hamburgers, hot dogs, and all the fixings filled the table. A small ice bucket held bottles of beer, and a carafe of white wine spritzer.

"What's his problem?" Ace asked, as Lizzie dropped her bag onto a chaise lounge.

"Nothing that a little swim couldn't fix," Lizzie said, walking over to the edge of the pool, and splashing some water in

Ritchie's direction with her foot. Ritchie's expression didn't change as he brushed the pool water off his face and his shirt.

"I like this girl," Ace said to Ritchie, laughing. "She plays with fire."

"No fire," Lizzie said, dipping her foot into the pool again. "Just water." This time, she sent a bigger wave of pool water in Ritchie's direction, drenching him completely.

Shocked, he wiped the water off his face, and stood up. "Maybe we should show her how we deal with troublemakers in Brooklyn," Ritchie said to Ace, the edges of his mouth curling upwards. He unbuttoned his wet shirt and threw it down on the chaise.

"Maybe you should," Lizzie said and, in one fell swoop, pulled off her cover-up and tossed it aside, revealing her bright red bathing suit. She shimmied her hips, daring Ritchie to come closer to the edge.

All at once, Lizzie and Ritchie were in the pool, laughing and kissing under the water.

"See," Ritchie said to Lizzie as they came up for air, "I had you pegged wrong. All this time I thought you were a good girl."

"I'm a very good girl," Lizzie said, pushing her wet hair back with her hands. "But sometimes it's fun to be a little bad."

Ritchie looked off to the side, and Lizzie turned her head, following his gaze. It led directly to a leggy redhead in a nude bathing suit. She practically looked naked.

"Eyes back where they belong," Lizzie said, using one finger to turn his head back toward her.

"Trust me," Ritchie said, looking down the front of Lizzie's bathing suit. "My eyes are exactly where they belong."

"I saw you staring at the redhead." Lizzie narrowed her eyes at Ritchie.

"What redhead?"

Lizzie wished that she'd worn sunglasses so that she could hide the jealousy in her eyes. She didn't expect a man like Ritchie to completely ignore other women, but she did expect him to stay focused on her when they were on a date.

"Her?" Ritchie said, gesturing toward the redhead. "I promise you, I was not looking at her. I was checking out the action, that card game, at the table behind her."

"You expect me to believe you were looking at a bunch of sweaty men playing cards, and not the gorgeous girl standing in front of them?"

"You can believe what you want," Ritchie said, shrugging his shoulders. "But I'm telling you the truth."

Ritchie leaned in for a kiss, but Lizzie splashed him and swam away instead.

"Hey," Ritchie said, following her to the deep end. "I'm here with you. I want to be with you."

"I know it's only our third date," Lizzie said, placing her arms along the edge of the pool. She closed her eyes and tilted her head back, felt the warm sun on her face. "That was silly of me."

"It wasn't silly," Ritchie said, moving next to her. Lizzie couldn't bear to open her eyes to face him. "I'm not looking at other women."

"You're not?" Lizzie said, her voice soft. She opened her eyes and turned to Ritchie.

"Can't you see that I'm drowning in you?"

Lizzie's breath caught in her throat. She didn't know how to respond. But she didn't need to. Ritchie leaned in to kiss her, and Lizzie closed her eyes once again and let herself drown in Ritchie, too.

18

Addy

"Courtney, do you know this man?"

Courtney looked like she was about to faint. The color had drained from her face, and she spun on her heel to walk back toward the elevator. Fight or flight. Courtney had chosen flight, it seemed.

"Courtney?" The old man didn't move. He simply watched as Courtney made her hasty retreat.

"I think you have my sister mistaken for someone else," Nathan explained.

"Courtney is your sister?"

"Yes."

"Hi, I'm Addy." Addy stuck out her hand. "Courtney's sister. How do you know Courtney?"

"I'm Sy Pierce. Lovely to meet you. Your sister and I met in LA."

"Nice to meet you."

"I'm Nathan Schneider, Courtney's brother."

"I thought I'd surprise Courtney."

"She certainly seems surprised." Addy looked to the elevator bank, where Courtney had already gotten into an empty car and gone back upstairs.

"I'm sure she just forgot something in her room," Nathan said.

"Join me for coffee while we wait for Courtney to return?" Sy sat back down on the couch, and a waitress materialized, ready to take their orders. Sy seemed like the sort of man for whom things materialized. Waitresses ready to take a breakfast order, young girls in the Caymans. "I hope you had a nice flight down."

"I'm only flying private from now on," Nathan said, smiling broadly.

"I'm glad you enjoyed it."

Addy looked at Nathan. Nathan looked back at Addy.

Sy filled the silence. "I've never done something like this before, you know. I don't want you to think I do this all the time."

"Come to the Caymans?" Nathan asked tentatively. They all knew that he was not talking about coming to the Caymans.

"That website," Sy said. "Meeting young women on the internet. But I'm glad I did, I tell you, because your sister is very special."

"She's definitely something," Addy said, as the waitress set down their coffees. Addy's cappuccino had an intricate design of a leaf in the foam. She hesitated to ruin it by adding sweetener. Nathan downed his espresso in one gulp.

"My wife died five years ago," Sy explained as he took a delicate sip of his cappuccino. Addy examined his face—his light blue eyes looked kind, and he had good skin, considering his age. Addy guessed he was around eighty. He had a full head of hair, completely white, but thick, not receding. "And of course, I have my kids and the grandkids, but it's different, isn't it? I want to have someone to take around town, you know? I have a wedding in Chicago next month, and it will be nice to have someone to dance with."

Addy looked at Nathan. Nathan looked back at Addy. Addy felt a pit developing in her belly. Addy recalled how her father,

before he died, asked Addy and Nathan to take care of Courtney when he was gone. Addy promised to do so, of course she
had, but at the time, she didn't think that it meant much more
than including her in the annual Christmas celebration (which
she had not even done last year) and a check-in phone call here
and there (which she had not really done, either).

"You want someone to dance with," Nathan said, under his
breath, as he motioned for the waitress. "I'm going to need
something a bit stronger," he said.

"I'm glad Courtney could be there for you," Addy said to Sy.

"It's only been one date," Sy said, laughing. "But as my grandkids tell me, YOLO!"

Addy and Nathan stared back at the man, slack-jawed.

"It means: you only live once."

"Right," Nathan said, but Addy found she could not speak.

Addy picked up her phone to avoid further conversation and
clicked onto Instagram. Her breath caught in her throat when
she saw the photo that was on the Lizzie and Ritchie's page.
Both girls, standing defiantly in the middle of a New York City
street in bouclé jackets, hands on hips. They weren't smiling;
they didn't even look like themselves. That wasn't the part that
was giving Addy pause, though. It was the fact that the girls
were wearing the jackets with lots of major attitude, but with no
actual pants. The bouclé jackets were clear copies of the iconic
Chanel look, only they hadn't paired them with demure skirts.
Instead, they wore lace boy shorts. Underwear. Emma in hot
pink, Olivia in neon yellow. To cap off the look, they each wore
white knee socks with black high-heeled Mary Janes. A pedo-
phile's dream come true.

Addy texted her daughters.

ADDY: Is this a joke? Take it down.

EMMA: tld u tht u wrnt gonna like

OLIVIA: ???

ADDY: IG. Take it down.

OLIVIA: biggest runway trend. gucci

ADDY: Now.

OLIVIA: Video: Gucci Runway Summer 2022

ADDY: Now.

OLIVIA: also chanel

OLIVIA: Video: Chanel Runway Summer 2022

ADDY: NOW.

Addy refreshed her Instagram over and over, waiting for the image to disappear. When it didn't, she texted Gary.

ADDY: What's the IG password?

GARY: What's IG?

ADDY: Instagram. Take down that photo of the girls.

GARY: What photo?

ADDY: Are you kidding me right now? Check!

GARY: I swear I didn't know about that.

ADDY: Take it down.

GARY: Done.

Addy refreshed her Instagram, and the photo was gone.

Nathan and Sy continued to make small talk, and Addy forced a smile as the truth came into closer focus. Her sister was not, in fact, a successful actress out in LA. Or in Japan, filming commercials. She was, in fact, a young woman who dated older, rich men from the internet for money. And private jets. Her vow to take care of Courtney would take much more than a phone call here or there to fulfill. Addy felt herself sinking into the couch when she considered the myriad ways she'd let her father down.

Sy used the term *sugar baby*, and Addy wondered if that was just a nice way of saying *call girl*. It immediately brought to mind those Elizabeth Taylor movies her mother used to watch on Sunday afternoons. *BUtterfield 8*, that was the one. Her mother loved the scene at the beginning, where the married man left Elizabeth Taylor's character two hundred and fifty dollars after spending the night together. Gloria Wandrous, her character was called. Gloria got so angry that she draped herself in his wife's fur and wrote *No Sale* in lipstick on his mirror.

Courtney seemed to be *For Sale*. And for a lot more than two fifty. The private jet alone probably cost five figures to charter. Maybe Addy should be proud of her sister. No matter your job, you should aim to be good at it. So, good for Courtney. After all, you only live once.

19

Nathan

No one spoke in the cab. Courtney had finally come back downstairs after two hours of hiding in her room. By then, Sy had left. By then, Nathan and Addy had eaten an early lunch, discussed how horribly they'd failed in their promise to their father to take care of Courtney. By then, Nathan and Addy had formulated a plan for what to do with their wayward sister: Courtney would come live with Nathan. She would work in the store with him all day, stay out of trouble, and after a while, maybe even go back to LA. Nathan planned to tell Courtney all this later that night, at dinner.

At the bank, they waited patiently for assistance.

Nathan produced his identification and his father's death certificate. He handed both the copy and the original to the banker.

"I'll just be a moment," the banker said, as he disappeared into a back office.

"Don't forget to get the original back," Addy said to Nathan.

The banker returned a few minutes later. "Now, I don't know what condition the box will be in," he told them, as they walked downstairs to the vault in the basement. The staircase was marble, and Nathan held onto the banister for support. "Some boxes have totally dried out. Some boxes were completely destroyed."

"We understand," Nathan said as they made their way down the stairs. The sound of the banker's leather soles echoed around them.

They walked through two sets of heavy doors before arriving at the area that contained their safe-deposit box.

The banker retrieved the box and led them into a private room to go through its contents. Nathan opened the top, and the smell was overpowering. Seawater lingered on the bottom, and a tiny jewelry box floated as if on a sea of sewage.

"There's nothing inside but this box," Nathan said to himself.

"Maybe the other stuff was destroyed? Cash would have disintegrated in all this water, right?" Courtney said.

"Gary leaves money in his jeans all the time. I run it through the wash, and it never gets destroyed," Addy said, moving closer to Nathan to get a better look. And then, muttering softly as if she were speaking directly to her father: "Why would you open a safe-deposit box for just one item?"

Nathan picked up the small box with two fingers. Setting it down on the counter, he attempted to dry it with the bottom of his shirt. He blotted slowly and methodically. Addy grabbed the box out of his hands and opened it.

Suddenly, no one cared about the smell anymore.

"Oh my God," Courtney said.

"It can't be," Addy said.

"But it is," Nathan said. "The Liz Taylor Ring." He reached for the box in Addy's hands and slipped the ring onto his pinkie finger. There was no mistaking this ring. It was his mother's ring, a D-color, eleven-carat diamond. Perfectly colorless, internally flawless. Given to Lizzie from Ritchie at the end of their nine-month separation in 1992.

"We cannot be looking at the same ring," Addy said, grabbing her brother's hand to take a closer look.

"But we are."

"This is not possible," Courtney said.

"Courtney's right. The ring was stolen in 2008," Addy said.

"I thought it was gambled away in 2006, though," Courtney said. "So, how could it have been stolen in 2008?"

"You're both wrong," Nathan said. "Mom had it in 2015. When Dad died, she slipped it into his casket. Something about paying the ferryman when you reached the underworld."

"Let me get this straight," Addy said. "You saw our mother put a priceless ring in our father's casket, and you didn't think to maybe talk her out of it?"

"I didn't see her do it," Nathan said. "She told me about it after."

"When her Alzheimer's was rapidly progressing."

"That's why she did it," Nathan explained. "I wasn't angry."

"The Alzheimer's is why she told you the story," Addy said. "It isn't true. She couldn't have done that, because the ring was stolen back in 2008. The night of the anniversary party. Mom woke the girls up with her screaming—I think she woke the whole hotel up. She didn't tell anyone, didn't want to worry anyone, but Gary and I both heard it."

"The ring was gambled away in 2006," Courtney said again. "I was there. There was no ring to be placed in a casket by 2015. Or to be stolen in 2008."

"Let me try it on," Addy said, motioning to Nathan's hand. "After all, I'm the oldest, so the ring would go to me anyway."

"I think that Mom would have wanted me to have the ring," Nathan said, curling his hand into a fist. He would not let Addy try it on. Once she put it on her finger, it would be over. She'd insist that the ring belonged to her, and there would be no turning back. But Addy didn't have the same reasons as Nathan for wanting the ring. Addy just wanted it for its value, an insurance policy in case she ever needed to cash in. But to Nathan, this ring was a symbol of his parents' love. Nathan remembered so vividly the day his mother got the ring. How he knew that the ring meant that things would finally change for them, for their family. How his father would finally stop gambling and they could be happy again. And they were.

Nathan thought about his parents' marriage, all the ups and downs. Then, he couldn't help but think of his own marriage.

Nathan looked down at the ring on his finger once again and had only one thought: it's mine.

20

The ring, 1992

"You're trying to make up for your gambling with the fruits of your gambling?"

Ritchie got up from bended knee. He'd thought it would work—he was positive it would. The second he won the ring, he was sure Lizzie would go for it. It was just so bright and shiny. What woman could say no to an eleven-carat sparkler?

But, true. He'd won it gambling. And gambling was the thing that had broken them up in the first place.

After being separated for nine months, Lizzie and Ritchie had been talking more lately, and not just about juggling the kids' schedules. They were enjoying each other's company again. Remembering why they'd fallen in love in the first place. What they had was more than just love, it was bigger than that. It was *fate*. Ritchie couldn't be the only one who felt that way, he was sure of it. (Lizzie felt that way, too, but she wasn't ready to let Ritchie know that just yet.)

"This is the last time," Ritchie said. "I promise."

"You said that the last time."

Ritchie had definitely said that the last time. And Lizzie had believed him, that was the horrible part. But attending the Gamblers Anonymous meetings had only lasted for three months. And now, here he was, fresh off a poker game with a massive diamond ring. What was Lizzie to think?

"It's probably stolen," Lizzie said, turning her back on Ritchie, turning her back on the ring. She didn't want to look at it. Couldn't look at it. She was sure if she looked at it, let herself get seduced by the endless facets of the Asscher cut, its depth, she'd cave. Both to the ring and to letting Ritchie come back.

"It's not," Ritchie said, remembering what Pete the Jeweler had promised, that he'd bought it at an estate sale. "It came with paperwork." He held it out for Lizzie to examine.

Lizzie grabbed the papers and read. She turned them over in her hands, reading every last line, like an accountant would. (Lizzie was not an accountant.) Then, when she'd let him stew for an appropriate amount of time, she put her hand out and let him put the ring on her finger.

"I'll try it on," Lizzie said. "But don't get your hopes up. This doesn't mean anything. I just want to try it on. I mean, when else will I have the chance to try on a ring this big?"

"Absolutely," Ritchie said, his eyes smiling, sliding the ring onto Lizzie's slender finger.

It is an irrefutable fact that when a woman puts a ring that large on her finger, something magical happens. The ring shines more brightly, washed in the glow of the woman wearing it. Her face lights up, brighter than a Christmas tree. And the ring reflects that feeling right back.

Lizzie was glowing. She tried not to smile. "This doesn't mean anything."

"Of course it doesn't."

Lizzie was lying. The ring meant something. The ring meant everything. Two weeks later, Lizzie took Ritchie, and the ring, back. One month later, she was pregnant with Courtney.

Ritchie knew it would work out this way all along. Had practically scripted it already in his mind. They'd get back together, they'd be a family again, and everything would be all right. With the money he'd won in the game, he could put a deposit down on a new house (a smaller house), take the first few steps to getting back to where they'd been before.

The ring would symbolize a new beginning. A fresh start.

But none of that would matter, because six months later, Ritchie would swap that diamond out for a fake.

PART TWO: CLARITY

21

Courtney

This was the solution. This would fix everything. All she really needed was some money. Just to get herself out of debt. Just to give herself a fresh start. The ring was the answer. Courtney asked Siri: How much is an eleven-carat diamond worth? The first website Siri spit out said: up to 2.5 million.

Courtney wanted the ring. So bad she could taste it.

She dressed carefully for dinner with her siblings. She would make a good impression, and show them that she was responsible, fully capable of dealing with the windfall of cash that would come from selling the ring.

"I'm the oldest," Addy said to Nathan for the millionth time.

Her childhood in a nutshell: her siblings having a conversation right in front of her, without including her. It didn't matter that they were at a gorgeous outdoor restaurant in the Caymans; it didn't matter that they'd be flying back to freezing cold New York, first thing in the morning. Being with Addy and Nathan could still make any evening unbearable.

"By eleven months," Nathan said. "You're barely the oldest." He lazily dipped his bread into a pool of olive oil.

"That's not what you said when I turned forty and you were still thirty-nine," Addy said, taking a sip of her wine. "But, seriously, Mom would have wanted me to have the ring. So, it's settled."

Courtney looked from one sibling to another. So, this was why Nathan insisted on putting the ring into his room's vault when they returned from the bank. He didn't trust Addy.

"It is definitely not settled," Nathan said.

"Well, then, let's put this conversation on hold until we get back to New York."

Nathan nodded, but then turned toward Addy, as if remembering something. "Are we about to litigate against each other?"

"I'm not going to litigate against my baby brother," Addy said, her voice singsongy, speaking to Nathan as if he were a child. Another sip of wine. "The girls' soccer coach used to always say—if you have a complaint, wait twenty-four hours until you email me about it. You'd be surprised how much you cool down over the course of a day."

"I'm perfectly cool."

"You seem very cool."

They stared at each other, daring the other to blink first. The waiter came over to the table, and Addy and Nathan gave him their orders.

"And for the young lady?"

Courtney's siblings turned to her, seemingly surprised she was still there.

"I'll have the house salad and the salmon, please."

"Very good. Another glass of wine?"

"I'd love one," Courtney said. And then, to her siblings: "Should we get a bottle?"

"Two glasses is my limit," Addy said. "I can't have more than two."

"We'll take a bottle," Courtney said.

"Court," Nathan said once the waiter was out of earshot, "what do you think we should do about the ring?"

"Easy. We should sell it and split the cash."

Nathan gasped. He actually gasped. Even though he no longer acted, her brother still had a flair for the dramatic. But he was so transparent. Perhaps this was why he'd never made it as an actor?

Addy rolled her eyes. Then, speaking to Nathan as if Courtney were not there: "We need to handle this."

"It's a family heirloom," Nathan said to Courtney. "So, selling it is out of the question. And anyway, we have more pressing matters to deal with. Like the Sy situation."

The mention of Sy's name made Courtney choke on her wine. "There's no Sy situation. I met him on a stupid website. It was a mistake. But he's completely harmless. And very nice. He's letting us take the jet home tomorrow. You're welcome."

"He does seem very nice," Nathan said, looking to Addy for validation.

"And you're lucky you didn't get hurt," Addy said. It seemed like they were speaking from a script. "But we don't want you out there, doing dangerous things like that. If you're having money troubles, why not just sell the apartment Mom and Dad got you?"

Courtney held her breath.

"Diego and I could help you out, tide you over."

"I'm not looking for a handout," Courtney said, but as the words came out of her mouth, she realized that a handout was exactly what she was looking for. Somehow if the handout came in the form of a payout of the ring, it would be different. An inheritance sounded better than a handout, didn't it?

"Well, I'd rather you take a handout," Nathan said, looking to Addy for confirmation, then continuing in a whisper: "than resort to...you know."

"No," Courtney whispered back. "I don't know."

"We're totally sex positive here," Nathan whispered. "We just don't want you selling your body for money, because you could get really hurt. We'll help."

"I went on *one date* from this sugar daddy website."

"Sugar baby, call girl, it doesn't matter," Addy said. "We're going to help."

"It *does* matter," Courtney said. "Those are two completely different things."

"Are they?" Nathan asked, under his breath.

"They are," Courtney said, sending an angry glare in her brother's direction. "I haven't even kissed Sy. He just paid me to take me out for a night."

"He paid you to take you out?" Nathan parroted back. "And then gave you a jet? For nothing in return?"

"That's how it works."

"That's not how the world works." Courtney flinched at Addy's words. It's not as if Addy had any idea how the world worked. She'd been a stay-at-home mom for the past sixteen years. What did she know about being on your own? Making a dream come true? Losing it all, only to have to start over again?

"It doesn't matter what we call it. Clearly, everything is not okay," Nathan said. "We're going to take care of you, just like Dad wanted."

"What's that supposed to mean?" Courtney asked.

"Before he died," Addy said, "Dad made us promise to always take care of you. Obviously, we haven't done a very good job of it, but we're here to help now."

Courtney wanted to say *I don't need your help,* but she found that she couldn't get the words out. She was struck by what Addy was saying to her, that her father had asked them to take care of her. As if she couldn't take care of herself. (It was completely beside the point that she, at present, could not.)

"You'll stay with Nathan and Diego for now. We'll know that you're safe, and to make a little money, you can work with

Nathan and Gary in the store. We'll help you get your condo sublet in the meantime."

Courtney didn't know what to address first: that she had no intention of living with Nathan and Diego, or that the condo their parents had bought for her was long gone?

"If we just sell the ring and split the money," Courtney carefully said, "then I think I can get back on my feet in LA, and we don't have to do this whole fake family intervention thing."

"It's not fake," Nathan said. "We care about you."

"We're worried about you." Addy reached across the table to grab her sister's hand.

"You're not worried about me," Courtney said, pulling her hand away. "You made it clear you don't care. You're just doing this because of some promise to Dad. And because you don't want to sell the ring."

"We're certainly not going to sell a family heirloom," Addy said, shrugging her shoulders, and looking around the restaurant, as if searching for someone to agree with her.

Nathan nodded. "One of us will keep the ring. The ring will stay in the family."

Courtney thought, but did not say: *Not if I can get my hands on it first.*

22

Addy

Addy wanted the ring.

The ring symbolized security. Security for her mother all those years ago, safe in the knowledge that she could always sell the ring, in case things ever got bad financially again. Security for Addy, too, all those years ago, because the ring meant her family was coming back together and the separation was only temporary, not permanent. Her family was intact.

Addy began to unpack. She brought her toiletries to the bathroom vanity and put her dirty clothes into the laundry basket. Every time she went back to her suitcase, she kept thinking the ring would be inside. And every time, she remembered that Nathan had insisted on taking it home himself, instead.

The ring was owed to her. It was really that simple, wasn't it? After all, Addy was the eldest sibling.

Addy was responsible for everything. And now that ring— her mother's ring—should be hers. After she got pregnant so young and couldn't take her rightful place in the business next to her father, she was owed. After having to deal with Nathan and Gary acting as if they were the ones who made the store profitable, she was owed. After raising their children and minding their home without ever a thank you, she was owed.

When her husband took over the family business, whose idea had it been to get her brother involved? When her mother's Alzheimer's had gotten bad, who took her to the endless doctor's appointments, who got her settled with in-home care? And now, upon discovering that Courtney was working as a call girl (sugar baby, call girl, was there any difference?), whose idea was it to take care of her, move her into Nathan and Diego's place, and fulfill the vow they'd made to their father?

Addy took off her diamond solitaire necklace and diamond stud earrings and placed them on the tray on her bedside table. Maybe she wouldn't put them back in the safe. Maybe she would start wearing them every day. Maybe she would wear the ring every day, too, once it was back in her hands.

At least Addy no longer had to wonder why there was a safe-deposit box down in the Caymans. The box hadn't revealed some new secret her father had kept hidden. Nothing had changed. Her father was still the person she'd thought he was. Flawed, yes, deeply, but also devoted to her mother. Devoted to his children, his family. There hadn't been an affair or some other seedy reason for the box. She didn't need to defend her father's honor.

The only thing that mattered now was what had been inside the box. The only thing that mattered now was the ring.

"Maybe you *should* sell it," Gary said as he lay down on their bed. "Maybe that's not the worst idea after all."

Addy stopped unpacking. She turned toward her husband, her face on fire.

"Whoa, truce," he said, throwing his hands up in the air, a surrender.

"I will not sell a family heirloom. That ring brought my family back together. When I look at it, I think about how it signaled the end of the worst period of my life. That ring made my family whole again."

Gary regarded her. "Three days ago, you had no idea the ring still existed."

"What is your point?"

Gary looked down at his hands. He spoke thoughtfully: "Neither you nor Nathan want to sell, but you both want it. You can't both have it, though. At least if you sell the ring, you both walk away with something."

Addy didn't answer. Suddenly, the idea of unpacking her carry-on bag seemed like an insurmountable task. She lay down on the bed next to her husband. He reached for her hand, but she instead used both hands to grab the comforter and drew it up to her neck.

"Hey, did you know that before Richard Burton gifted the ring to Elizabeth Taylor, it was owned by Vera Krupp?"

Addy didn't respond.

"I just Googled it. The Krupps were German arms manufacturers who supplied weapons to the Nazis. Elizabeth Taylor loved this little factoid. She said that the ring belonged with a nice Jewish girl like herself."

Addy poked her head out from the blanket. "Is that true?"

Gary smiled and handed Addy his phone. "See for yourself."

"Anybody home?" Olivia's voice rang out from the mudroom downstairs.

"Up here!" Addy and Gary called out in unison. They listened as Olivia stomped up the back staircase. Addy could always tell which child was coming up the steps—Olivia's heavy footsteps made her presence known, but Emma was quiet, like a cat.

"Welcome back," Olivia said, as she hugged her mother and then nudged her over so that she could lie down beside her.

Emma followed closely on her sister's heels. "So, was there anything good down there?"

Addy groaned in response.

"So...no?"

"Wemissedyou,"Oliviasaid."DidyouhaveanyfunintheCaymans?"

"No." Addy answered truthfully. The trip had not been fun.

"Did you find anything good?" Olivia asked.

"Dibs!" Emma said.

"You can't call dibs on something before we even know what it is," Olivia said.

"Oh, really?" Emma said. "I think I just did."

"It was my mother's ring," Addy said quietly.

"I thought you said the ring was stolen?" Emma said.

"Apparently, it was not," Addy said.

"What was it doing down in the Caymans?" Olivia asked.

"I don't know how it got there," Addy said. "But the important thing is figuring out who it belongs to."

"Me," Emma said. "I just called dibs. Hand it over."

"Uncle Nathan has it," Addy said.

"You gave it to Uncle Nathan?" Emma said. "You said you would give me anything you found in that box!"

"Do you really think she's going to give a sixteen-year-old an eleven-carat diamond?" Olivia asked. "Use your brain for a minute."

"Girls," Gary said. He typically just said this one word and waited for Addy to fill in the rest. But Addy was too tired. Sometimes Gary would say it a second time, waiting for Addy to deal with the conflict. "Girls!"

Addy ignored him again. She closed her eyes and rubbed her bare feet against her fluffy comforter, her soft sheets. Maybe she would just stay in bed for the rest of the afternoon.

"Let's give your mom some time to unpack," Gary said, corralling the girls out of the bedroom and down the stairs. He didn't close the door behind himself, so Addy could hear them situating themselves downstairs, turning on the television, and carrying on a conversation about what was in the vault.

Addy kept her eyes closed. Her thoughts drifted as she took a deep breath in. Maybe they *should* just sell the ring. Maybe Gary was right. (A smaller thought, pushed away: maybe Courtney was right.) She certainly wasn't going to fight with her brother over a ring. And in a true compromise, no one is completely happy. For either sibling to end up with the ring, that would make one sibling wildly happy and the other incredibly disappointed. If they split the proceeds, they'd both be slightly unhappy, but at least have some money to split.

And this idea that she deserved it. It was somewhat childish, wasn't it? Did anyone really deserve an eleven-carat ring? It was a ridiculous extravagance, one that Addy didn't need. After all, she didn't need it as an insurance policy like her mother had— Addy didn't have a husband who gambled. And, being the product of a father who did, Addy had a number of small nest eggs stashed away. She had 529 college savings plans for both girls, fully funded. She had money in savings accounts, CDs, and a few other conservative investments, too. She certainly didn't need a ring to prove that her husband loved her, or that she had enough money in the bank, or to make her more secure than she'd already made herself.

Still, Addy couldn't help it: she wanted the ring. It was a piece of her father. A piece of her mother. A physical symbol of their family coming back together as a unit again after the separation. Addy wanted that feeling of wearing it, of her parents still with her, by her side.

And if a pair of diamond studs made her feel invincible, imagine what an eleven-carat sparkler could do.

23

Courtney

The fire started innocently enough.

After they all settled in at Nathan and Diego's place, Courtney suggested that she cook dinner. She had planned to make the steaks she'd found in the freezer. Courtney pulled up a recipe on her phone, and it seemed easy. *Step one: heat up a good olive oil in the pan before adding the steak. Steaks can be cooked from frozen without defrosting first.* Nathan and Diego had a completely stocked kitchen, so she got the good olive oil heating up while she got the meat out of the wrapping paper. As soon as the first steak was ready to go, Courtney turned to the burners and saw that the pan had caught fire.

What she should have done was to call for help. Nathan and Diego would know what to do. But how could she admit she couldn't heat up a few steaks? What she should have done was to cover the pan, rob the fire of oxygen. Simply placing the pan's cover on top would have done the trick. But how was she supposed to know that? What she should have done was to douse the fire in baking soda, which would have put it out immediately. There was a large box of baking soda in the cabinet to the left of the stove, and another one in the fridge. But she did not do that. Courtney did not do any of those things.

What she *did* do was the opposite of what you are supposed to do when you have a grease fire: she panicked. She used the pot filler on the wall to fill the pan with water. Cold water, she reasoned, would immediately put the fire out.

It did not. The water from the pot filler made the fire rage completely out of control, and before Courtney had a second to blink, the fire had leapt up to the range hood and climbed past it. Flames engulfed the hood and the surrounding cabinets, and then made their way up to the twelve-foot ceiling, traveling across the length of the loft. By the time Nathan and Diego heard Courtney screaming in the kitchen, their loft was on fire.

Diego grabbed Courtney, and brought her down to the ground. Nathan ran back into the bedroom, and Diego screamed at him to leave everything, nothing was worth dying for. With Nathan now at their side, they crawled out of the loft. Once in the hallway, Nathan pulled the fire alarm and then used the Emergency Call feature on his phone. Diego dragged Courtney down the stairs while Nathan made sure that their downstairs neighbors got out.

By the time they made their way out into the street, the fire trucks were already there.

"I'm so sorry," Courtney said, still dazed as she sat on the sidewalk across from their building.

"It's okay," Diego said quietly. "As long as everyone is all right, that's all that matters." He looked over at Nathan, who was accounting for all the people and pets who lived in their six-story building. Everyone who had been home had made it out safely, it seemed. And the fire had been contained to their apartment only.

"We're going to check the walls for hidden fires," the fire chief told Nathan, "but it looks like we were able to get here in time."

"Thank you for everything," he replied.

Courtney tried to catch Nathan's eye, tried to apologize directly to him, but he would not acknowledge her. He was staring down at his hand. Specifically, the huge sparkler that he now wore on his pinky finger. They say that when people lose their homes in a fire, the thing they run back for is family photographs. But that wasn't what Nathan had gone back for.

Nathan had saved the ring.

An hour later, the building was cleared for reentry. By then, their downstairs neighbors had already decamped to their place in the Hamptons. But the fire chief assured everyone that the building was safe to enter and safe to sleep in that night.

As they made their way slowly back up to the loft, Courtney tried to apologize again, but Diego simply nodded and told her that accidents happened. Nathan closed his eyes and took in deep breaths through his nose, out his mouth. Diego seemed willing to forgive her, but Courtney wasn't looking for his forgiveness. She needed Nathan's.

The door was still open, the way they'd left it. The entire loft was covered in soot. Courtney saw Diego's shoulders stoop slightly as he took it all in. The smell was overpowering. Like burnt cashmere, or a dog that's been left out in the rain.

"I'm so sorry," she said. Why did she think she could cook a gourmet meal for her brother and brother-in-law in their gorgeous Soho loft? The last three meals she'd made at Chrissy's tiny one-bedroom had been mac and cheese out of a box.

"Accidents happen, sweetheart," Diego said. And then, to Nathan: "Didn't Simon have that company he used when his Fire Island bungalow flooded? A restoration expert?"

"Texting him now." Nathan started typing away on his phone. He refused to look up at Courtney, busying himself with the work at hand. The enormous ring on his pinky finger shone, even through the dust that settled all around the loft. With the apartment on fire, Nathan had run back for the ring. Why hadn't Courtney thought of that?

Diego opened the windows. "Courtney, why don't you go and wash your face, freshen up?"

"I don't want to freshen up," she said. "I want to help clean up."

"You have oil splatters all over your face," Diego said, walking over to her. He brushed his thumb across her cheek. "You need to get some bacitracin on this. These burns are small, and don't look serious, but you need to treat them. Your pretty face."

"Simon says he'll text the owner for us," Nathan reported, face still buried in his phone, typing away.

"Wonderful," Diego said, attempting to smile. Diego trying to smile while his beautiful loft was completely destroyed made Courtney ache deep in her belly.

"I don't care about my face," Courtney said. "I want to help."

"There's nothing to do," Diego assured her. "It's sad, but we're so lucky that no one was hurt. That's all that really matters."

"The owner texted me back," Nathan said, his voice monotone. "He'll get a team here tomorrow. He said to just leave a key downstairs with the doorman."

"That's a great idea. Maybe we should stay at my parents' place for the night?" Diego said, his face lighting up at the idea. "They could have the guest quarters ready for us by the time we get uptown."

Courtney felt herself perking up, too. The idea of staying at Pedro Garcia Flores' Central Park West penthouse sounded like heaven.

"Oh," Nathan said, finally looking up. "I already texted Addy."

24

Courtney

Duke did not like Courtney. Wasn't that a thing, Courtney thought, animals being good judges of character? Her sister's eight-year-old rescue dog, a mastiff mix with a rich chocolate brown coat, had not stopped bothering her, jumping all over her, since Courtney had walked in the door. Her friend Chrissy's dog had loved her. What was this dog's problem?

"You should change," Diego whispered to Courtney. "The grease on your shirt is making the dog go crazy."

"You can shower in my room," Emma said.

"Duke's just hungry," Addy explained. "C'mere, boy!" She clapped her hands twice, and Duke followed her happily into the kitchen. Courtney could have sworn she'd seen Addy use the same trick with Gary.

"There are towels in the closet," Emma said. "And you can borrow anything you want from my closet."

"That's so sweet," Courtney said. Even though she hadn't seen her niece in two years, it was as if no time had passed.

"I'm happy you're here," Emma said, as she quietly closed the door to the bathroom to give Courtney privacy.

Courtney turned on the shower. It was a bit cold and would need time to warm up, and she realized that she'd left her bag downstairs in the hallway. She left the water running as she went downstairs to retrieve it.

"Jesus Christ," she heard Addy say. "What a shitshow."

Courtney realized, all at once, that Addy was talking about her, assuming that she was upstairs in the shower. Courtney stood in the foyer, frozen in place, listening to her siblings talk about her in the family room.

"I know," Nathan said, his voice filled with anger. He had tried to keep his cool on the drive out from the city, but Courtney knew he was furious. How could he not be? She only wished he would have talked to her about it. Let her apologize. "Could you believe this?"

"Accidents happen," Diego said. "We're lucky no one was hurt."

"I think we all could use a drink," Gary said. Courtney heard the glasses clink over at the bar cart.

"Agreed," Addy said. "Nathan, let's get the ring into the wall safe."

"I'll just hold onto it, if you don't mind," Nathan said.

"It's an eleven-carat diamond," Addy said, laughter in her voice. "We can't just leave it sitting out."

"Addy's right," Diego said, his voice soft. "It should be in the safe."

"What's the code to the safe?" Nathan asked. He sounded like a petulant child.

Addy laughed again, louder this time. "Are you kidding? You don't trust me?"

"The code is Ritchie's birthday," Gary said. "Now, who's ready for a drink?"

Courtney stood in the hallway, next to the large console, listening as Gary opened a bottle of wine and served it to her siblings and brother-in-law. She then heard the singsongy tones of a keypad. Addy must have put the ring into her wall safe. She heard six chimes ring out, not just four, so the code was her father's full birthday: 04–28–51.

"What are we going to do with her?" Addy said.

"There's nothing to do," Diego said. "She's a grown-up. We just help her get back on her feet."

"She was selling herself on the internet," Nathan said. "She needs more than just to get back on her feet."

"Why don't we sell the LA apartment and move her back out here where we can keep an eye on her?" Gary said.

"We can't tell her what to do," Diego said. "She's not your child. She's your sister-in-law."

"Diego's right. We need to make her think it's her idea," Addy said.

Courtney held her hand over her mouth so that she wouldn't gasp out loud. She knew her sister was a bitch, but thought she was more of a garden-variety bitch. She hadn't realized Addy was capable of this level of deviousness.

"I think if we just explain—" Gary began, only to be cut off by Nathan.

"She burned down our apartment," Nathan said, raising his voice. "She's out in LA working as a sugar baby. She's putting herself in danger. This is a train wreck."

"Let's keep our voices down," Gary said.

"Nathan's right," Addy said. "That guy who showed up in the Caymans was nice, she lucked out. But what other men has she been out with? She could have been hurt. She could have been killed. We promised our father we'd look out for her."

"She just needs a little love. A little TLC," Diego said. "She doesn't even look like herself. A few weeks with us is exactly what the doctor ordered."

"She needs a lot more than that," Addy said. "She needs—"

Olivia's heavy footsteps came hurling down the staircase,

making the adults go silent. Courtney remained frozen in place, hoping her niece wouldn't notice her standing there.

"Aren't you in the shower?" Olivia asked. Emma followed close behind, with Duke on her heels. Duke barked like crazy as soon as he saw Courtney.

"Your dog does not seem to like me," Courtney said, laughing self-consciously. Olivia raised her eyebrows in lieu of a response.

"He just needs to get to know you, is all," Emma said. "Here, give him a treat."

She showed Courtney to the pantry while Olivia ran upstairs to turn the shower off. Emma pointed to a big box on one of the higher shelves, and Courtney got on her tippy-toes to reach it. She gave Duke one of his favorite treats. And just like that, he was putty in her hands.

"It's settled," Addy said to Courtney, walking into the kitchen, nursing a glass of red wine. Like she was the mama duck, everyone followed Addy. "Everyone will stay with us for a while. Get things back on track."

"Everything's perfectly on track," Courtney said. "I think maybe I should head back to LA."

"Do you have another private jet waiting for you?" Nathan asked, looking at Addy instead of at Courtney. "Or do you need a night or two to set something like that up?" Diego placed a hand on Nathan's shoulder and Nathan shrugged it off.

"I can make my own way home," Courtney said. She thought about the code to the safe. How easy it would be to simply grab the ring and then hop on a red-eye back to LA.

"Can you?" Nathan asked, his eyes narrowing.

"I think that's enough," Diego said quietly to Nathan.

"You're all staying here," Addy said. "You can spend time with me, spend time with the girls, and we can figure out how to move forward with everything. Make sure you're all taken care of."

Courtney looked around to each of the adults, practically

begging each one to take her side, to back her up. But it was clear that they were all on the same side, united, and Courtney stood alone, a team of one. Even Duke had moved away from her and stood firmly at attention at Addy's side.

"What can I do to get you settled in?" Addy asked Courtney.

"I'll have a glass of wine."

25

Lizzie, 1978

"Try this," Ritchie said, and he held out a slice of mango for Lizzie to taste.

They sat on a large blanket in the middle of the park. Ritchie had found a spot under a huge tree, one with the perfect amount of shade. This was something Lizzie would come to appreciate about Ritchie—he always knew the best spots to go, always knew where to sit, be it a concert, a restaurant, or even just the park, and he always knew how to find a fun time. How to make the best out of every situation. It was such a contrast to her home life, where her parents couldn't be happy unless everything was in its perfect place, everything going according to plan.

"Good, right?" Ritchie asked, as Lizzie murmured in delight. "They're hard to come by, but I know a guy who gets them shipped up from Florida."

"I've never tasted something like this," Lizzie said. The mango was sweet and juicy. She could still taste it on her lips.

"Tastes like heaven, doesn't it?"

"It does."

Ritchie took a piece of mango from the Tupperware con-

tainer and popped it in his mouth. Lizzie could see the edges of
his lips curl as the sweetness reached his tongue.

"Want another bite?" Ritchie asked, holding out another piece
of mango.

"Yes," Lizzie said. As she bit down, the juice ran down her
chin, and she quickly brought the napkin up to her face.

Ritchie leaned over and gave her a gentle kiss. His lips were
sticky and sweet. "Tell me something true."

Lizzie couldn't think of a thing to say. No one had ever asked
her something like that before. In her experience, the few boys
she'd dated only wanted to try to make out with her, see how
far she'd let them go. They certainly didn't care about learning
anything about her, much less something true.

"What?" Ritchie asked, laughter in his voice. "You don't
know anything true?"

"I do," Lizzie said, laughing along despite herself. "I just can't
think of anything."

"You can't think of anything?" Ritchie said. "I can think of
a million things—it's a beautiful day today. I'm sitting with a
beautiful girl. I feel good. All stuff that's true."

"Well, aren't you a poet?"

Ritchie looked down at his lap. "Maybe I am."

"I adored the letter you wrote me after our second date,"
Lizzie said. "I've never gotten a love letter before."

Ritchie held Lizzie's gaze, but didn't immediately speak. He
took a deep breath. "Can I show you something?"

"Sure."

"Read you something, actually," Ritchie said, as he wiggled
a bit to grab something from his back pocket. He pulled out a
notebook.

"Another love letter?" Lizzie asked. "A whole notebook of
them?"

"I bring a notebook with me everywhere I go. A little habit
I started years ago, when a teacher suggested it to the class as a

way to document your life, see where you've been. Writing every day was a class assignment, but I guess I just never stopped."

"Really?" Lizzie was surprised she hadn't noticed it before.

"Yeah, I write everything down. Sometimes it's a sentence or two about my day. Sometimes it's a draft of a love letter," Ritchie said, a sly smile playing on his lips. "I have something I want to read to you."

Ritchie read from his notebook:

Sometimes, when I see you, I think it's not real
That someone so fair, so beautiful should be mine.
But then you look at me, with those bright eyes of yours
And I feel like I could conquer the world.
How do you do this thing you do to me?

"So, you *are* a poet," Lizzie said, feeling a flush in her cheeks. Somehow, Ritchie reading his poem out loud seemed more intimate than anything else they'd done together. "It's beautiful."

"I wrote it the day after we met. For the second time, I mean."

"It's lovely."

Ritchie ran his hand through his hair and looked away. "You don't think it's stupid?"

"No. Can I see more?" Lizzie grabbed the notebook from Ritchie's hands and flipped to the page after the poem he'd just read. "*Spinks vs. Ali, 9–15–78. Ali 2 ½ to 1 favorite.* What's that?"

"Like I said, I use the notebook for everything. My poems, random thoughts—"

"Boxing matches you plan to gamble on?" Lizzie knew that this was part of the reason her mother called him a *degenerate*, because Ritchie and his friends liked to gamble, but Lizzie found it sexy. Exciting. And anyway, her sister had married the *right* sort of man from the *right* sort of family, and look where that had gotten her.

"Yeah, that, too." Ritchie smiled at Lizzie, and in that smile, she could see her future unfold with him: a big, beautiful wedding that would be the envy of her mother's friends, exactly two perfect children—a girl and a boy—and then growing old together, side by side, still holding hands the way they did now.

"Let's see what else is in here," Lizzie said, as she flipped the page. "This is just a list of words: *pulchritudinous, bewitching, resplendent, sublime.*"

"Sometimes if I hear a word I like, I write it down," he said, running his hand through his hair again. "Those are words that remind me of you."

"Lemme get this straight: under this tough exterior, you're just a softie?"

"I am *not* a softie," Ritchie said, taking the notebook away and putting it back into his pocket. "If you had a list of words to describe me, *softie* would not be on the list."

"Hey, I wasn't done reading!"

"You're done."

"Come on," Lizzie said, leaning in toward Ritchie. The edges of his mouth were turned down, even though he tried to give off his usual devil-may-care attitude. He was trying to hide it, but she could tell she'd hurt his feelings. "I can't be the first girl to tease you about these romantic notebooks."

"You're the first one I ever let look at them," Ritchie said quietly, as if in prayer.

"You've never shown these to another girl?"

"I've never shown them to another living human."

"Not even Ace?" Lizzie joked.

"You think I don't like you more than I like Ace?"

Lizzie laughed. "I don't know."

Ritchie pulled her closer. "Not even Ace. Not even my own mother."

Lizzie leaned in. Ritchie put one hand onto her cheek, and she drew her arms around his neck.

"Why did you let me read it, then?"

"I wouldn't say I let you," Ritchie said, the edges of his lips pulling upward. "I'd say you grabbed it out of my hands forcefully."

Lizzie laughed. "You read me the poem. And I loved it. Can you blame me for wanting more?"

"There's something about you," Ritchie said quietly. "I don't know what it is. But being around you makes me want to lay myself bare. Makes me want to know everything about you. And I want you to know everything about me."

"Is this just a line?" Lizzie asked, narrowing her eyes. "Is this something you say to all the girls?"

"This is not something I've ever said to another girl."

Lizzie didn't answer. She didn't know what to say. Then: "There's something about you, too. I've never felt this way about any other man."

Ritchie leaned in to Lizzie slowly. His kiss was tender and soft. Lizzie thought that if the world were to end at that very instant, she would feel she'd lived a very full life, having experienced Ritchie's kiss.

When they kissed, it felt like the whole world narrowed down to the tiny space between them. When they kissed, Lizzie felt it go through her heart, down her spine, into every last nook of her body. When they kissed, Lizzie never wanted it to end.

26

Ritchie, 1978

Ritchie courted Lizzie the only way he knew how: the old-fashioned way. The way his father taught him. He hadn't taught him much, but his father did show him the proper way to woo a woman: love letters. So many love letters. He wrote them all the time. Scribbled in the tiny notebooks he carried in his back pocket, wherever he went, then rewritten in script on crisp linen notecards he bought at the fancy stationery shop in town. He composed them in his head when he was at the racetrack, taking notes on the backs of his tickets. He jotted down his thoughts on the backs of bowling scorecards, when the guys weren't looking. If he thought of the perfect word or learned a new one to describe Lizzie—*pulchritudinous*—he'd write it on the back of his hand, and later record it in his notebook.

Ritchie knew that Lizzie's family didn't approve of his lifestyle. The gambling, the pool halls. The jumping from job to job, never settling on a career. He knew that if he wanted Lizzie's family to accept him, he'd have to stop gambling, start making an honest living. So that was the plan. Ace had a lead on a job at an advertising firm in Manhattan. Ritchie knew he'd be a pro at it, make lots of money.

Ritchie had told the guys that he wouldn't be gambling at Ace's bachelor party in Atlantic City (it would be the first of four bachelor parties he'd attend in his lifetime for Ace, first of four weddings to women all named Susan). Drinking, sure. Partying? Most definitely. But at that exact point in time, Ritchie had fallen head over heels in love with Lizzie, and was going to clean up his ways.

But it was one of those perfect nights, when the stars come into alignment, and you just can't do any wrong. The group had decided to hit the craps table before dinner. Poker was his bread and butter, but even Ritchie had to admit, craps was more fun. More social. And a craps table accommodates sixteen—the exact number of men in Ace's bridal party.

Ritchie immediately sensed that the table was hot. For starters, he knew the pit boss who was on that night, and he'd already comped Ritchie's room and lunch at the buffet. The boxman at the table was also named Ace, which was lucky, and the two dealers calling the game were guys Ritchie knew well. Dealers he'd always won with.

Ritchie stood behind Ace, delivering a Dark and Stormy, his favorite drink, to the groom. See, Ritchie thought, casinos can be fun even if you're not gambling! Fourteen of the guys from the wedding party stood at the table with Ace.

"Only one open spot, Ritchie," Ace said. "It's got your name on it."

Ritchie resisted at first. But after Ace threw six opening sevens in a row, earning all of his buddies money over and over again, Ritchie couldn't hold off any longer. You'd be a fool to let Lady Luck go when she came calling for you.

"If I hit one more seven—that's seven sevens in a row—it's a sign. It means you have to play," Ace said. Ritchie could not argue with this logic.

Ace hit another seven, and Ritchie slid in next to him, ready to play. Who could argue with a sign from above? He threw five one hundred dollar bills onto the table, and watched as the boxman made those bills disappear. The dealer slid the chips Ritchie's way and wished him good luck.

"I don't need luck," Ritchie said. "I've got the groom."

Ace smiled and threw another seven. Ritchie immediately doubled his pass line bet, turning fifty bucks magically into one hundred. Next, Ace threw a six, and that became the point for the rest of the game. All the men backed up their bets, and placed bets on the other numbers on the table. They just needed Ace to throw a six again before he threw another seven.

Ace threw number after number. Eights, fives, fours, and nines. No sixes, but no sevens, either. As he threw the dice, his friends won more and more money. The table began to attract a crowd: a hot table with sixteen young guys all hooting and hollering and getting drunker by the minute on free drinks will do that in AC.

From across the table, Ace's cousin yelled to Ritchie, "I'm feeling a Yo. How about you?"

The Yo Eleven. One of the riskiest bets on the table. The payout was 15 to 1. A sucker's bet. But a fun bet.

"I'm feeling Yo," Ritchie called back, and he threw a one hundred dollar chip onto the table. Ace's cousin did the same.

Ace threw the dice, and the dealer called out the number. "Yo Eleven."

He'd just won fifteen hundred dollars.

The stickman passed the dice back to Ace so fast, Ritchie could barely process that he'd won. He picked up his winnings as Ace got ready to throw again.

"I've got another Yo in me," Ace said. "I feel it in my bones. If the waitresscomesbackwithourdrinksbeforeIroll,it'sasign.ItmeansI'll rollanotherYo."Asthewordsescapedhislips,thewaitressroundedthe corner. Ace laughed out loud. He threw a hundred dollar chip onto the table and Ritchie did the same.

Ace threw the dice, and the dealer called it out again. "Yo Eleven."

"Yo Eleven!" the table cried out in unison. Most of the men had won fifteen hundred dollars on their hundred dollar Yo bets.

"Press it?" the dealer asked.

"Press my Yo!" Ace's cousin screamed from across the table. He was planning to leave the fifteen hundred he'd just won on the Yo Eleven on the table, and let it ride. How drunk was he? Ritchie had already downed two gin and tonics, but he still had it together.

"Sir?" the dealer asked Ritchie.

"Okay," Ace said to Ritchie, "if the next woman that walks by this table is a blonde, it'll be another Yo."

Ritchie looked up, and sure enough, a blonde walked right by their table. "Holy shit."

"I'll throw you another Yo," Ace assured him, and Ritchie believed him.

"Why the fuck not?" Ritchie said. After all, it was a bachelor party, and he was there to have fun.

Ace gathered the dice in his hands and blew on them, before letting them rip across the table.

"Yo Eleven," the dealer announced.

The crowd erupted in cheer. Ritchie looked down at the table. He'd just won twenty-four thousand dollars. Coupled with the winnings from hitting his number over and over, Ritchie was now up over sixty thousand dollars for the night.

A reasonable person would have gathered his chips and left the table. But that was not something Ritchie could do. It was not something Ritchie ever could have done.

Ace threw the dice again, and the dealer called out the number. "Seven out."

"I was ready for dinner, anyway," Ace said with a laugh.

The men grabbed their chips and made their way to the cage to cash out.

But Ritchie wasn't done. On the way over to the cashier, he made a detour at the roulette pit.

"If the guy with the vest hits one of his numbers," Ritchie told Ace, "it means I'll win if I play."

"Not gonna happen," Ace said, and they watched the metal ball spin around the roulette wheel.

"Thirty-four, red," the dealer announced. The guy with the vest cheered as one of his four-way bets paid off.

Ritchie looked at Ace. Ace looked back at Ritchie. "I stand corrected."

Ritchie threw down a thousand dollar bet on twenty-two, his lucky number. A single number has 37 to 1 odds, paying out at 35 to 1. The guys all watched to see what would happen next. Some cheered and encouraged him to make the bet. The ones who weren't as drunk told him he was crazy to try it.

But Ritchie wasn't listening to them. He was listening to that little voice in his head, the one that always said: *more*. He did it for fun. He did it to show off, *look at how little a grand means to me*. He did it because he couldn't *not* do it.

"No more bets," the dealer said as he sent the ball spinning. The roulette wheel spun round and round. Ritchie couldn't take his eyes off it, mesmerized. The ball teetered before falling into its final spot.

"Twenty-two black," the dealer called out.

Ritchie paid for dinner that night, barely making a dent in the additional thirty-five thousand dollars he'd won at roulette. And the pit boss comped all the bachelor party's rooms.

Ritchie would clean up his act another day.

27

The ring, 1993

Ritchie needed to clean up his act. It had been two months since he'd swapped Lizzie's diamond out for a fake, and so far, Lizzie was none the wiser. He just needed one big score to buy the diamond back. Make things right again.

At a wedding, one should focus on the bride. Lizzie had her eye on the bride, ready to throw her bouquet. All the other guests had their eyes on the bride. But Ritchie did not. Ritchie could not stop staring at Lizzie's ring.

Here's what we know: Ritchie had sold the diamond back to Pete the Jeweler six months after giving the ring to Lizzie. He'd had to—he couldn't come up with the money for a down payment on the new house without it, and after their nine-month separation, he wanted things to go smoothly. He figured he'd just temporarily use the diamond as a piggy bank, buy it back once he was flush again.

Lizzie was completely in the dark. She didn't know the ring she'd been wearing for the past year hadn't been real. Well, the ring was real, it was the diamond that was fake. Pete insisted that Ritchie keep the setting and only sell the stone. He put a high-quality cubic zirconia in its place and promised Ritchie that Lizzie would not be able to tell the difference.

Pete the Jeweler was correct.

Still, Ritchie wanted to buy back the real diamond. Even though there was only a small chance she'd figure it out, he didn't like those odds. He didn't think he could survive her leaving him again. Their nine months apart had been torture. He needed Lizzie. Needed her like he needed oxygen.

"A dime says the brunette catches the bouquet," Ace said to Ritchie. Lizzie overheard and threw both men a dirty look.

Lizzie and Ritchie had been having a great night together—dancing and smiling, their nine-month separation a distant memory. Their bond even stronger, now that Lizzie was pregnant with their third child. But Ritchie had promised his gambling days were over, and just the mention of gambling, the mere whiff of it, put Lizzie in a mood. And here was Ace, offering Ritchie a bet.

"I don't gamble anymore," Ritchie said, making a big show of it. "You know that, Ace."

"Oh, I'm so sorry. Yes, you told me that, and I respect that decision," Ace said, theatrically, wife number three, Sookie, standing dutifully by his side, oblivious to the conversation going on beside her. "I forgot. Forgive me, Lizzie."

Lizzie pursed her lips. It was her tell, and its meaning was clear: she was pissed.

Lizzie crossed her arms and directed her attention to the dance floor, where the bride tossed her bouquet. One of the bridesmaids caught it, and Lizzie clapped along with the rest of the wedding guests.

Ritchie felt a tiny ping when the brunette didn't catch it, knowing he could have made an easy thousand off Ace if he'd taken that action. He rubbed his temples and let out a sigh.

"Say our goodbyes?" Lizzie asked Ritchie, spinning on her heel to leave before Ritchie had a chance to respond.

"Don't you want a slice of cake?"

"No."

"They say it's good luck to have a bite of wedding cake," Ritchie said in a singsongy voice. His flirty voice that used to melt Lizzie right down to the floor.

Lizzie looked back at her husband, expressionless. The voice didn't work. She did not melt. Quite the opposite, in fact. Ice in her voice, she said, "I don't believe in luck."

"Well, I need all the help I can get," Ritchie said, flagging down a waiter who was passing out cake. He grabbed a plate and offered it to Lizzie, who refused. He cut a bite of cake and offered his fork up. Reluctantly, she let Ritchie feed her. He smiled and took a bite for himself.

A half hour later, they said their goodbyes and made their way to the valet station. Ritchie handed his ticket to the kid manning the keys and then took out his wallet to find a few singles for a tip.

"It's gonna be huge," one valet said to the other. "You up for it?"

"I don't know," the other replied. "I can't really afford to lose any of this cash I just made."

"You need to spend money to make money."

"Says the person with more money than me."

"Come back to the club once they've cleaned up from the party. It's going to be a fun game, and I bet you'll make money."

The first valet looked up and saw Ritchie listening. "Your car will be out in a minute, sir."

"No problem," Ritchie said, smiling. He glanced back at the vestibule, where Lizzie stood inside, chatting with Ace and Sookie. Quietly: "Say, is that game open to anyone?"

"Anyone who can buy in."

Ritchie smiled again. If he could get the diamond back, it

would solve everything. He wouldn't gamble anymore. He wouldn't have to lie to Lizzie. Everything would change for him once he won one more big score. "I'll be back in under an hour."

28

Courtney

Courtney had won over the dog, but not her niece, Olivia. Emma was much more open, much more willing to let Courtney in, but Olivia? Olivia was a rock.

Emma had welcomed Courtney with open arms, no questions asked, as if no time had passed. Olivia acted like they'd just met, and she hadn't heard good things.

"So, your mom says you're super into math?" Courtney asked Olivia, entering her bedroom slowly. Courtney had only missed one Christmas, but it was like starting over again. It was like Olivia was a different kid. A different person.

Courtney hadn't thought she'd be at her sister's house for more than one night. Her plan had seemed foolproof at the time: grab the ring, get on a red-eye back to LA, pay off her debts. But that idea wasn't as easy in reality. First, she couldn't book a flight back to LA, since her credit card was overdrawn. She hopped onto sweetdaddy.com to try to get a date, get fast cash, but her sister and brother had gotten into her head—what if she *had* just gotten lucky with Sy? What if she met someone who wasn't as kind? What if she got hurt? Maybe her father had been right. Maybe she did need her brother and sister to help take care of her.

She told herself she didn't care—after all, living at Addy's house was like being back under her mother's roof. A fully stocked kitchen, laundry service, and the house seemed to magically clean itself. Courtney had a new plan: she would ride things out at Addy's in comfort, while she convinced her siblings to sell the ring and split the proceeds.

"Into math?" her niece said. "No. Good at it? Yes."

"What are you into, then?"

"I don't know. What are *you* into?" Olivia asked. She looked Courtney directly in the eye. "Besides sex work, that is."

"Did your mother—" Courtney began, before catching herself. She saw the sly smile and realized that her niece had goaded her into getting angry, defensive. And she's fallen directly into her trap. Courtney adjusted her posture. "I mean, I'm not a sex worker."

"Word around town is that you are."

"Well, I'm not. I was a little hard pressed for cash, and my friend got me onto this dating site. I just did it to make some fast cash."

"So, you have sex with old dudes, and they give you money? And private jets? What do they call those—BJs? I mean, PJs."

"No, my God. Who told you that? You know what, it doesn't matter," Courtney said, walking over to the window seat to sit next to her niece. "I didn't sleep with that guy. I went on one date with him. He's a nice guy. He's lonely. He was willing to take me out and pay me for it."

"If it looks like a duck…"

"I thought your generation was supposed to be sex positive."

Olivia picked up her phone. "Siri, what's the definition of a prostitute?"

Courtney grabbed her phone away from her. "Stop that." And then, seeing her niece's reaction, she reluctantly handed it back.

Olivia read aloud: "Dictionary.com says: *a person who willingly uses his or her talent or ability in a base and unworthy way, usually for money.*"

Courtney took a deep breath and looked around Olivia's room. She still had a row of spelling-bee awards from elementary school on her wall. A plaque from Student Council. Olivia was just a kid.

"Are you done?"

"I guess," Olivia said. "But my mom's right. You could have been killed."

Courtney pressed her fingers to her temples. This was something she hadn't considered: her niece was scared. "What do you want to know? Ask me anything."

"Why did you do it?"

"I told you, I needed the money. I'm completely broke."

"You could have sold the LA apartment. You own it free and clear."

"Who is telling you all this stuff?"

Olivia shrugged. "I hear things."

"I did own it free and clear, but I lost it, too."

"How do you *lose* an apartment?"

"It's complicated." Courtney looked at her niece. Olivia's appearance was so much more controlled than Emma's. Her hair, blown out straight, her nails, clipped short, without polish that might dare chip.

"Like, you took it to the beach one day and left it there?"

"No."

"Try me."

"I gambled it away."

Olivia sat up at attention. "You gambled your apartment away?"

"Yes."

Olivia's shoulders released. "Look, if you don't trust me, I get it. But don't make up some weird lie."

The late-afternoon sun came through the window, blinding Courtney. She reached back to adjust the blinds, enveloping the room in darkness.

"It's not a lie. And you're the only one in the family who knows. Auditions weren't going well, and I started gambling to make extra cash. First, it was just little stuff. College football through a bookie, the occasional trip to Vegas. But then, it got a bit out of control, and the more I lost, the more I tried to win it back. I could be just like your grandpa, get a big score and make everything okay. But the house always wins."

Olivia got up and turned on the light. "Didn't Grandpa Ritchie have a massive gambling problem?"

Courtney squinted as her eyes adjusted to the light. "No. I mean, yes. But he had so many nights when he was on a heater. I just needed one good streak to make everything right."

"And how did that work out for you?" Olivia walked across the room to sit back down in the window seat next to Courtney.

"I was in so deep to one of your grandpa's old bookies that I had to sell the apartment just to pay him back."

"You're doing sugar daddy dates to try to win back your apartment?"

Courtney noticed that Olivia's nails weren't just clipped short. Her left thumbnail had been bitten down. "I lost a bit more than that."

"How did you lose more? Once you lost the apartment, didn't you stop gambling?"

Courtney looked down at her hands. "Not exactly."

"I thought you said you had no money?"

"I started gambling on markers, playing at underground games."

"And?"

"I didn't win."

"So, how much?"

Courtney could not bring herself to look back up to face her niece. "I wanted to stop. I really did. But then I hear about this big poker game. Poker was always my game, and I figured that it was my chance. My chance for that one big win. I had to take out another marker, but I was up. I doubled the marker in the first hour, but I got greedy. I wanted to try to erase the hundred and twenty-five grand I owed, *and* get the apartment back."

"Let me guess—you lost."

Courtney tilted her head up to face her niece. "I lost."

"So, no apartment, and you're in debt to one of Grandpa Ritchie's old bookies for a hundred twenty-five thousand dollars."

Courtney could hear her sister down in the kitchen, starting to get dinner ready. She whispered, "It's a little more than that."

"More?"

"Yes," Courtney said. "With the juice and everything."

Olivia mimed drinking from a glass, and Courtney shook her head. "The juice is the weekly interest on what you owe."

"So that's why you want to sell the ring."

"How do you know that I want to sell the ring?"

"I hear things."

"Right," Courtney said, laughing, despite herself. "Well, yeah, that's why I want to sell the ring."

"But it's a family heirloom," Olivia said.

"A lot of good a family heirloom will do me when I don't have anywhere to live," Courtney said, her voice louder than she intended. She took a beat before continuing. "Anyway, that's your mother talking, not you. She just wants it so that I can't have it."

"She wants it because it's a symbol of her parents getting back together, the nine-month separation ending," Olivia said.

"No, that's why your uncle wants it."

"Uncle Nathan wants it because it's a symbol of the epic love story of Grandma and Grandpa."

"How do you know all of this?"

"I overheard Mom talking to her therapist on the phone,"

Olivia said. "To her, the ring represents security. To Uncle Nathan, the ring represents love."

"You hear a lot," Courtney said, doing a mental calculation of what Olivia might have overheard her say.

Her niece shrugged. "So, tell the truth. Is this a real story or made up? Do you really owe all this money? Are you just messing with me so that I'll tell Mom to sell the ring?"

"Real," Courtney said. Her lips curled into a Cheshire cat smile. "You don't think a girl resorts to prostitution if she has money, do you?"

Olivia laughed. "Right. But then, how come none of the adults know about this?"

"I can't bring myself to tell them. They think I'm this huge fuckup. They think I need them to take care of me. It's easier if I just do my time out here, and then get back to LA and figure things out on my own."

"Maybe if you just tell them the truth, they'll sell the ring to bail you out."

"Have you met them before?"

"So, you're just going to lie your ass off to get them to think that you're not a giant fuckup?"

"Don't use curse words. Your mom would kill me."

"Your words."

Courtney thought about that. Those were her words. They were true, though, weren't they? That's what she did. She fucked things up. She could have been living in LA, waiting tables and auditioning, but instead she got herself in so much debt that she'd never get out of it. She lost the apartment her parents had bought for her. The last thing she had from them. Why was she like this?

Emma walked into the room without knocking. "You guys want to play cards?"

Courtney couldn't think of anything she wanted more.

29

Addy

"Where's that cabernet Nathan brought back for us from Napa?"

"Didn't we finish the case?" Addy asked, as she put pasta into a large pot to boil. "I didn't think we had any left."

"I know we had one bottle left," Gary said.

"Girls, ten minutes until dinner!" Addy called out.

"I was saving it for a special night."

"And this is a special night?" Addy asked, laughing. Nathan, Diego, and Courtney had been staying with them for three nights, and much like the Benjamin Franklin quote about fish and houseguests, they were starting to stink.

"Not special," Gary conceded, "but it will be nice to have people who appreciate wine to share it with me."

"I appreciate wine."

"You can't tell the difference between a pinot grigio and a pinot gris."

"Well, yeah, I'm not a sommelier."

"And you only ever have a glass or two. Nathan and Diego will really enjoy it with me."

"I never have more than two glasses, sure," Addy said. "But I always enjoy—no, *appreciate*—those two glasses."

"Did you open it without me?" Gary regarded his wife.

Addy sprinkled some salt into the pot and stirred the pasta. "Yes, honey. I opened it without you and then drank it by myself at home, in all my spare time."

Gary laughed. "Right."

"Maybe you opened it without noticing."

"You don't think it was—" Gary didn't finish his thought. He didn't need to.

"They're only sixteen."

"Think about the things you were doing when you were sixteen."

Addy preferred not to.

"What can I help with?" Diego asked as he walked into the kitchen.

"The girls will set the table, so you can just relax," Addy said. "Girls, five minutes until dinner!"

"You can help me find the last bottle of cab you guys brought back from Napa."

"Where should we start?" Diego asked, and then went off with Gary to the basement.

Nathan came in next. "Where is everyone?"

"Gary and Diego are downstairs, looking for a lost bottle of wine. The girls are upstairs with Courtney."

"Should we leave them alone with Courtney?" Nathan asked. "Wouldn't want her teaching my nieces all the tricks of the trade she learned out in LA."

Addy laughed, but Nathan had planted a seed. Was her little sister a bad influence on her girls? If Gary was right and the girls were drinking already, what would be next once Courtney taught them how to reel in old dudes and get them to loan you their private jets? She shook her head, as if to release the thought from her mind. She looked over at her brother and saw it.

"What are you wearing on your pinkie?"

"I needed a pick-me-up," Nathan said. He held his hand out to look at their mother's ring, shiny and bright.

"You went into my wall safe without telling me?"

"It's not your ring," Nathan said, matter-of-factly. "It doesn't belong to you."

"But the wall safe is mine—" Addy began, before deciding to drop it. Getting into a fight with Nathan about her wall safe was not going to be productive for anyone. It wasn't about the safe, anyway. It was about the ring. Addy changed the subject. "How's the restoration going?"

"Really well," Nathan said. "It's amazing how much they were able to get done in just a few days. Diego was in the city this morning. They did all the heavy cleaning, apparently there was oil everywhere, and they've sent out the upholstery and window coverings. Tomorrow, they'll drywall the ceiling."

"That's great," Addy said, as she took the green beans out of the oven and placed them into a serving dish.

Without being asked, Nathan added a serving spoon to the bowl and moved it to the kitchen table. They worked in sync like this anytime they entered a kitchen, a remnant of the nine months their parents were separated, when they tried to do anything they could to get their mother to smile, to cheer her up. It wasn't something they ever discussed; it was just something they did on autopilot.

"Then, they'll repaint, and we'll move back in."

"That's great," Addy said again, as she turned the oven to broil and watched as the chicken cutlets turned a golden brown.

"You ready to get rid of us already?"

"No," Addy said. "Not at all. That's not what I meant. I love having you here. And hasn't the short commute been nice for you?"

"It has."

"If you moved out here, I could see you more often."

"There's no reason to move out to the burbs if you don't have kids," Nathan said, the same way he always did when this topic came up. "And we don't have kids. I don't even know how much longer we'll be married."

"This again?"

"This again."

"Why don't you try couples therapy?" Addy opened the oven and took out the tray of chicken cutlets. Each one was a perfect, golden brown, and Addy smiled, pleased to have completed a task so well.

Nathan grabbed a spatula and plated the cutlets onto a platter. As he brought it to the table, Addy drained the pasta.

"You literally think therapy is the answer to everything."

"I do. Therapy has changed my life. So, yes, maybe I'm a bit emphatic about it, but it's been good for me. I believe in the power of it."

"Do you ever think that our parents' marriage messed us up for other relationships?" Nathan asked.

"I thought you thought Mom and Dad had the greatest love of all time? That their love story was one for the ages?"

"I do," he said. "I did. I mean, I do. I don't know what I mean. I mean, how can I live up to that relationship?"

"Their relationship wasn't perfect. No relationship is perfect."

"These chicken cutlets are perfect," Nathan said. Addy smiled at her brother. "But my relationship problems are bigger than therapy. I think Diego is cheating on me."

"What?" Addy turned to face her brother.

"The new clothes… He's been getting into shape lately…"

"That doesn't mean he's having an affair."

"His father is almost as famous for his many extramarital affairs as he is for his music."

"So?"

Nathan held out the theater receipt, and Addy grabbed it. "What am I looking at?"

"It's a receipt for a show," Nathan said. "But when I asked him about it, he said he wasn't at the theater, he was working out."

"So maybe he bought tickets for something in advance," Addy said. "Maybe he wants to surprise you."

Nathan didn't respond.

Addy was about to fill the silence when Gary and Diego came back upstairs with a bottle of wine.

"Couldn't find the cab," Gary said. "Will pinot noir work?"

Nathan took the bottle and set about opening it.

"Girls!" Addy called out. "Dinner!"

Olivia and Emma flew down the stairs, with Courtney close on their heels. They set the table, with Courtney assisting with the glasses and a pitcher of water. Duke took his usual place near the head of the table, next to Addy's seat.

Addy couldn't help but laugh to herself. She and Nathan, standing at the counter, the grown-ups, and her girls and her baby sister, doing their chores like good little children.

30

Nathan

"Aren't you going to put that back in the safe before we go to bed?"

Nathan hadn't even realized he was still wearing the ring. Well, of course he realized—the thing had heft, it was heavy on his finger—but he was getting used to the feel of it. He didn't want to take it off.

"I find it comforting to wear."

Diego smiled. "Well, if you come to bed, I can think of other things that are comforting."

The guest room at Addy's house had two single beds, but Diego had pushed them together on their first night. Now, it was like one big bed, but there was a gap in the middle where the two bed frames met. The mattresses didn't touch.

Anyway, Nathan didn't feel like being comforted like that. He knew the only thing that would make him feel better would be to talk to Diego, to confront him about the affair, but he couldn't bring himself to do it.

Still, how long had it been since they'd had sex? Nathan couldn't recall. That wasn't a good sign. If you couldn't recall the last time you had sex with your husband, then it was too long since you had sex with your husband.

Nathan remembered a time when he didn't have to wonder when the last time they'd had sex was. When they'd first started dating, they'd done it all the time. At night, in the morning. In their bed, in the bathroom of the restaurant where Nathan waited tables. (And once, even, in the pantry at Addy's house during a particularly boring barbecue.)

But it wasn't just sex. Nathan and Diego used to touch each other more. Walking from one room in the apartment to the next, there would be a hand brushing his shoulder. When they lounged together on the couch at night, Nathan would burrow his cold feet beneath Diego's warm legs. At dinner with friends, Diego would lazily throw his arm around the back of Nathan's chair, his fingertips grazing his husband's arm.

Forget sex, when was the last time they even touched?

Nathan walked over to the twin beds and got in. He climbed over to Diego's side, and his knee fell into the space between the two beds. They both heard it—his knee slammed into the wood bed frame with a thump.

"Are you okay?" Diego said.

"I'm fine," Nathan said. "Fine." But when he moved his leg, he yelped out in pain.

"Let me go get you some ice," Diego said, and jumped out of bed.

Nathan slumped back and cried quietly. He had thought that staying at Addy's would make him more comfortable than staying at Diego's parents'. Something about a home-court advantage. But it hadn't helped.

He looked down at his mother's ring on his finger. A symbol of his parents' love. Was that why he was wearing it? Was that why he didn't want to sell it? He was still holding on to his parents' epic love story, while his own love story was ending.

Nathan's phone dinged with a text. He picked it up, and was confused by the message:

FRANK: When can I see you again?

Nathan was about to text back to tell this man that he had the wrong number, but then he realized: he wasn't holding his phone. He'd accidentally picked up Diego's. Nathan dropped it, as if it were on fire.

"I've got ice!" Diego called out, as he slowly walked into the room, carrying a tray. "And tea, too!"

Diego gently placed the baggie filled with ice onto Nathan's knee, and then offered him a cup of tea.

"Thank you," Nathan said, still stunned. Why hadn't he just shown Diego the text message? Why couldn't he ever stand up for himself when it counted? Nathan started to quietly cry again.

Diego put his arm around Nathan's shoulders. "Still mad at Courtney?"

"No," Nathan said. "She's apologized a million times."

"So why the tears, then?"

Nathan looked at Diego. This was it. The moment he would tell Diego the truth. "I'm in pain."

"The ice isn't helping?" Diego asked, rearranging the baggie so that it fully covered Nathan's knee.

"It's helping," Nathan said. He searched Diego's face for answers. *Are you cheating on me?* But Nathan found that he couldn't get the words out.

"Is something else bothering you?" Diego asked, wiping a tear from Nathan's eye gently with his finger.

Nathan felt Diego's warm hand grab onto his own. Diego asked, "Do you want to talk about it?"

Nathan took a long sip of his tea. It was a mix of black tea leaves, that much he could tell, though he wasn't certain which blend it was. The tea was strong, but had a sweetness to it. Coupled with the honey, it was delicious and soothing, just what he needed. He shifted the baggie with the ice. His knee didn't hurt anymore. It was numb. But still, he couldn't stop crying. "That's actually the last thing I want to do."

31

Addy

"Do you hear that?"

"Hear what?" Gary looked up from the book he was reading in bed.

Addy sat on her side of the bed, furiously rubbing lotion onto her hands, like she was punishing them for some unknown offense. "Courtney," she said. "Courtney is hanging out with the girls again. This is their new thing—hanging out together in Olivia's room, late at night."

"Well, that sounds like fun," Gary said, smiling. "Maybe you should join them."

Addy looked at her husband's face. Wide open, eyes welcoming. He smiled at her. She felt the sudden urge to punch him.

"I can't just go in there," Addy whispered. "Are you joking?"

"Well, it's *your* house. They're *your* girls. And you're clearly jealous that Courtney is spending time with them. Why not just join in? You'll get time with the girls, and time with your sister. It's a win-win."

Gary put his head back down into his book, seemingly pleased with himself for having solved Addy's problem. He had not solved Addy's problem. Addy wasn't sure where to begin. Everything Gary had said was wrong. Wrong, wrong, wrong. She decided on the most obvious point. "I'm not jealous."

"Oh." Gary did not look up from his book.

"Why would I be jealous? I have nothing to be jealous of. I'm concerned, that's what I am."

Head still in his book, Gary murmured, "Concerned?"

"Yes, concerned. You should be concerned, too." Addy grabbed Gary's book out of his hand, forcing him to look at her, and her sticky hand cream made marks all over the book's cover. "Courtney is a bad influence. She could be a bad influence on our girls. Aren't you worried about that?"

"Well, I wasn't," Gary said, and furrowed his brow. "But now I am."

"I mean, just look at Courtney's Instagram," Addy said, leaning over to her bedside table for her phone. "Look at this. And this. And then, look at the Lizzie and Ritchie's page. Today's post was supposed to be about spring dresses. Instead, it's a picture of all three of them in a bathtub. Did you know about this?"

"It's supposed to reference an iconic '90s supermodel photo," Gary replied. "Are you angry about the photo or about the fact that your sister is spending time with them?"

"The photo!"

Addy's phone in his face, Gary instead chose to look directly at Addy. "You could just go down the hall and see them in real life."

"These photographs are them in real life."

"Not really."

Addy turned away from her husband. He didn't understand. He didn't understand any of it! Addy pulled the covers off the bed. Duke looked up from his perch at the edge of the mattress. She slowly lowered her legs down, quietly put her slippers on, and then tiptoed toward the bedroom door. She opened it carefully, so carefully, so as not to make a sound. Addy remembered how sound carried through the upstairs hallway.

When the girls were babies, she could hear, from her bedroom, if either of them so much as rolled over in bed. Standing in her doorway, Addy smiled as she thought about that time in her life. It seemed like a lifetime ago. Addy recalled that feeling she used to have after the nighttime ritual, the house quiet, the day complete. That was when she'd felt most at peace. Once they were tucked firmly in their beds, she could take a deep breath, secure in the knowledge that her girls were safe. She could go to sleep herself. How different things were now. Sixteen-year-olds didn't need to be put to bed anymore. Most nights, Addy went to sleep before the girls. Addy hadn't slept well since their curfew had moved up to 11 p.m.

Addy closed her eyes—hadn't she read something recently that said if you were robbed of one sense, your other senses were heightened?—and listened to what was happening down the hall. Duke joined her at the door, and all she could hear was his steady breathing. "Shh," she told him. He whimpered and made his way back to the bed. Addy closed her eyes again; she could tell that the three of them were gathered in Olivia's room, the one closest to the master.

She heard the unmistakable sound of a deck of cards being shuffled. Addy flew back toward the bed in just three steps, like a gazelle being chased by a cheetah. Duke jumped off the bed as Addy hopped in. "Can you hear that? They're playing cards!"

"Okay, good," Gary said, his eyes trained on his book. "So, completely innocent."

"Not innocent," Addy said. "When someone in my family plays cards, it's not innocent. I told you she was a bad influence!"

"So, go in there and tell them to stop," Gary said quietly.

"I can't go in there and tell them to stop!" Addy whisper-yelled. "You can't tell sixteen-year-old girls not to do something! That only makes them want to do it more!"

"So, then go in there and play with them," Gary said, followed by a deep exhale. "You can monitor what they're playing. It's probably Go Fish."

"Maybe she's teaching them poker. Or how to be a sugar baby."

"She did that one time. It's not her full-on profession. And I think she learned her lesson. And even if she is teaching the girls how to play poker, that doesn't mean they're going to become degenerate gamblers."

Addy didn't respond. It was one thing when she referred to her own father as a *degenerate gambler,* but it was always quite another when she heard the same words coming out of her husband's mouth. "Right," she said quietly.

"I shouldn't have said that about your father," Gary said. He rubbed his eyes. "I'm sorry I said that. You know that I loved your father."

"It's fine," Addy said. "This isn't about my father."

"You're worried about the girls gambling. Who else is this about?"

Addy collected herself. She took a deep breath in, quieted her thoughts. "Right."

Gary leaned over and gave Addy a gentle kiss on the lips. "Honey, no matter how many hands of cards Courtney plays with the girls, you're not going to lose them. They're not going to trade you in for your sister. They're not going to fall under Courtney's spell just because she shows them a little attention. They're smart girls. They've got good heads on their shoulders."

Gary was right. Of course he was right. Olivia and Emma were smart girls. Good girls. They might play the part of bad girl on Instagram, but Addy knew who they really were, deep down. That wasn't going to change overnight. Addy didn't have to break up an impromptu card game just to prove that. She handed Gary his book and picked up her own.

32

Courtney

"Ready?" Olivia asked, and started dealing the cards without waiting for an answer.

Emma slunk down to the carpet, across from her sister, and got ready to play. She patted the spot next to her, signaling her aunt to sit down. Courtney did as she was told.

"Go Fish?" Olivia asked Courtney.

"Why don't we play something fun?" Courtney asked.

"Go Fish is fun," Olivia said. "Wasn't last night fun?"

"Being with my nieces is always fun," Courtney said. She loved spending time with Olivia and Emma. Getting to know them had been the best part of staying at Addy's house the past week. They were smart and beautiful and sweet, rough start with Olivia notwithstanding. How had her sister managed to raise such lovely human beings?

"So, what do you want to play instead?" Emma asked.

"Your grandfather loved poker," Courtney said, barely able to keep the excitement out of her voice. She wanted to show them something that would bind them together, teach them part of the family history Addy had surely neglected to share. "Want me to teach you how to play poker?"

"Yes," Emma said quickly.

"No," Olivia said, just as fast. Then, after a beat, "I don't feel like learning a new game."

Emma stuck her tongue out at her sister.

"Hearts?" offered Olivia. Gary had taught them to play hearts on a family trip to the Grand Canyon a few years back, and Olivia and Emma loved it. They'd taught it to their friends, and it became a sleepover party essential.

"Sure," Courtney said, and they began to play. Minutes later, Courtney placed her cards down on the floor. She'd shot the moon, right under their noses, and won the whole game.

"Oh my God," Emma said. "How did you do that? You have to teach me to do that."

"I can show you," Courtney said, smiling widely. "Or I can show you how to play some *real* card games. By the time I was your age, your Grandpa Ritchie had already taught me every table game in Vegas, and I could calculate the odds on any bet in my head. I'm teaching you blackjack."

"I don't want to gamble," Olivia said.

"I do," Emma said.

"Doesn't matter," Courtney said. "Don't think of what I'm teaching you as gambling. It's not like I'm dragging you to Atlantic City. Even though I *had* been to an Atlantic City casino by the time I was your age."

"I want to go to Atlantic City," Emma said. "Would you take us?"

"Your mother would kill me. Dead."

"We are not going to Atlantic City," Olivia said.

"Forget Atlantic City," Courtney said. "I'm just going to teach you about life."

"Byteachingustogamble,"Oliviasaid.Shesat,backramrodstraight, and refused to pick up her cards. Then, whispering, "But Grandpa Ritchie…"

"Your Grandpa Ritchie was a wonderful man and father," Courtney said forcefully. "He doted on you when you were a kid. Spoiled you silly."

Olivia's lips pursed.

"I remember Grandpa Ritchie," Emma said. "I used to love going with him to the park to feed the ducks."

"Remember that time we forgot the bread and he paid some kids on skateboards twenty bucks to go to the market and get us a loaf?" Olivia laughed at the memory.

"No," Emma said. "He gave them a ten, because he wasn't sure if they'd actually come back. When they came back with the bread, he gave them each an extra ten bucks."

"No," Olivia said. "He gave them twenty."

"Remember he said that it was a good life lesson? Never pay in full until the job is done?" Emma looked to her sister for confirmation.

Courtney cleared her throat. "Playing cards will teach you how to read people. It's math, psychology. Important life skills."

"We're all about good life skills," Emma said.

"As long as Mom doesn't get mad again," Olivia said. "She's still mad about Instagram."

"I could help you with that, too," Courtney said. "I'm good at Instagram. Wasn't yesterday's post great?"

"She hated the bathtub pic," Olivia said. "She said it was inappropriate."

"It was an homage to a really famous photograph of the '90s supermodels," Courtney said. "It was super artistic and clever."

"She just wants us to go back to what we were doing before," Olivia said.

"But we want to push the envelope," Emma said.

"But we don't want to get in trouble," Olivia said.

"I have an idea," Courtney said, as she was formulating one in her head. "I know exactly what to do. Just wait right here."

33

Lizzie, 1978

"I can't believe we're here," Lizzie said, taking in the lights and sounds all around them. "I've never been to a casino before."

Ritchie held Lizzie's hand as they walked through the lobby of Resorts in Atlantic City.

The show they'd driven three hours to Atlantic City to see: Pedro Garcia Flores. The hottest ticket in town. Sold out. And Ritchie had gotten them first-row seats. Well, his pit boss had, anyway.

"I still can't believe we're going to see him live," Lizzie said. "I am the envy of all of my friends. And my mother."

"Your mother wanted to go? I could've gotten another two tickets for your folks, easy."

Lizzie wasn't sure how to respond. Her mother certainly did not want to go anywhere with Ritchie Schneider—she'd made that clear repeatedly, anytime she saw her daughter. A man like Ritchie wasn't good enough for her. She wanted nothing to do with him. But yes, she was, like most women in America, a huge Pedro Garcia Flores fan. And anyway, Lizzie knew that

eventually her mother would come around to Ritchie. Just not
yet. Lizzie settled on the truth. "She loves Pedro Garcia Flores."

"All I care about is whether *you* love the guy."

"I do," Lizzie said. Then: "Oh, no! I shouldn't have said that.
How rude of me. I don't love him. I love—I mean, I'm on a
date with you."

Ritchie laughed deeply. "I'm not threatened. Every woman
in America is in love with Pedro Garcia Flores. Why should
you be any different?"

Lizzie smiled coyly. "Well, in that case, if he asks me to come
up onstage, you're finished."

"Did I say front-row seats?" Ritchie asked, as they got closer
to the theater. "I meant back row. Nowhere near the guy."

Lizzie laughed, and Ritchie drew her in for a kiss. She'd never
done this with a boyfriend before, all these public displays of
affection that Ritchie seemed to have no problem with, and
she wasn't sure if it was proper. She could practically hear her
mother chastising her in her head: *how vulgar.*

Lizzie walked toward the long line, already queuing up at the
theater, knowing they'd have to wait to get in, since it was a
sold-out show. Ritchie shook his head, and tugged her arm in
the other direction. "This way."

He led her to the front of the line, where another red velvet
rope was set up. "Schneider," Ritchie said to the man in the suit
who stood as the gatekeeper. The man glanced down at his clip-
board, then opened the ropes for them to pass. Ritchie shook
the man's hand as they walked by.

"We don't have to wait in line?" Lizzie whispered to Ritchie.

"They know me here," Ritchie said, shrugging and offering a sly smile as a well-dressed woman met them at the doors.

"Mr. Schneider, we're so glad to see you this evening," she
said. "Follow me."

"Didn't this casino just open?" Lizzie whispered.

"They opened in May."

"It's August."

"I think a few months is long enough to get to know some-one," Ritchie said, his hand resting on the small of her back as they walked toward the front of the theater. "Anyway, it's not the amount of time you know someone. I think it's about the connection you share. Don't you?"

Lizzie felt her cheeks flush as she considered what Ritchie was saying to her—they'd only known each other for a few months, but they had a connection. It was clear. When they'd checked into the hotel, Ritchie had gotten them two rooms. Was he suggesting otherwise?

"Does this table work for you?" the well-dressed woman asked.

"It's perfect," Ritchie said, as he took the hostess' hand in his.

Lizzie's eye followed Ritchie's hand as it lingered on the host-ess' hand for a moment too long.

"Want me to teach you?"

"Teach me what?"

"You were staring at me, how I gave her a tip."

"Oh, I…"

"That's not what you were looking at."

"Of course it was."

"Did you think I was flirting with her?" Ritchie asked, his face full of mischief. "Don't tell me you were jealous?"

"Of course not," Lizzie said. But she *had* thought that he was flirting. Why had he held her hand for so long?

"Listen," Ritchie said. "I was not flirting with that hostess, I was palming her a tip, same way I did to every other guy in this casino. That's how you do it, you fold the bill up, really tiny, in your hand, and you pass it off."

Every gambler had a tell, and Lizzie knew Ritchie's: a squint in the eyes that was imperceptible, if you weren't looking for it. She regarded him. Ritchie didn't squint. "Show me how."

"Well, you take a bill and fold it over three times," Ritchie said, taking her hand and turning it over. He kissed her palm. "And then you put it there."

A waitress came over to take their drink order. "The lady will have a white wine spritzer," he said, "and I'll have a beer."

The table was so tiny, their knees couldn't help but bump underneath.

"Look, there it is," Lizzie said. The stage was already set up with a small stool, and Pedro Garcia Flores' famous red guitar, the one gifted to him by a nurse when he'd crushed his hand in an accident. The guitar that had brought movement back. The guitar that had made him an international superstar. Seeing the guitar was almost as exciting as seeing the man himself. (But not quite.) Lizzie could practically reach out and touch it from where they sat.

Ritchie held her hand across the table. "I'm happy to be here with you."

Lizzie smiled, but he must have seen something in her eyes.

Ritchie asked, "What's wrong?"

"My sister," Lizzie said. She hadn't meant to bring it up, and certainly not now, but the words fell from her mouth, unbidden. The jealousy she'd felt earlier hadn't gone away. Somehow, it had multiplied. "When we first started dating, she said that she could have you, if she wanted you. Is that true?"

"Look, I'm going to tell you the truth," Ritchie said, staring Lizzie directly in the eye. "If I wanted Maggie again, I could have her. After her divorce, she made that very clear. But I don't want her. I want you. The thing with her, all those years ago, it wasn't real. It wasn't serious. What I have with you…well, I don't want to scare you off, but what I have with you is real. I can feel it. Can't you feel that, too?"

Lizzie nodded in agreement.

"What we have is true love. It's fate," Ritchie said.

Lizzie watched Ritchie as he spoke. He didn't squint, not once. He was telling the truth.

34

Lizzie, 1978

All eyes were on them.

Lizzie had been so excited to bring Ritchie to her cousin's wedding—what could be more glamorous than a wedding on a yacht at sunset? Ritchie had taken her on so many fabulous dates. Now it was her turn to impress him.

"I thought you said things were better with your family?" Ritchie asked Lizzie. "I wouldn't have come if I'd known that things still weren't okay."

"Everything *is* okay," Lizzie replied. "Everything's better than okay. Let me tell you something true: I'm here with you, we're at a beautiful wedding, and we're on a marvelous yacht."

"Also true: I feel like everyone's staring at us," Ritchie said. He ran his hand through his hair and looked around at the party.

"Are they?" she asked casually, grabbing a flute of champagne from a passing waiter.

The ceremony had taken place out on the deck, and the weather was clear and crisp. The water was as smooth as glass, making for a serene ride, no bumps. Delicate fairy lights were strewn across the guardrails, and the tables were covered in lush linens with delicate floral arrangements. The smell of the gardenias mixed with the salty sea air in a way that made Lizzie feel intoxicated.

But Lizzie couldn't deny it: Ritchie was right. Everyone was staring at them. Had been since they'd first stepped foot on the yacht.

Lizzie had thought her cousin's wedding would be the perfect place to show off her boyfriend. Together for over three months already, this was no longer a fling. Her parents would have to admit this was the real thing. They'd have to get over their initial impression of Ritchie, get to know him better. And Maggie would have to drop the fiction that Lizzie had "stolen" him from her.

But none of that had happened. Lizzie had thought that with time, the family would come to accept Ritchie. But just because you are ready for something to happen doesn't mean that it actually will.

The yacht was named *Eternity*, which was fitting, since it felt like they'd been at the wedding for a lifetime. But only the ceremony and cocktail hour had passed. Lizzie and Ritchie still had three hours left to go.

"It's worse than the paparazzi," Ritchie whispered. He was right. It wasn't just Lizzie's parents and sister who seemed to disapprove of them, the whole extended family seemed to be looking their way. Whispers of *"is that him?"* and *"I heard he dated the sister first"* and *"Katharine says he doesn't have a job"* filled the air.

"Why don't we dance," Lizzie said, and held her hand out.

Once on the dance floor, she closed her eyes and tried to lose herself in the moment. It didn't matter what others thought— she was dancing with the man that she loved.

Lizzie felt a tap on her shoulder. "May I cut in?" For a brief moment, Lizzie let herself believe it was her mother, that this was the olive branch she'd been waiting for. Her mother would dance with Ritchie, dissolve the family tension, and things could move forward. She'd continue to date Ritchie with her parents' blessing, and the rest of the family would gossip about some other family member.

But when she opened her eyes, it wasn't her mother. It was her sister. Maggie wore a pale pink dress, with delicate straps that fell off her shoulders. Lizzie had thought the dress was so inappropriate, the light color so close to the bride's white dress, but now she realized how sexy her sister looked. Lizzie felt foolish in her navy party dress, with its high neckline, bracelet-length sleeves, and billowing skirt.

"I always have a dance for an old friend," Ritchie said, putting his hand out for Maggie.

"No," Lizzie said, grabbing his hand before Maggie could take hold, "you don't."

"We don't need to make a scene," Ritchie said. Then, in a whisper, "How would it look if I refused to dance with your sister?"

"How would it look if you did?" Lizzie replied. Lizzie turned to her sister. "Maggie, you may not dance with my boyfriend. All this stops now."

"It's just a little dance," Maggie purred. "I didn't mean to threaten you."

"Threaten? No," Lizzie said. "I'm clear on where I stand with Ritchie. But it seems as if you are not. Let's settle things once and for all. Ritchie, tell us—who do you love?"

"Lizzie?" Ritchie's eyes searched Lizzie's.

"It's a simple question, really," Lizzie said. "Who do you love? Is it me? Or is it my sister?"

"You," Ritchie said simply. "You know that. I only love you."

"And I love you," Lizzie said quietly. And then, turning to face her sister once again: "Is this matter settled? Ritchie loves me. And I love him. So please stop pretending that things are otherwise."

Just then, the bride and groom walked into the reception,

and the crowd began to cheer. They glided toward the center of the room and immediately began their first dance, as the party guests all moved to the edge of the dance floor to watch. After a few minutes, the band invited everyone to join them. Ritchie held his hand out for Lizzie, and they made their way back onto the dance floor.

"You know that you're the only one," Ritchie whispered into Lizzie's ear.

"I do know that," Lizzie said.

"Then, what was that silly thing with your sister?"

"You were right all along," Lizzie said. "Everyone *was* staring at us. As much as I wanted my mother to approve of you, of us, she clearly still does not, and now she and my sister have poisoned everyone at this wedding to think poorly of you. To think that I stole you from my sister, to think that you're not good enough for me. I just want my family to see what I see, and adore you the way I do."

"I want that, too."

"But my family doesn't have to love you, I suppose. I love you, and that's what's important."

"Maybe we should make it official."

Lizzie stopped dancing. She pulled back. "What are you saying?"

"I think you know what I'm saying." He drew her close, once again, and they danced.

"Have you asked my father for permission?"

"Do you think he'd give it to a degenerate like me?" Ritchie asked.

Lizzie considered this. "You're not a degenerate."

"I don't care what anyone else says," Ritchie said. "I only care about you."

"And I only care about you," Lizzie said, her voice soft.

Ritchie spun Lizzie around, and brought her back in his arms. He leaned in to whisper in her ear: "Marry me."

35

The ring, 2004

The hardest thing a gambler could do was to set aside money and then not use it for gambling. But it was time to cash in the chips.

Lizzie had no idea that the ring she'd been wearing since 1992 was a fake. How could she? The cubic zirconia was gorgeous. Shiny and bright. She wore the ring all the time, to clubs and dinners out, to weddings and birthday parties, and even once to the grocery store because she simply "didn't want to take it off." And why shouldn't she enjoy a little everyday glamour? She'd worked hard to make her marriage succeed, to keep her family together. When she'd turned fifty the year before, she'd vowed that this would be her best decade yet.

In all that time, Ritchie had never stopped thinking about replacing the diamond he'd sold with a real one again. The Liz Taylor Ring, made whole again. The symbol of their love.

Pete the Jeweler understood. In 1993, Pete had called Ritchie to tell him he had a potential buyer. He'd contacted Ritchie as a courtesy—if Ritchie had the money, he would sell it back to him instead. But Ritchie did not, so the stone was sold. Ritchie was crushed, but Pete the Jeweler assured him that he'd be able to find a similar stone, a perfect match, when he was able to afford it.

Ritchie started saving, determined to replace the fake. It wasn't easy at first, Ritchie still gambling, still falling out of business after business, but now that he had the store, he had steady money coming in each week. For the past two years, he'd carefully deposited a portion of his earnings every month into a savings account. The next time Pete the Jeweler called, Ritchie would be ready.

The call came in 2004. Lizzie's diamond was back—the original stone. The guy he'd sold it to was getting divorced, and the wife quietly came to Pete the Jeweler to sell the ring behind her husband's back. (Lots of wives quietly came to Pete to sell things behind their husbands' backs.)

Ritchie had lost his chance to buy back the diamond once. He wasn't going to lose it again.

He drove to the tiny storefront in Manhattan, the cash he'd just taken from the bank flush against his chest in the inside pocket of his sport coat. Ritchie said he would wait while Pete replaced the stone. When Pete brought it out for him, Ritchie could barely tell the difference between the real stone and the fake. Both were beautiful and complex, due to the Asscher cut. As Pete the Jeweler held up the ring, newly polished and reset, Ritchie could swear it looked exactly as it had the day before.

"You messing with me?" Ritchie said, holding the ring. "Looks exactly the same as before."

"Use this," Pete said, and passed his loop to Ritchie. Ritchie held the loop up to his eye, and examined each stone. He had no idea what he was looking at. But he could tell they were different. The one that was set in the ring had tiny black dots in the center.

"This one's the fake," Ritchie said. "It's got black dots in it."

"That's how you know it's real, actually," Pete said, motioning with his pinkie finger to the stone. "The black dots are spots of carbon that have not crystallized. They're natural flaws. That's why the fake stone doesn't have them. It's man-made."

Ritchie looked again. The loose stone in his hand did not, in fact, have the dots. He would ask Addy to check the internet about this later.

"How many years have I known you, Ritchie? I wouldn't lie."

Ritchie considered his words. It was true, Pete the Jeweler wouldn't lie. He couldn't bluff to save his life; that's how Ritchie had ended up with the ring in the first place. Ritchie brought the ring home.

The following weekend, Lizzie could feel Ritchie's eyes on her as she dressed for a night out. He watched her as she opened the wall safe in her closet and took the ring out. She slipped it onto her finger and put her hands on her waist, a smile playing on her lips. When Ritchie didn't react, she shimmied her hips, beckoning her husband. The diamond glowed on her finger, lit from within.

Before Ritchie could respond, the phone rang.

"It checks out," Addy said. "You can tell a real diamond from a fake by its flaws."

"Thank you for looking it up for me."

"No problem," Addy said. "But why did you ask? Is Mom's ring a fake?"

"Of course it's not," Ritchie said.

"Sorry, I shouldn't have said that," Addy said, clearing her throat. "I assume this is about the new jewelry line for the store?"

"Of course," Ritchie said, hoping his words sounded smooth and self-assured. "My clever girl, always one step ahead of her father."

"Email me pictures. I'm dying to see it."

"Will do, kiddo."

"I'm sorry about what I said about Mom's ring," Addy said, her voice softer, quieter, as if she knew that her mother stood only fifteen feet away. "After all, you always say it's a symbol of your love. If the ring were fake, what would that say about your relationship?"

36

Addy

Addy could always tell her twins apart. Always. Even as infants, when they looked the most alike, she had no problem. She always could tell Olivia from Emma.

People had tricks for telling their twins apart—different color bracelets on their wrists, letting one kid's nails grow longer, color coding their wardrobes. But Addy never needed anything like that, and she took pride in that fact.

They were always just Olivia and Emma, two distinctly different beings. Everything about them was different. And even though they were identical twins, they looked physically different. Olivia was thinner, for one. Emma had more of an hourglass figure. Olivia cut her hair shorter and blew it out straight every day, whereas Emma's fell in long, loose carefree waves down her back. Olivia had a small mole in the shape of a star on the inside of her right wrist. (A mother once asked her if it was a tattoo. A tattoo! On a child!) Emma had a birthmark in the shape of a heart on her left shoulder.

It wasn't just the way they looked. It was their energies, their auras. Sometimes, Addy could swear that she could feel Olivia's presence before she walked into a room—that nervous buzz she could always feel coming off her daughter's skin. But Emma could be like a ghost. You wouldn't know she was there until she wanted you to know. Until she announced herself. Olivia spoke a mile a minute; Emma barely spoke at all. Olivia seemed like she was always on a treadmill, even when she was standing still; Emma seemed like she barely had a pulse, like her heart beat just a little bit slower than everyone else's.

But now she couldn't tell which girl she was looking at. She had gone to the Lizzie and Ritchie's Instagram page to make sure they hadn't posted any more inappropriate photos. What she saw made her breath catch in her throat.

All Addy could see was *it*, sparkling against the sunlight, bold and bright. That was the point of the photograph, after all, wasn't it? To only see *it*? The picture was audacious, beautiful. Artistic and gorgeously composed—a close-up of one of her daughters' faces (Emma, she could now see clearly that it was Emma), covered completely by her hands, one on top of the other. And on the top hand, on the third finger, there it was: her mother's ring, the Liz Taylor Ring, glistening in the sun, for all the world to see.

37

Nathan

Nathan was happy to be alone. Sure, he loved his big sister, but after two weeks under Addy's roof, he needed his space. The car ride into the city offered just the right amount of silence.

He loved the late nights he spent at his office, long after Gary would go home to Addy and the girls. There was something so meditative about the monotony of paying bills, doing administrative work. He could shut that part of his brain off, the one that was filled with anxiety, the one that was filled with doubts. It was just him and the numbers, figuring out how it all added up. He would watch his thoughts come and go, always fascinated about what managed to pop up when he was balancing the company checkbook or entering inventory into a spreadsheet.

Nathan was excited to see his apartment. Their apartment, he should say. The home he'd shared with Diego for ten years.

Their apartment reflected a life shared together. Every time Nathan and Diego took a vacation, they brought something back to memorialize the trip. Their expansive bookshelves displayed stoneware they found during a walk through town in Tulum, wood bowls they'd bought on the beach in Jamaica, a

hand-painted guitar from a street vendor in the Canary Islands.
On the walls: a vintage Pedro Garcia Flores poster they'd found
in Old San Juan, a painting from an exclusive gallery in Italy,
a drawing from a street artist in Barcelona. In their bedroom,
linens they'd picked out from a family-run boutique in St. John,
a matching set of lamps from a small shop they'd discovered in
Paris, and the binoculars they'd bought for their African safari,
which were placed on a countertop and never moved, eventually becoming part of the decor.

The contractor said that the place looked brand-new. You
couldn't even tell that there'd been a fire. How strange yet
comforting, Nathan had thought, for things to go back to the
way they were, exactly. That was what he wanted, of course
he wanted his apartment to be saved, but wasn't that strange?
Shouldn't the apartment bear some mark of what it had been
through? Some way to show its history?

Humans have scars. A way to remember where they've been.
Nathan rubbed the underside of his chin. When he'd gotten into
a fight in high school and been rushed to the ER, he'd needed
seventeen stitches, both inside and out, which left a scar across
his jawline. Nathan didn't mind it much. It was part of his story.

But the apartment would have no such scars, thanks to the
restoration expert's team. It was as if the fire had never happened. A special coat of primer had been applied to the walls to
remove the smoke smell, and they'd matched the existing paint
color on the walls and the ceiling. The damaged cabinets had
all been replaced, and the window treatments and furniture had
all been sent out. Everything had been cleaned, scrubbed, and
reassembled. Brand-new again.

Nathan found a parking spot on the street, right in front of
his building. Surely that had to be a sign. His luck was about to
change. Things would start working out now.

"Are you Nathan Schneider?" someone asked. Nathan looked
up and saw a young guy, dressed in jeans and a sport coat.

"Excuse me?"

"I found your headshot in my boss' old stuff. Were you auditioning on Broadway in the early aughts?"

Nathan couldn't help but run his fingers through his hair to put it in place. He turned his head ever so slightly to the left, his best side. "Who's your boss?"

The man held up a photocopy of an old headshot of Nathan's. It was over ten years old. Did Nathan look ten years older, he wondered? He didn't feel ten years older. In some ways, he felt no different than that kid he'd been, waiting tables and auditioning relentlessly. But the headshot was proof. His face was unlined, plumper. His hair was thicker. He looked more relaxed. Happier.

"This you?"

"Yes." Nathan smiled at the man. Yes, that was him. It was him ten years ago, but it could be him again. He vowed to talk to Diego, have a real conversation with him, and have it out. He could be that young, carefree person again. He was sure of it. And if, in the process, he scored a nice little side acting gig (a national commercial, maybe?), all the better.

The man held out a nondescript manila envelope. "You've been served."

PART THREE: CUT

38

Maggie, 2015

He was mine. He was mine before he was hers; he was mine long after he was hers.

Don't you know who I am? Haven't you heard the stories? I was a legend back in my tiny Long Island town. Everyone knew me. Everyone knew *of* me. Everyone, and I mean everyone, wanted a piece of me. And I can't say that I blame them. I was beautiful. I was bold. I was brash. In fact, when I look back at who I was then, it pains me in a way I can't describe.

I'm an old woman now. And the world has no use for an older woman. The world is nicer to a beautiful, young woman. Now that I'm older, even though I'm still beautiful, the world doesn't treat me the same way it did back when I was younger. It's not as accommodating. It's not as kind.

But back then, oh! The world treated me like a queen.

I was the girl with the long black hair. I was the girl with the body that made men look twice. Three times. I was the girl whose laughter was like a song. And money? My family had loads of it. I never thought I'd have to worry for a day in my life. And that kind of security does something to you. It seeps deep into your pores, it becomes part of the fabric of your being, giving you an overall sense of feeling carefree that is not easily taken away.

And when it is, it destroys you.

No one ever glanced at my little sister, Lizzie. When people spoke of the Morgan girls (and they always talked about us), they meant me.

Lizzie wasn't beautiful. And don't kid yourself, beauty matters. Lizzie had her head in the clouds. She never lived in reality, always rushing off to the movies, obsessing over movie stars and their private lives. Especially Elizabeth Taylor. As if she could ever live like that. I was too busy living my life to be bothered with silly fantasies like that.

I looked like a movie star. Acted like one, too.

I first met Ritchie back in 1969. Just like any other girl with half a brain, I didn't want him. You should've seen him. His hair unruly, his face in desperate need of a shave. And he was sweaty. Like he was hiding something. Like his whole life was one big secret that he would kill to keep buried. He reminded me of Nixon in that debate with Kennedy. (Couldn't he tell? I didn't want a Nixon. I wanted a Kennedy.) And the accent. Oh, that accent! He spoke in Brooklynese so thick, I could barely understand half of the words that came out of his mouth.

When he approached me, I gave him a look that said: *stop*. But he didn't stop. In fact, he went faster. He had the air of the type who got every woman he wanted. And maybe he did in his obscure part of Brooklyn, but this was Long Island. His whole routine wouldn't fly out here.

"Hey, you wanna get outta here?"

I glared back at him. "Do I know you?"

"I'm Ritchie Schneider, nice to meet you." *Nayce t' mee chew.* He held his hand out, and I honestly had no idea what he expected me to do with it.

"Excuse my friend here," a similar-looking Brooklyn type

said, coming up from behind Ritchie and putting his hand on Ritchie's shoulder. Was he trying to be cute? Bail his friend out? Get me for himself? I couldn't figure out what these two were doing. And I didn't want to. "He knows not what he does."

I didn't respond. I simply turned away, back to my friends, his signal to leave. We all had a good laugh about it.

But then, the following week, I saw Ritchie again at one of the beach clubs out on the South Shore. He looked different that day, and certainly better when he was in a pair of swim trunks. He and his friends stood out like a bunch of sore thumbs, but the way they all threw around a football on the beach made me take notice. This Ritchie was different from the one I'd met at the party. He looked handsome, for one, without the five-o'clock shadow that had made him look shifty. His hair, which had looked a mess the night I'd met him, now blew in the breeze, and it looked sexy. Purposeful.

"Are you going to go over there and talk to him?" my friend asked.

"No," I replied, as if it were the most obvious thing in the world. "I'm going to walk by them in my swimsuit."

I tossed my cover-up onto a chaise lounge and made my way onto the beach. As I walked toward the water, it was as if time had switched into slow motion. The football game came to an immediate halt as I walked by, every man stopping to look at me. When I saw Ritchie look my way, I was sure to stare him dead in the eyes. He was at my side before the first wave lapped my toes.

"Hi," he said.

"Do I know you?"

"I think we met. At a party last week."

I shrugged my shoulders.

"I'm Ritchie Schneider." There he was again, introducing himself, as if it was supposed to mean something. As if I was supposed to know what that meant. As if I was supposed to care.

"I'm Maggie." I walked deeper into the ocean, away from him, knowing he'd follow.

"Morgan. I know."

"Do you, now?" I raised an eyebrow. Most guys I knew pretended they didn't know much about my family. But here was this Ritchie Schneider, laying all his cards on the table. I was intrigued.

"It's not every day I get rejected by a beautiful woman. I needed to know more."

I smiled, despite myself. And the game was on.

We dated secretly. It was the only way, really. My mother would never approve of this brutish lout. This man who wasn't suited for a Morgan girl. But I didn't care. There was something pulling me to him, his animalistic charm. When I was with him, all I could imagine were his strong arms pulling me close. The sensation of his body pressed up against mine. His lips all over my body.

Dating secretly was so much more delicious than dating out in the open. Dating secretly lent an air of excitement, made everything more dramatic. We found ourselves in places that were dark. Places that were secluded. Everything felt more romantic, sexy.

And I suppose it was. Because the truth is, even though we broke up in 1969 and then Ritchie started dating my baby sister in 1978, he was dating me in 1978, too. And we've carried on our affair since then. For our entire lives. Don't believe me? I've got the love letters to prove it.

39

Addy

"We need to call Rudy Katz. He's still our lawyer, right?" Addy saw her husband give a furtive look to her brother. They always did that whenever she used the word *our*. Whenever she tried to express any ownership over the family business. She knew she didn't work at the store anymore, of course she did, but would it kill them to give her any acknowledgment of her contribution?

"Called him the second I got served," Nathan said.

"And?"

"We're being sued by a woman named Holly Morgan," Nathan said. "Apparently, she's our late Aunt Maggie's daughter."

"She's our cousin?" Addy puzzled this over in her head. "But Aunt Maggie never had children."

"That's what I said," Nathan said. "Apparently, she had a secret daughter. Who is now claiming that our father is her father. Which would mean that Maggie's daughter isn't just our cousin. She's our half sister."

"That can't be." Addy squinted her eyes, as if trying to remember something. A secret daughter. How could someone have a child and not want to scream it to the world? Addy couldn't imagine a scenario where she'd given birth to a child and didn't want to celebrate it. Gary walked over and put his arms around her shoulders.

"Yeah," Nathan continued, "and I guess she's been stalking our family or something, or just following the store, since she saw the Instagram post that Olivia and Emma did with the ring, so now she believes she has a valid claim on it."

Addy felt her insides harden at the mention of her daughters. What they'd done. Surely Courtney was culpable here, too, since the post had been her idea, but it was Emma's face on the post. And it was both of her daughters who had said yes. Her daughters were no angels, she would never be one of those parents who believed her children could do no wrong, but the thought that they may have set something in motion that couldn't be undone made Addy feel like there was a weight dragging her down to the ground. "Does she?"

"If she can prove that she's one of our siblings, she may have a claim on Dad's estate."

"But he died seven years ago."

"Yes, but the ring," Nathan said. He rubbed his temple. The next words came out slowly, like the honey at the bottom of the jar: "And the store."

Addy felt Gary's shoulders flinch at the mention of the store. She gave her husband a tiny squeeze, an affirmation that she was there for him. She said, "But we'll fight it."

"Yeah, he's getting us in touch with a good estate guy."

"How do we even know she is who she says she is?" Gary asked.

"That's step one," Nathan said. "Demand a DNA test. Katz has already sent a request to her lawyer. They have thirty days to get it done."

"Good," Gary said.

"Thirty days is way too long," Addy said, and Nathan nodded.

"There's no way this is real, so does it matter?" Gary asked. "These are just the things we need to do to make this go away."

Addy nodded her head in agreement—after all, her head told her that her husband was right. There was no way this was real. There was no way her father had carried on an affair with her aunt. A woman she'd never met. Her parents' love story was epic, the stuff of legends. To admit that he had a secret love child with her mother's sister, of all people, would be to crash down everything that she believed about her parents and her family. She couldn't bear it.

But still, a little voice in her head remembered all the lies Ritchie had told over the years. He lied about the gambling. He lied about the money. He lied every time he didn't tell Lizzie the exact extent of his gambling problem.

To be a gambler was to be a liar.

40

Nathan

Addy invented the internet, and now she was going to fix this. It was a good plan. Of course it was. All of Addy's plans were good plans. Except maybe this one wasn't. Nathan looked to Gary, for some sort of backup, but Gary found something very interesting to look at, outside the window.

"The plan is to feed her?" Diego asked, reading Nathan's mind.

"Well, that makes it sound dumb," Addy said. "The plan is to invite her over for dinner and charm her, get her to drop the lawsuit. Once she gets to know our family, she's not going to want to litigate."

There were so many things wrong with what Addy was saying, Nathan honestly did not know where to start. Nathan decided to stick with the truth. "Our lawyer said not to contact her."

"Lawyers aren't always right," Addy said, shrugging. "Especially when it comes to family matters."

"Her family is *suing* our family," Nathan said.

"And anyway, how would we find her?" Courtney asked.

"Simple," Olivia said. "She obviously saw the Instagram post, so we just check who's following us."

Emma immediately put her head down in her phone.

"We don't even know who she is," Nathan said. "She could be our half sister, or she could be a random on the internet who will come to your house and kill us all."

Nathan wasn't sure what he was more upset about—this alleged new sibling, or the fact that he was still stuck at Addy's house. After two weeks, the restoration of the loft had been almost complete. But then Nathan had gotten served. He immediately ran up to the loft to get his bearings. To be alone. To figure out what had just happened.

That's when the roof had caved in on him.

One minute, Nathan was standing in the loft, trying to catch his breath after getting served. The next, the ceiling of the loft, newly painted and perfectly put back together, collapsed. An explosion of drywall rained down in front of him, along with the roof of the entire building. All onto the floor of his living room. Nathan had looked up at where his ceiling used to be, and he could see clear through to the bright Manhattan sky.

He had to laugh—the metaphor of what had just happened in his life, literally coming true.

Turned out, the fire had damaged more than just the ceiling of his loft. It had also damaged the roof of the building. After the fire, and then construction, and then a week of rain, the roof was simply not strong enough to hold itself up any longer. It had called it quits.

Nathan and Diego would be camping out at Addy's house for an indefinite amount of time.

"I don't think she's going to kill us," Addy said, but without her usual confidence. Nathan could tell he'd rattled his sister. "She's still our cousin, isn't she? Or do you think she's lying about being Maggie's daughter altogether?"

"Maybe we should try to meet at a restaurant," Courtney said, "in that case."

"That sounds safer," Diego agreed. "Public place. And we wouldn't have to give her your address."

"She already knows where we live," Nathan said to Diego. "She had us served at our apartment."

"True," Diego said, as if turning this over in his head. "But she doesn't know where we're staying now, at Addy's house."

"She definitely knows where we all live," Gary said. "She obviously had a private investigator figure it out. We should be hiring our own private investigator."

Nathan considered his brother-in-law's words. Maybe a private investigator wasn't a bad idea. They could find out who this Holly Morgan really was, for one. And then maybe the investigator would give Nathan a discount to find out more about this man Diego was having an affair with. A two-for-one type thing?

"A private investigator sounds so salacious," Addy said, wrinkling her nose, as if she'd smelled something bad. "I thought we were assuming that Holly is our cousin, but not our half sister."

"Who knows who she really is?" Nathan wondered aloud, throwing his arms out dramatically. He sighed out loud.

"This is starting to sound a bit overdramatic, like one of those old movies we used to watch with Mom on Sundays," Addy said. "What was that one with Elizabeth Taylor where she has a breakdown after spending the summer in Europe? I only caught the ending, but it scarred me for life."

"*Suddenly, Last Summer,*" Nathan and Diego said in unison.

"Yes," Addy said. "That's the one. She plays a girl who gets committed to a mental institution."

"Because her cousin was using her as bait to lure men in for himself!" Nathan said. "That white see-through bathing suit!"

"White see-through bathing suit?" Gary said and then immediately put his head into his phone, no doubt to Google *Elizabeth Taylor, white see-through bathing suit.*

"Yes!" Diego said. "She lures men in for her cousin to prop-osition for sex, and they attack and cannibalize him! Katharine Hepburn tries to get her lobotomized to keep it all secret!"

"But old Monty Clift wouldn't let her do it," Nathan said.

"No, he would not," Diego said. "That movie was filmed after Monty Clift had that horrible accident and his face had to be completely reconstructed."

"He still looked dreamy," Nathan said. "And did you know that Elizabeth Taylor was the one who saved his life after the car accident?"

Diego looked his husband in the eye. "How dare you ask me such a question. Of course I knew that."

Nathan couldn't help but laugh. For a split second, he was able to forget all of the doubts he'd been having. This was the man he'd married. A man who could make him laugh. A man who could casually discuss Monty Clift's film career. A man who loved Nathan's family as unconditionally as he loved his own.

Emma picked her head up from her phone. "Hold up. Did you say *cannibalize*? Like, they ate him?"

"Yes!" Diego said. "It's a must-see."

"Ew," Olivia said. "Do they show him getting eaten?"

"No. It's very artistic," Nathan said. "Apparently, Tennessee Williams wrote it after he underwent psychoanalysis to cure his homosexuality."

"As you do," Diego said, and they both laughed.

"Can we get back to the dinner invitation?" Addy asked.

"So, basically," Nathan said, "the first thing that pops into your mind about cousins is a movie about cannibalism. What, pray tell, will be on the menu for such a dinner?"

"It wasn't the cannibalism," Addy said, shaking her head. "Anyway, I'll make a vegetable lasagna, if you insist."

"Not your famous pot roast?" Diego asked. "If anything will make her drop the lawsuit, it's your pot roast."

"How would we even find her?" Nathan asked.

"Right," Gary said. "First, we can get some recommendations from our lawyer for a good private investigator. Then, it'll take him some time to track her down. So, at the earliest, we're looking at—"

Emma looked up from her phone and cut her father off. "Found her."

41

Lizzie, 1980

Lizzie couldn't believe this was happening. She'd driven past the house countless times, always imagining what it looked like on the inside. Who lived there, what sort of family they'd be. Lizzie was sure they were a happy family. She could tell.

They'd taken to calling it *the dream house* when they drove by, since Lizzie always asked Ritchie to slow down as they passed so she could admire it. Each time he slowed down, there was another detail she noticed, another reason to fall in love with it. There was something about the house, something that felt like home.

It was nothing like the house Lizzie had grown up in—overly formal, stuffy, uncomfortable. The house where Lizzie grew up had rooms she was not allowed to spend time in, couches she was not allowed to sit down on. And Ritchie had lived in apartments his whole life. He'd never had a house to call his own. Lizzie and Ritchie talked about the day they'd be able to buy a house like this one. Something warm and inviting, a place to create their life together.

The house was a two-story craftsman that looked lived-in.

Loved. It had a generous front porch, with two rocking chairs, and a big red door. Large windows faced out onto the street with shutters painted a rich navy blue. There was a brick path that led directly to the front door, and a mailbox with a painting of a pineapple on the side.

Lizzie imagined cool fall days, wrapped in a throw blanket as she and Ritchie sat on the rocking chairs. She envisioned buying a swing that would hang on the end of the porch, and then drinking coffee as she watched her future children playing in the front yard. She could see herself hanging a Christmas wreath on that beautiful red door, a sign that everyone would be welcome at her house for the holidays.

She indulged these little fantasies anytime they drove by the house. Lizzie knew that Ritchie was listening to her—he always hung on her every word—but she hadn't realized what he was planning.

And now, here she was. Not only was she finally inside her dream house, but it belonged to her.

"I can't believe you did this," she said to Ritchie, as she stood in the front foyer. Even though she'd used the key to get in, even though they'd signed the papers that very morning, she could still hardly believe that it was theirs.

"You always said it was your dream house," Ritchie said. "So, I figured we should buy it." He smiled widely at her, and she kissed him in response.

"Can we look around?"

"It's yours now," Ritchie said. "You can do anything you want."

Lizzie paused as she walked into the dining room. Oh, the meals she would serve in this room! Sunday night dinners, like her mother used to do, and big holidays with tons of friends and family. Would her parents agree to come to their house for dinner? She had barely spoken to them since she'd eloped—once a month on the telephone, tops—but perhaps now that they had a respectable house, it would signal a respectable life. Perhaps now they would be ready to be a part of her life again. Yes, that would be the first thing she would do, Lizzie thought. As soon as she got a dining room set, she would invite her parents to dinner.

"I made sure they left the chandelier as part of the deal," Ritchie said with pride, pointing up at the light fixture that hung in the dining room. It was beautiful. It was just like Ritchie: dazzling and chaotic and brilliant. It caught the light that filtered in from the window, and made the room feel bigger. Brighter.

"That's incredible," Lizzie said. "I hope it didn't cost too much."

"Nothing is too much for you."

"Where did you get the money for this?"

"Don't worry about that," Ritchie said, wrapping his arms around her waist. "You just worry about decorating it."

Years later, once Ritchie's gambling problem had come to light, Lizzie would wonder why she hadn't pressed him further on how he'd gotten the house. Where the money had come from, when he could only hold down a job for a few months at a time. Why hadn't she asked more questions? Was it because, deep down, she knew the answers, but just hadn't wanted to admit it to herself? Lizzie truly didn't know.

42

Lizzie, 1981

"Now, that's a name you don't hear very often." The nurse read off the card on the bassinet as she leaned down. "Adelaide. Old family name?" The nurse carefully picked two-day old Adelaide up and handed her to Lizzie for the afternoon feeding.

"No," Lizzie said, getting Adelaide comfortable in her arms. Lizzie had never seen a more beautiful baby in her life. Just at that moment, Adelaide looked up at her, all big eyes and open heart, and it was as if nothing else in the world mattered. "It's from the show *Guys and Dolls*."

"Never heard of it."

"Broadway show? They made a movie out of it?" Lizzie didn't know why her statements were coming out as questions. "With Frank Sinatra?"

"Not familiar. Anything else I can help you with before you get started, Mom?"

Lizzie wondered how long it would take for her to get used to being called Mom. Was it something instinctual? Did you feel it the moment you gave birth? She didn't feel like a mom. Not yet, anyway. Sure, she had a baby in her arms, and that baby was undoubtedly hers, but she wasn't used to the name. Why couldn't the nurse just call her Lizzie? Or Mrs. Schneider (another name she had yet to get used to, but still preferable to the anonymous *Mom* that all the nurses seemed to use at the hospital)?

"What does your mother think of it?" The nurse's question broke Lizzie from her reverie. Lizzie hadn't even realized she was still in the room.

"Think of what?"

"The name."

"Oh, I don't know yet," Lizzie said, and put her head down to focus on Adelaide, a signal she hoped the nurse would interpret as her cue to leave. When Lizzie heard the gentle click of the door, she knew it was safe to look up. Who was that nurse, and how dare she comment on the name Lizzie had given her child?

Lizzie shook her head, as if to brush off the nurse's comments. She began feeding Adelaide, impressed by how heartily she ate, how hungry she seemed to be. This would be a healthy baby. Lizzie couldn't stop looking at her. This magical being. Did another baby ever look like this, ever? Sheer perfection. All she ever wanted, wrapped up in this tiny human.

Lizzie now understood what people meant when they spoke of the miracle of birth. It *was* a miracle, truly. How else to explain this tiny thing in her arms? Lizzie was exhausted from giving birth the day prior, but exhilarated by this baby she now held close. She could hardly believe this was something that women did every day. It felt so momentous. But everyone treated it like it was nothing, like filling a cavity, because it was a thing that women did, not men.

But, still, the nurse's question. Lizzie didn't know what her mother thought of the name, because her parents hadn't come to the hospital yet. Lizzie had hoped her mother would be there when she got out of the operating room. She knew that Ritchie had called them.

Lizzie was disappointed. How could her parents not want to

meet their first grandchild? She knew that they disapproved of Ritchie, but surely the birth of a grandchild would supersede any bad feelings?

Lizzie was among the last of her friends to have her first child, so she was familiar with how things usually went. Friends told stories of their mothers waiting patiently in the waiting room, desperate to meet their grandchildren. Fathers excitedly handing out cigars to everyone in the hospital. She even knew one girl whose mother had come into the delivery room with her, to hold her hand while her husband cut the umbilical cord.

Lizzie's story was a bit different. She'd woken up in the middle of the night in labor, only to find that Ritchie had gone out for a poker game. Lizzie had been lucky that one phone call to Ace's house was all she needed to track him down, and he was pulling into the driveway by the time she'd dressed and gotten a bag together with a few essentials.

They joked with the nurses about how Ritchie had almost missed the birth of his first child over a poker game. When the doctor arrived, he told his own story about being on an epic roll one night in Vegas, and once the baby was born, Lizzie had decided to pay homage to her favorite movie about gamblers by naming her daughter Adelaide.

Adelaide cooed as she fed. Lizzie ran her finger against the softness of her baby's face. Was there anything softer than a baby's skin? Anything more perfect than a baby's gentle breath? It was a miracle, pure and simple.

Adelaide stopped feeding. When this had happened yesterday, the nurse had suggested that the baby needed to burp. Careful to support her head, Lizzie lifted Adelaide up, and slowly patted her back. Having Adelaide pressed against her body, Lizzie felt her warmth and thought that maybe she could stay like this forever.

It was so primal, this need to touch and feed and take care of your baby. Lizzie had hardly noticed when it had kicked in. She rubbed Adelaide's back, and could hear her slightly gurgling. No burp yet. Then, Lizzie remembered how the other nurse had coached her yesterday: *"A little stronger, Mom. You won't hurt her!"*

Lizzie increased the pressure on the ball of her hand, and gave Adelaide a stronger bump. And then, just like the nurse had promised, she burped. Lizzie felt a flush of relief.

Maybe it was her first lesson in parenting: sometimes you have to be a little tougher than you'd like to be. You want to be gentle, but it's for the good of the child to be a bit firmer.

Was that what her own mother was doing to her by not coming to the hospital? Perhaps this was her mother's way of being firm.

Adelaide snuggled herself onto Lizzie's chest, her face right over where Lizzie's heart would be. Lizzie leaned down and planted a kiss on her daughter's head. It was soft, and smelled of baby powder and goodness. She let her lips linger on the top of her downy head for a few moments before her thoughts drifted back to her own mother.

No, Lizzie did not need her own mother now. She was a mother herself, and all she needed was Ritchie and their baby. As Lizzie herself began to drift off to sleep, Adelaide already napping on her chest, Lizzie could almost believe it.

43

Lizzie, 1985

Christmas Eve. A magical time.

One of the things Lizzie loved most about the house was creating new memories in it. Memories that would last her children a lifetime. Lizzie couldn't wait to throw a big Christmas Eve party, like her mother used to do. But she would make her Christmas Eve party even bigger, even better than the ones her mother used to host. Make it warmer, welcome even more people. In fact, Lizzie had invited her parents to sleep over after the party, so that they could enjoy Christmas morning all together.

The house was lit from within. Ritchie had insisted on getting Lizzie the biggest tree she'd ever seen, and they'd spent every weekend since Thanksgiving making it beautiful. Addy was only four, Nathan only three, but Ritchie picked the kids up, one by one, and helped them hang ornaments all around it. Lizzie's mother had a system for how to decorate a tree—the lights went first, wrapped evenly throughout the tree, and then the ribbons. The bright glass ornaments went toward the inside, making the tree glow, while the more delicate and intricate ornaments went toward the outside, for everyone to see and admire. A huge velvet ribbon went on top, and then picks were added to any spots that needed more fullness. (Her mother used red poinsettias, but Lizzie had bought a set of green-and-white mistletoe, covered in glitter.) Lizzie's tree skirt was made of a white fur that she thought impossibly glamorous.

Ace's family was the first to arrive.

"Everything looks so beautiful," Ace's second wife, Suzie, said, their two-year-old son, Donnie, in her arms.

"Thank you," Lizzie said. "Why don't you drop off Donnie in Nathan's room? The babysitter is entertaining the kids with a puppet show."

"You think of everything," she whispered to her friend, and rushed off up the stairs.

Lizzie put the music on—the CD player had been an early Christmas gift from Ritchie. It held five different CDs, and Lizzie planned to play her favorite Christmas albums on shuffle as many times as her guests would allow her to get away with it: *Once upon a Christmas* by Dolly Parton and Kenny Rogers; *Christmas Is Here* by Pedro Garcia Flores; *The Christmas Album* by Neil Diamond; *Elvis' Christmas Album*; and *A Jolly Christmas* from Frank Sinatra.

Within the hour, the house was filled with friends, old and new. Neighbors, other parents from the children's play groups, and Ritchie's coworkers from the car dealership. Lizzie's high school friends all made an appearance, and the guys from Ritchie's weekly card game all showed up, wives and children in tow. Ritchie poured glass after glass of his egg nog (secret ingredient: a splash of cognac), and Lizzie held court over by the Christmas tree.

The babysitter brought the kids downstairs, and they caroled the party guests, while the neighborhood teenagers tried to sneak egg nog.

Lizzie almost missed the phone ringing entirely. The music was loud, the guests even louder, and Lizzie wasn't expecting anyone to call. After all, nearly everyone that Lizzie knew was already there. But as the kids finished up their rendition of "Rudolph the Red-Nosed Reindeer," she ran into the kitchen before the last ring.

"I'm afraid we won't be able to make it." Lizzie had to press a finger inside her ear to hear the voice on the phone. It took a moment for Lizzie to realize it was her mother, and that she was not coming.

"Who was that?" Ritchie asked, as he came into the kitchen to refill the ice bucket.

"It was my mother," Lizzie said. She spoke quietly, holding back tears. "Seems she isn't feeling well this evening, so she can't come."

"Oh, Lizzie," Ritchie said, putting down the ice bucket and gathering Lizzie in his arms. "I'm so sorry."

"It's all right," Lizzie said, breaking from his embrace and grabbing a napkin to dab at her eyes. "It's no problem at all. And we have a house full of guests. We should tend to them."

"I know how much it meant to you," Ritchie said. "I'm sorry."

Lizzie looked at Ritchie. She cupped his face in her hand. "All I really need is you."

44

Ritchie, 1992

It was the hardest conversation he would ever have. Ritchie didn't know how to tell Lizzie. How to say it. How to admit the truth.

But he had to, since they would need to be out of their house by the end of the month. Ritchie had fucked up. Sure, he'd screwed up plenty of times in the past, lost tons of money over the years, but this one couldn't be undone. This time, he'd lost it all.

It was bad enough that he'd made the call he never thought he'd make—to Gamblers Anonymous. He spoke to a very nice person on the phone who told him that everything would be okay. Most family members of gamblers never knew how bad the problem was, so the conversation would be rough, but they'd all been through it, and they'd all come out the other side. It was important to tell Lizzie the truth, and then start working the program.

"I don't know how to say this to you," Ritchie said to Lizzie. He knew this was the moment that would separate his world into before and after. Lizzie would never look at him that way again, so carefree. So unconditionally loving. "Can we sit down?"

"I've got to get dinner going," Lizzie said, shuffling around the kitchen. She took some vegetables out of the fridge's crisper and began to chop. "Can this wait?"

"It can't wait."

Lizzie looked up from the counter. "What can't wait?"

"It's all gone."

"What's gone?"

"The money. The house. Everything. We need to move out by the end of the month." Ritchie was speaking fast, so fast, as if delivering the information at record speed would lessen its impact.

"What on earth are you saying? Is this a joke?" Lizzie laughed and then continued chopping the vegetables.

"It's not a joke."

She looked up at Ritchie. "So, then, why would we need to move out of our house?"

"I lost the house. I lost everything."

Lizzie's hands froze over the cutting board. "What? How?"

"Gambling."

"How could you possibly lose that much money gambling? I know you and your friends like to have fun, but you're smart about it." She waved her arms around, the knife in her right hand, as she spoke. Ritchie watched Lizzie's arms, her hands. The knife.

"Usually I am," Ritchie said, his head bowed down. "But this time, I wasn't. This time, it got completely out of control."

"But it's just a hobby. It's just for fun, those poker games. Do you owe Ace money or something?"

"It's not Ace."

"You're serious."

"As a heart attack. I'm so sorry."

"I'm just confused," Lizzie said, shaking her head. She gripped the knife harder. Her knuckles turned white. "How could you lose so much money at one time?"

Ritchie didn't answer. He watched as the realization slowly came over Lizzie's face.

"You didn't lose it all at once."

Ritchie found himself unable to respond.

"So, this is something that's been going on for a long time?"

Ritchie hung his head. "Yes."

"But you never told me," Lizzie said, placing the knife onto the cutting board. "Why didn't you tell me?"

"I thought I would get it back. That you'd never have to know."

Lizzie laughed, but her face told another story. "Well, now I know."

"I mean, you knew that I liked to gamble."

"Gambling is one thing. Having fun at a casino, playing poker with friends. *Losing our house* is another."

"I'll win it back," Ritchie said. "I promise you. It's just for now, the bank—"

"What do you mean, you'll win it back?" Lizzie furrowed her brow. "You can't gamble anymore. You obviously have a problem. A huge, raging problem."

"It's not a problem. I can stop anytime I want. I just got myself into a jam—"

"A jam?" Lizzie's voice got louder. She almost never yelled, and it threw Ritchie off his game.

"I'm going to fix it. Let me fix it, and then I'll stop. I can stop anytime I want."

"If you can stop at any time," Lizzie said, her voice now full-blown thunder, "then, why didn't you stop before you lost our house? Our goddamned home? The place where we're raising our children?"

"I know. Look, I—"

"What are we going to tell Addy and Nathan?"

"If you'd just calm down—"

"Calm down?" Lizzie shouted. "You want me to calm down? I gave up everything for you. My family, my sister, my mother—"

"Lizzie, please," Ritchie said. "This is the last time, I promise."

Quietly: "Get out of my house."

"Lizzie, I—"

Louder: "Get out of my house. It's still mine until the end of the month, isn't it?"

"Well, yes, but—"

Louder still: "Get out!"

"Lizzie, you don't mean that."

"I do mean it. You kept this from me. A secret. For how long, Ritchie? How long have you been lying to me? A month?"

Ritchie looked down at his shoes.

"Longer? Three months? Six?"

Ritchie didn't answer.

"Get out!" Lizzie screamed. "Get out!" She screamed it over and over, louder and louder, until Ritchie left the house. And even after he slammed the front door shut, he heard her screaming. He started his car, and backed out of the driveway. He could still hear her screaming.

Even as he got to the end of the block, at the stop sign on the corner, Ritchie swore he could still hear Lizzie screaming.

45

Courtney

Why must you always mess things up? Courtney asked her reflection in the mirror.

Courtney looked at herself and couldn't help but think about all the things she'd done wrong. Losing the LA apartment. Getting herself into debt with a bookie. Burning down Nathan and Diego's loft. And now this.

Courtney had always resented the way Addy swept in and tried to fix everything all the time. If Sy hadn't shown up in the Caymans, Addy wouldn't think she needed help. If Courtney hadn't burned down the loft, Addy wouldn't have to host everyone at her house. If she hadn't told the girls to pose with the ring for Instagram, there wouldn't be this lawsuit. Courtney hit her head lightly on the mirror. Then, a bit harder. Her head throbbed, but she did it again. It hurt, but it felt good. Like she deserved it, somehow. She would have hit her head against the mirror a fourth time, if the doorbell hadn't rung. She froze where she stood—she did not want to go downstairs.

Duke began barking furiously at the sound of the doorbell. Courtney heard Addy rush across the house, screaming: "She's here! She's here!" By the time Courtney got down the stairs, she found her entire family gathered, all standing by the door, ready to meet their Aunt Maggie's daughter.

Addy arranged her face into a huge smile and opened the door wide. "You're here!"

The woman on the other side of the door looked terrified. Maybe it hadn't been such a good idea to greet her all at once?

"Come in," Addy said. "Come in! I'm Adelaide, but everyone calls me Addy. This is my husband, Gary, and our girls, Olivia and Emma. This is my brother, Nathan, and his husband, Diego. And this is our sister, Courtney. You must be Holly."

Holly Morgan stood frozen at the door, her mouth arranged in an *o*, as if she'd been surprised by what she saw when Addy opened the door, and had not yet gotten over it. Quietly, she said, "There are so many of you."

Duke jumped up into Holly's arms. "Oh, and this is Duke!"

"Why don't we give her some room," Gary said, motioning for the family to move into the house, away from the door.

Everyone followed his lead, but Courtney did not. She felt that as a sibling, she should stay. After all, this lawsuit concerned her, concerned the ring that belonged to her family, so she should face this matter head-on. Nathan seemed to have had the same idea, because he didn't budge, either.

"I feel like I should hug you," Addy said. Courtney was having trouble deciphering if this was Addy's fake voice or if she genuinely wanted to hug this person. Then, she saw the slightest twitch of her sister's eye and realized, all at once, that it was nerves. Addy was nervous. "Should we hug?"

Holly put her hand out.

"Forgive my sister," Nathan said, stepping in front of Addy. "She's just really excited to meet you. I'm Nathan. Can I take your jacket?" He shook her hand, and so Courtney followed suit, introducing herself. Holly handed Nathan her jacket, and he hung it up in the front closet.

Addy led the group into the living room, where she'd set out appetizers: a platter of cheese and crackers with a bowl of mixed nuts on the side, a bowl of chips with a smaller bowl of salsa on the side, and yet another bowl filled with her homemade guacamole. Courtney marveled at the sheer number of bowls. Was a bowl a symbol of welcome, like a pineapple? "Can I get anyone a drink?"

"I'll take a—" Nathan tried to answer.

"I meant Holly," Addy said, cutting him off. "Holly, what can I get you to drink?"

"No, thank you."

Holly sat down on the couch. Courtney felt Addy's eyes on her as she sat down next to Holly. Was she not supposed to have done that? Addy wasn't the boss of her. This girl was her family, too. Courtney could charm her just as easily as Addy could. Maybe Courtney would be the one to fix things, for once, and get Holly to drop the lawsuit.

"So," Nathan said, as he settled onto the opposite couch with two glasses of wine, handing one to Diego as if on autopilot. Diego tapped his lips with his index finger, twice, but Nathan didn't seem to notice. Courtney had seen them do this before— send each other taps on the lips—and Nathan usually responded back in kind. But this time, he didn't even notice Diego doing it. "Tell us about yourself."

"Oh, I, uh…" Holly looked like a deer caught in headlights. She stared blankly at Nathan, seemingly unable to speak.

"This must be overwhelming for you," Addy said, walking over from the bar cart to the couch. She stood over Courtney until she got the message—this was her dinner, her night. Courtney would have to move. Courtney slid to the edge of the couch, allowing Addy to sit between her and Holly. Courtney immediately chastised herself—she should have scooted toward the middle, leaving Addy on the end. Courtney got up and refilled her wineglass.

Addy made herself comfortable in the middle of the couch, the center of the room. Turning to Holly: "We're just excited to get to know you. We're shocked that we didn't even know that our Aunt Maggie had a daughter."

"She was estranged from the family, yes," Holly said, her voice thin and difficult to hear.

"I always thought it was *our* mother who was estranged," Nathan said, seemingly only to Addy. Courtney watched as Addy raised her shoulders. Nathan responded in kind. Courtney considered leaving the room and going upstairs for the evening— would anyone even notice? She turned this thought over in her mind once, twice. Instead, she filled her wineglass to the tippy-top and sat back down on the couch.

"I didn't even know that I was a part of your family," Holly said, her voice still quiet.

Courtney wondered if she did the quiet voice on purpose. When she'd met Sy, he did it at dinner. She asked him to speak up, and he told her that very important people always talked quietly, since they knew they commanded the room. He suggested that she never raise her voice, either—eventually people would realize that they needed to listen carefully if they wanted to hear what she had to say. So far, this advice had not worked out for Courtney. Courtney wondered if you needed to be a master of the universe, like Sy, for this trick to work. The most powerful person in the room. Courtney was not the most powerful person in the room, ever. She was not even the most powerful person in her family.

"For most of my life, I had no idea who my father was," Holly said.

"Well, we're just glad you're here now," Addy said, facing Holly, her back to Courtney.

"For all those years, we had no one," Holly continued, as if Addy hadn't just spoken to her. "It was just the two of us."

"You've got tons of us now," Nathan said, smiling. Courtney

saw Diego try to take Nathan's hand, only to find it unrecipro-cated. Nathan was so wrapped up in the Addy/Nathan show, that he hadn't even noticed his husband, sitting right next to him.

"We didn't really know your mother," Addy said. "But we saw our mother's photo albums, and your mother was beautiful."

No one said the obvious thing, the fact that Holly herself wasn't beautiful. She was plain. The edges of her mouth seemed to be turned downward, as if set in a permanent frown.

"Yes," Nathan chimed in. "Maggie was so beautiful."

"My mother was a lot of things," Holly said, looking down at her shoes.

This was painful. Courtney took a long sip of her wine. How long did they have to do this? Pretend to be making nice, when the only reason Holly was really there was because Addy thought she could get her to drop the lawsuit. Courtney was amazed at how highly her sister thought of herself. She thought she was so much smarter than everyone else, so able to make the world bend to her will. Courtney should pull Holly aside and tell her the truth. That would show her. Courtney brought her wine-glass to her lips, just another tiny sip, but found that the glass was already empty again. She got up to refill it.

"I'm trying to see if there's a family resemblance," Addy said. "I definitely look like our mother, but Nathan and I don't look that much alike."

"You look like your sister," Holly said, and Courtney could feel all eyes in the room land on her back as she stood at the bar cart. "Courtney."

"Courtney and I have the same hair," Addy said. "So, Na-than, I guess that makes you the odd man out."

"Well, luckily, your daughters seemed to have inherited my good looks," Nathan said, "so you're welcome."

"It's nice that the three of you are close," Holly said.

"We're not close," Courtney said, turning away from the bar cart to address Holly.

"Tell us more about your mother," Addy said, drawing Holly's attention back to center.

"It was complicated," Holly said.

"Oh," Addy said. The room filled with the silence.

Holly dabbed a napkin to the side of her eye. "She kept things from me. But then, a month before she died, I found a box filled with these letters. Love letters. And I knew. I just knew they were from my father. I confronted her, and she admitted the truth. That my father was Ritchie Schneider. That was when I started following you on Instagram. I got a bit obsessed, I guess you could say."

"I get it," Courtney said, sitting back down on the couch. If she'd looked at her sister, she would have noticed that Addy's face had lost all color. But Courtney was focused on Holly. "I'm sort of obsessed with Instagram, too."

"You look different than your pictures on Instagram," Holly said, furrowing her brow.

Courtney struggled to keep the smile plastered on her face. She might have looked different than her Instagram photos, but Holly Morgan looked different than Courtney had pictured her, in her mind's eye. She thought Holly would look more like her Aunt Maggie, which was to say, impossibly sexy, and a little dangerous. Courtney only knew her Aunt Maggie from old photo albums, but even in two dimensions, Maggie was a force.

Holly was not a force. She sat hunched over, as if in defeat. Courtney may have been a giant fuckup, but at least she didn't look like it.

Courtney reached over to put her wineglass down onto the coffee table, but missed the coaster. Addy cried out and tried to grab it as the glass fell to the rug. Courtney watched this happen, but was too slow from the wine to react. Luckily, the glass had been empty.

Just then, the oven's timer went off. "Dinner's ready," Addy said. "Should we all go to the kitchen?" Addy did not wait for anyone to respond. She led the charge, everyone following her, like baby ducks in a row. Courtney wondered what would happen to the many bowls they'd left in their wake.

Addy removed the pot roast from the oven, and Nathan got the sides plated and onto the table. Gary and Diego disappeared downstairs to pick out a bottle of wine, and Courtney set the table with her nieces.

"What can I do?" Holly asked Courtney.

"You're our guest!" Courtney said. "Please, just have a seat."

"Yes," Addy said, wrestling the pot roast onto the butcher block so that she could slice it with her electric knife. "You're family. Please, just sit."

"Shouldn't family help out?" Holly asked. "Looks like the siblings take care of the meal, the spouses pick out the wine, and the kids set the table. Let me help."

"I think we've got it covered," Nathan said.

Courtney stared at the cloth napkins in her hand. *The kids set the table*. Even Holly could see it—Addy and Nathan treated her like a child. And what was worse was that Holly had cast herself in the sibling role so easily. Why hadn't Courtney done that? Her thoughts tumbled around, making her feel light-headed. Courtney threw the napkins down on the table. She spun on her heel to go upstairs.

"Court," Addy said. "Where are you going? Dinner's ready!"

"I'm going upstairs," Courtney said.

"Your dinner will get cold," Holly said.

Courtney turned to face Holly. Holly stood next to Addy, holding a bowl filled with warm breadsticks. "*You* are not a sibling," Courtney said to Holly. As soon as the words were out of her mouth, she regretted them. She shouldn't have said that. After all, the whole point of the evening was to get Holly to like them, to get her to drop the lawsuit. Not to antagonize her. But Courtney couldn't stop. So, instead, she doubled down. "I'm barely a sibling here, so that makes you… Well, I don't know what it makes you, but you are not a sibling. So, you can just put those fucking breadsticks down."

Holly placed the breadsticks back on the island. Her face flushed red. "I'm sorry, I shouldn't have come."

"Why would anyone want to willingly join this family, anyway?" Courtney said, the edges of her vision blurring, ever so slightly. "I've been a member all my life, and let me assure you, it's not that great."

"Courtney," Addy said, with the same intonation she used to chastise her girls.

"She's kidding," Nathan said, laughing nervously. "We tease a lot in this family. So, you'd better get used to it!"

"I'm not kidding," Courtney said, looking at her brother. His forehead was beginning to glisten. Then, bringing her attention back to Holly: "If you want to be a part of this family so badly, go ahead, take my spot!"

"Aunt Courtney," her nieces said in unison. Then, Emma: "You don't mean that."

"I think we've all had enough to drink for one night," Addy said, laughing nervously. "I think maybe we should bring those breadsticks to the table to soak up some of the alcohol! Let's eat, shall we?"

"No, I think I should go," Holly said quietly. "This was a mistake."

"Please stay," Addy said. "You're our Aunt Maggie's daughter, our cousin, and we'd like to get to know you."

"*Cousin,*" Holly repeated. She laughed a hollow laugh. A sad laugh. "You don't believe me."

"Our father would never have cheated on our mother," Nathan said.

"Nathan!" Addy said. "Let's table this discussion for now."

"There's no discussion," Holly said. "I have the letters. I have the proof. Ritchie Schneider was my father."

"No, he was not," Nathan said, more forcefully this time.

"Maybe you should leave," Courtney said. Addy threw a death stare in her direction, but really, wasn't Courtney just saying what everyone else was thinking?

"Was that the plan all along?" Holly asked. "You're trying to scare me off from being a part of your family?"

"The opposite!" Addy said, throwing her arms out wide. "Quite the opposite! We're welcoming you to our family!"

"So, you want me to drop the lawsuit. That's all this is about."

"That's not the reason we invited you," Addy said. "But yes, we don't think a lawsuit is necessary for an issue we can handle within the family."

"You're no different than my mother," Holly said, her hands balling up into fists. "I never knew the truth about anything. Everything was a manipulation."

"We're not trying to manipulate you," Nathan said. "Until two weeks ago, we didn't know that you existed. We're just trying to get to know you."

"Please stay," Addy said.

Holly shook her head, back and forth, as if having an internal debate with herself. Then, she rushed out of the house, leaving her jacket behind.

46

Addy

Addy used to be good at things. Addy used to fix things, make things better. All she'd done now was make things worse. It was as if the longer Courtney stayed at her house, the more she rubbed off on her. Addy had thought that the opposite would have happened. But no, the rubbing off seemed to be happening in the wrong direction.

Addy sat quietly, waiting for her name to be called for the DNA test. She'd forgotten the novel she meant to throw into her bag, and so she sat staring at the walls of the waiting room instead, alone with her thoughts. The lawsuit would be going forward, just as if the dinner had not happened. (Or maybe more forcefully now?) She had been sure that her plan would work—after sharing a lovely family dinner, the lawsuit would be dropped and the DNA test would be unnecessary. Only now she could see that she hadn't been optimistic. She'd been foolish.

A lab tech called her name. "Addy, hi!"

Addy looked back at the tech and smiled.

"It's me," she said, "Rebecca O'Connor! Courtney's friend?"

Addy followed her back to the examination room and tried to place her.

"It's so good to see you!" Rebecca said. "I haven't seen your sister in years. How is she?"

"Oh, she's fine," Addy said and jumped up on the examination table. She wondered if she should take off her shoes? Or stay dressed? All they really needed was to swab her cheek, right?

"Addy Schneider," Rebecca said, smiling brightly. "It's been so long. What are you up to these days?"

"Oh, you know," Addy said, still trying to place who Rebecca was. Surely she should have remembered one or two of Courtney's friends? But, no. When it came to Courtney's childhood, Addy was drawing a blank. "Married, two kids…"

"Me too!" Rebecca said, taking her phone out of her scrubs pocket to show Addy pictures.

"They're adorable," Addy said, as she looked at Rebecca's toddlers. She searched their little baby faces for something that would remind her of who Rebecca was. But she couldn't remember a thing. Addy laughed nervously.

"Okay, enough of my kids. Let me go get the nurse for you."

"Thank you."

Addy closed her eyes. She wished she hadn't forgotten that book. She had the sudden urge to grab her phone, to waste time by scrolling through Instagram, but that was what had gotten her family into this trouble to begin with. She thought about the post—how one little photo could cause so much trouble. How one humongous ring could change the dynamic of her family. Bring one sister home from the West Coast, invite a new maybe-sister in from God-knows-where, and lead the whole lot of them to start fighting. Things would have been better if they'd never found that ring in the first place. How different things might have been if they hadn't taken that trip down to the Caymans. If they'd just told the banker to get rid of the safe-deposit box, sight unseen. If she hadn't retuned the telephone call. None of this would have happened. She could have gone on with her life just the way it had been before.

But she'd returned the call.

Addy replayed last night's conversation in her mind: Courtney offering Holly her spot in the family. Courtney was lucky to be a member of their family. Didn't she know that? Addy was the one who should be kicking Courtney out of the family, not the reverse. After all, if not for her and Nathan, who would have helped her out of her sugar baby situation and brought her home? Of course, Courtney hadn't asked for their help. (Better not to think of that.)

There was a knock on the door. "Come in," Addy said, just as the nurse was letting herself into the room.

"Just a DNA test today?"

"Yes," Addy said. "It's silly, really. This lawsuit…" She trailed off as she realized the nurse didn't really care why she was there. Addy was babbling.

"Addy's sister was my childhood best friend," Rebecca said to the nurse. "So, we need to show her the VIP treatment."

Addy smiled uneasily. *The VIP treatment.* When Addy couldn't recall who Rebecca even was.

"VIP treatment it is. So, open wide, and we'll swab your cheek," the nurse said, and Addy closed her eyes, like a child trying to be invisible. Just close your eyes and pretend that it wasn't happening. Like her relationship with Courtney. Just close your eyes and pretend that she didn't exist.

"And that's it."

"Thank you."

"The lab will report the results directly to the court," the nurse said. "Any questions?"

Addy laughed. Addy had many questions. Did she really wish that she could go back to the time before they found the ring? Would that make things better? Sure, she would go back to never speaking to her sister, except for Christmas (well, most Christmases), but was that better?

Perhaps it was time for Addy to reevaluate her relationship with Courtney. Was it too late to take a lifetime of hurt and turn it into a real relationship? Was that something Courtney even wanted? How could she even begin?

Yes, Addy had many questions. But none that the nurse could answer for her.

47

Nathan

Nathan drove down to the beach to take a jog before work. It was something he hadn't done since high school—run off to the beach to escape for an hour—but for some reason, it was like his body was taking him there without his mind listening.

The beach always reminded Nathan of his parents. Their first date took place down near the beach, and he would always think of their romantic story anytime he was there.

But now all he could think about was what Holly had said at dinner. As he gave his legs a stretch, he wondered: Could this story be true? Did his father have an affair? Could he have a half sibling he knew nothing about? If he had a half sibling out there in the world, wouldn't he have known it? Sometimes it felt like he had a cosmic connection to Addy, like if she fell down, he would feel it. If she was having a bad day, he'd know.

Then he remembered Courtney. He went weeks without thinking about her. Remembering she even existed. Nathan's face flushed with shame.

He checked his shoelaces and set off on the sand. He began with a slow jog, letting his legs get into a groove. Holly had thirty days to comply with the court-ordered DNA test. Dinner hadn't gone well, but Nathan hoped she wouldn't drag her feet, hoped they could resolve this soon. Nathan needed to know the truth.

His father would never betray his mother like that. He could never be with another woman. His mother's sister, no less. Nathan wasn't a religious person, but he'd worshipped at the altar of Lizzie and Ritchie since he was a kid. How many of his life's choices had he made based on the search for that one perfect love? That ultimate love story?

Nathan ran harder, faster. The sand gave way beneath his feet, so he moved toward the water, where it was packed more densely.

His parents had never divorced. They'd had many ups and downs, but they'd managed to get through all of them. The nine-month separation. They fought hard for their love. They'd made it through everything, their love not just intact, but stronger.

Was the love he shared with Diego strong enough to make it through anything? Could Nathan forgive him for an affair? After all, he worked late at the office nearly every night. Maybe it was his fault for not being around enough?

But it was more than the affair, wasn't it? They didn't speak anymore. Didn't really hear each other. Case in point: this ridiculous fortieth birthday party Diego was planning for him.

Nathan smiled and nodded as he passed other runners on the beach. He recalled the advice of an old friend—sometimes if you start to smile, your body catches up and you start to feel happy. But all Nathan felt was angry, confused. He ran faster, and didn't even notice it when the waves hit his sneakers.

He would be forty years old in just a few months. By the time his mother had turned forty, she had already lost her house, separated from her husband for nine months, and then taken him back and started their whole lives together again. What had Nathan done in his forty years? What did he have to show for it?

Nathan slowed his pace, finally coming to a stop as he got to the end of the beach. He sat down in the sand and put his head in his hands.

Nathan began to cry.

The waves came up to his feet, and as they licked his ankles, Nathan leapt up. He'd forgotten how cold the ocean was, off season. Wiping the tears from his eyes, he walked back toward his car. He would just solve his problems like he did any other—with a list. He'd put it onto an Excel spreadsheet, if he had to. What were the problems bothering him most?

1. His marriage.
2. Turning forty.
3. The possibility of a half sister.

Turning forty couldn't be changed, and the mess with their half sister would take a while to untangle. And they'd already done the first step—the DNA test. As for his marriage, a bit of advice from his father popped into his head: the way to woo a lover is through an old-fashioned love letter. Ritchie had encouraged Nathan to write one after the break-up with his college ex. (He hadn't listened.) And then, he remembered.

Ritchie wrote Lizzie love letters. Nathan had a hatbox full of them. And those were just the final versions. There were more. Ritchie wrote drafts of them in his notebooks, those falling-apart things he always carried. He wrote them on his hand and he wrote them on receipts from the track. The final versions were written on beautiful scented paper that he'd take hours to pick out at the stationery store. When Nathan was a kid, this was the most romantic thing he'd ever heard, and it colored the way he viewed his father. Here was this man, this strong-looking Brooklyn tough guy, and he wrote love letters. Poems.

But now Maggie's daughter was tarnishing that memory. She claimed Ritchie wrote love letters to her mother, too. If a man writes love letters to many different women, doesn't that make them less important? Less romantic? After all, how could you mean everything you wrote to two different women?

Nathan needed to get his hands on those love letters. Needed to read his father's notebooks, needed to get inside his father's mind and find out what he was thinking, what he was doing, for all those years. He ran, as fast as he could, back to his car. There was no way Ritchie would have thrown out the notebooks. He saved each one, like a collector would save a piece of fine china. Gamblers saved good luck charms, and these notebooks were about to be Nathan's good luck.

With each step on the sand, Nathan thought: When was the last time he'd seen the notebooks? Where had those notebooks gone when Ritchie died? Lizzie had refused to clean the house out after Ritchie's death. Nathan remembered this. Lizzie said there were too many memories attached to each thing, and she wouldn't let Addy get a cleaning crew in to help her figure out what should be trashed and what should be donated. Nathan had fought with Addy—Addy suggested that perhaps they do it one day when Lizzie was out, but Nathan insisted they respect their mother's wishes.

So, the notebooks were in the house when Ritchie had died. That much, Nathan knew for sure. But then when Lizzie died, Addy had gotten her wish—she brought in a cleaning crew to help her go through the house, ready it for selling. Nathan was there that day. Did he see the notebooks? Surely if he'd seen one, he would have taken it. But then he remembered the boxes in the attic. Any boxes marked *Ritchie* were just brought to the store, without even being opened. At the time, Nathan told Addy that they might come in handy one day, and she accused him of being a pack rat. Called him a sentimental fool.

"You haven't needed those boxes marked *Ritchie* in all of the years that you've been running the store," Addy had said at the time. "What makes you think you need them now?"

Nathan hadn't answered his sister then, but he knew that he shouldn't throw them away. For some reason, he just knew.

Nathan couldn't wait to get to his office, find the old notebooks, and then say the thing that he loved saying to his know-it-all sister: *I told you so.*

48

Ritchie's notebook, 1992

She is my love
She is my everything
I wish she could see what I see when I look at her
How I long to be back in my bed, next to her
~~How I long to make things right, go back to the way things were~~
GONNA NEED MORE THAN SOME STUPID LOVE
POEM

49

Ritchie's notebook, 1992

9-30-92: Skipped GA meeting. Do I really need them anymore?

10-1-92: Wrote a love letter for Lizzie. Maybe this time she'll accept it? Lost count of how many she's thrown away.

10-2-92: Picked kids up from Lizzie's rental house. She needed help with a leaky sink. I offered to help, and she let me do it.

10-3-92: Took kids to the movies, pizza afterward for dinner. Miss those kids like crazy when home during the week.

10-4-92: Lizzie invited me in for coffee when I dropped the kids off. Things looking up?

10-5-92: Lead on a job at a brokerage firm.

10-6-92: Card game at Ace's place. New guy joined the game, a jeweler.

10-7-92: Thinking about getting into jewelry business—that guy seems loaded. Too bad he can't play cards to save his life.

10-8-92: Saw Lizzie at back-to-school night. Knees bumped when we got into those tiny chairs at Addy's English class.

10-9-92: Went to pick kids up for the weekend. Lizzie had pizzas waiting. Got to have dinner as a family.

10-10-92: Took kids to a Broadway show in the city. Ace's friend got us backstage. Those cats are goddamn terrifying up close.

10-11-92: Dropped kids off at home, and Lizzie suggested we all go out for Sunday night dinner. After dinner, I suggested that maybe I could see the kids during the week, too. Lizzie said yes.

10-12-92: Lonely day, lonely dinner in front of the TV.

10-13-92: Can't stop thinking of Lizzie.

10-14-92: Went to Lizzie's rental to see the kids, brought in takeout from the Italian place Lizzie loves. Worked like a charm. Got to have dinner again like a family.

10-15-92: Made appointment to see Ace's jeweler friend from the card game. Calls himself "Pete the Jeweler." Beautiful stuff, just need a big win to take something home.

10-16-92: When I went to Lizzie's to pick up the kids for the weekend, the kids came running outside to see me, and Lizzie said: "what's the rush?" Invited me in for coffee.

10-17-92: Took kids to the mall. Addy ran off with a bunch of friends. Nathan doesn't seem to have as many.

10-18-92: Dropped kids at home, Lizzie had a home-cooked meal waiting. Invited me in.

10-19-82: Interview for job at brokerage firm.

10-20-92: Got the job. Can't wait to tell Lizzie.

10-21-92: First day on the new job—couldn't wait. Boss says I'm a natural at selling stocks.

10-23-92: Picked kids up for the weekend, took everyone out to dinner.

10-24-92: Lizzie agreed to come with us into the city for a matinee of Phantom.

10-25-92: Dropped kids back at home, could've sworn Lizzie wanted me to invite myself in. I didn't.

10-27-92: Won big at poker game at Ace's house. Pete the Jeweler said he'd pay me with something from his store.

My love,
You asked me to tell you something that was true.

    I know only this—I love you. Let me say it again: I love you.
Only you. You say that I love the cards and the chips more than
you, but that's not the truth. It's you. It's always been you. It
will always be you.

    Ours was not an ordinary love, ours was a mad, furious love.
A love that was stronger than either of us could even know at the
time, an all-consuming thing. The kind they write novels and love
songs about, musicals and operas. Our love is monumental, epic,
extraordinary. Our love is the stuff of legends.

Love,
Ritchie
1992

50

Lizzie, 1992

This was a mistake.

Lizzie and Ritchie had been back together for a month, but Lizzie felt it in her bones. She'd made a mistake. Lizzie turned the business card over in her hands. She would make the call today. She'd meant to do it yesterday, of course she had, but she hadn't been able to bring herself to even take the card out of the back of her wallet, where she'd hidden it safely behind Addy's and Nathan's school pictures.

But today she would do it. Today, she would call the divorce lawyer.

How could she have gone back to Ritchie? What had she been thinking? She'd sacrificed her relationship with her family for him. He'd lost their house, gambled it away, and she'd taken him back. Had it been the ring that had swayed her? Did she really think the ring symbolized a change in Ritchie? That it meant that things would be any different this time?

Her mother was right. She never should have married Ritchie. But it was too late, wasn't it? She was almost forty years old. She was thirteen years in. She had two children with him, a life. How do you extricate yourself from that? Lizzie didn't know how.

Lizzie thought of Elizabeth Taylor and Richard Burton. Their Hollywood namesakes, she called them. When Liz and Dick got back together again, it was a disaster. They'd gotten divorced again a year later.

Lizzie had been hopelessly, madly in love with Ritchie since she was sixteen years old. How do you stop yourself from wanting your first love, still needing him? It simply wasn't possible. The pull was physical, chemical. Impossible to stop. *Fate.* When she thought about their first kiss, about any kiss from Ritchie really, she felt it all over her body. The way his lips felt on hers. The way his body pressed up against hers, as if they were perfectly matched. As if they were made for each other. A lock and a key. When she was near him, her body betrayed her. Even if her mind said: *run!* Her body was right there, saying: *come closer. Closer.*

But today she would make the call. Today she would take the first step in doing what she knew she should have done almost a year ago, when Ritchie had told her he'd lost their home. She was going to divorce Ritchie Schneider. She'd start a new life, a better life. Maybe even a life that included her mother and her sister again.

Lizzie lay in bed, turning the business card over in her hands. She'd gotten back into bed after breakfast, after getting Addy and Nathan on the school bus. Exhaustion had overcome her, and it wasn't even 9 a.m. Since getting back together with Ritchie, she hadn't gotten much sleep.

As she thought about being with Ritchie the night before, a feeling came over her. Usually, such thoughts set her body on fire, like she could still feel his touches on her skin, but this was different. For some reason, the feeling wasn't lust. The feeling was nausea.

Lizzie jumped up and ran to the bathroom. She made it to the toilet in time to get sick. Horribly sick. What had she eaten for breakfast? Had she eaten the kids' leftovers again? It was a horrible habit she'd developed in the nine months that she lived alone with them. Never eating a full meal, just eating whatever Addy and Nathan left behind, over the kitchen sink as she washed the dishes. What had she served them this morning? Surely a leftover frozen waffle couldn't make her ill. Lizzie tried hard to remember. But then, instantly: she knew it wasn't anything that she'd eaten. She knew why she was sick. And she knew that she would get sick again.

She was pregnant. She knew it, clear as day. She had made a mistake, many mistakes, and this time, she couldn't get herself out of it.

51

The ring, 2006

What Courtney thinks happened in 2006: Ritchie gambled the ring away.

What really happened in 2006: Ritchie gambled the ring away.

Ritchie had completely forgotten it was poker night. And he was set to host. Poker nights usually happened on Mondays, but Ace had asked to switch it to Sunday that week.

Lizzie was out at a friend's daughter's bridal shower, and Ritchie had planned to eat pizza and watch a movie with Courtney. Lizzie loved how Ritchie had such a close relationship with Courtney. Even at age thirteen, her daughter delighted in spending time with her dad.

When the doorbell rang, Ritchie assumed it was the pizza. Even though he'd just ordered it ten minutes prior, it simply did not dawn on him that he had made other plans. But when he saw Ace standing on his doorstep with a six-pack and a smile, he remembered.

"Hey, Uncle Ace," Courtney said, standing behind Ritchie. "We just ordered a pizza. We rented *Ocean's Eleven*. Want to watch with us?"

"Sinatra?"

"No," Ritchie said.

"You know we got a game, right?"

"Forgot," Ritchie said. "You want to round up the guys and bring them to your house instead?"

"Sure, boss."

"I don't mind," Courtney said. "We can order more pizza, and you can teach me some poker tips."

"This isn't your kind of game," Ritchie said.

"Not your kind of crowd," Ace said, just as three other cars pulled up to the house.

"Please?" Courtney pled. "You'll barely know I'm there."

"The game's off," Ritchie said.

"I'll feel bad if you cancel it because of me. I'll just watch the movie upstairs while you guys play," Courtney said as a plan began to take form: she'd watch her movie (a movie about gambling, the irony), and then sneak down to watch some of the game, pick up some poker tips. "After all you do for me, you should have a few hours to yourself."

Ritchie considered this as the men got out of their cars and walked up the driveway. "You'll watch the movie upstairs," Ritchie said, as Ace nodded in agreement.

Courtney smiled and then ran up the steps.

Ritchie and his friends set up in the kitchen. As Ritchie made his way into the family room to grab the cards, he heard Ace saying to the men quietly: "Don't speak to her. Don't even look at her. If you get within five feet of the staircase, I'm not responsible for what I might do to you."

An hour later, the pizzas were gone, and Ritchie was up five hundred. Two hours later, Courtney's movie had ended, and she came downstairs for a glass of water. The men all put their heads into their cards, afraid to be caught even glancing at Courtney.

Courtney announced to the table that for her twenty-first birthday, she and Ritchie were driving to Atlantic City. It was true—they'd been planning the trip ever since she could remember, and Ritchie was excited about it. Lizzie refused to go—she didn't think they should be glamorizing gambling to their child, even though she'd come to terms with the fact that Ritchie still dabbled—but Ritchie thought it was harmless. After all, it had been a long time since something really bad had happened because of gambling. He didn't even need to attend the meetings anymore. He was fine. And anyway, the only gambling he really did was this friendly poker game once a month, the occasional visit to a casino while on an island vacation.

Ritchie loved how close he and his daughter were. Sure, he had a great relationship with Addy and Nathan, too, but his relationship with Courtney was different. He was older, for starters, and he was a new man. A better man. He knew who he was in a way that he hadn't when he'd first become a father. But it was more than that. With Courtney, everything felt fresh. When she looked him in the eye, Ritchie didn't see all his past mistakes, all his past humiliations. Addy and Nathan had forgiven him for all his past trespasses—losing their family home, almost tearing their family apart—but Courtney hadn't lived through any of that. There was no residual pain. No worry that there was something still simmering. Some old resentment. Some old hate.

Courtney held a perfect poker face as she looked down at her father's cards, and then gently tapped her father's foot with her own. Ritchie looked down at his cards—a straight flush. The second-best hand you could get. Ritchie wasn't surprised. After all, he'd been on a roll all night. Of course he had a perfect hand dealt to him, laid out all pretty and ready for the taking.

"Back upstairs you go," Ritchie said. "This is our last hand of the night. So, get another movie ready to go, and we'll watch it when I'm done here."

Courtney groaned as she left the room. She already knew the rules of poker, but she also knew that the only way to get better at a card game was to play it, or watch it be played. She wanted to watch her father win.

Lefty, Pete the Jeweler, Ace, and Ace's cousin all went out immediately. It was between Ritchie and a guy they called the Captain. He worked for Lefty, who was now working as a bookie, and was so named because he owned a boat, and never let anyone forget that he owned a boat.

"How high are you willing to go?" the Captain asked.

Ritchie moved all his chips to the middle of the table. He had a hand that was practically unbeatable. The Captain could only win if he had a royal flush, and Ritchie was sure he'd seen all the picture cards go out already.

"How about we make it interesting?"

"More interesting than all of the chips on the table?" Ritchie laughed.

"I'll take that big diamond your wife wears."

"That's not mine to gamble," Ritchie said, squinting his eyes as he looked at the Captain.

"Word on the street is that it is," the Captain said. "But if you're not up for this kind of action, I understand."

Without thinking: "I'm up for it." Ritchie had a practically unbeatable hand. What were the odds that the Captain would have the one hand that could beat Ritchie's?

The odds, it turned out, were very good.

He turned his hand over, and Ritchie's face fell.

Ritchie wondered for a split second: in his heart of hearts, had he always known that he'd one day gamble the ring away? Was that the reason why he'd held onto the fake stone all these years? Just in case he needed it again?

Ritchie's only consolation was the fact that Courtney hadn't been here to witness his undoing. Little did he know, she saw the whole thing go down from her perch at the top of the staircase.

52

Courtney

"Those are all filled with notebooks?" Courtney said, as her brother walked in with a giant banker's box. He dropped it down onto the floor of the entrance in Addy's house.

"Yup."

"That's a lot of poetry." Courtney lifted the lid off the box and peeked inside.

"There's more."

"There's another box filled with notebooks?"

"There are *seven* more boxes filled with notebooks." Courtney followed Nathan out to his car to help. Over the past few weeks, he seemed less angry with Courtney about her slipup to Diego, about starting the fire, but she still apologized every chance she got. Slowly, she was rebuilding Nathan's trust in her.

Nathan opened the trunk. Courtney couldn't believe her eyes—she always remembered her father carrying his faithful notebooks, but she never thought that he'd saved them. Never considered how large a lifetime of notebooks could be, how a daily habit of writing could add up.

"This is kind of incredible, if you think about it," Courtney said, as they stacked the last of the boxes in Addy's front hallway. Their father's every thought, entered in these books. Everything that passed through his mind. Everything that he thought was worth remembering, all in one place.

"Addy's going to kill us if we leave these there," Nathan said, motioning to the stack of boxes that now filled the front entryway. "We need to find them a home. Is there room in one of the upstairs closets?"

"Or we could just leave them here and see what happens." Courtney could tell that Nathan didn't want to laugh. He never liked to laugh at Addy's expense. But he couldn't help himself, it seemed. He put his hand over his mouth, but then began laughing uncontrollably.

"Dinner's in ten minutes!" Addy called out from the kitchen.

Courtney brought her hand to her forehead in a mock salute. "Yes, Captain!" she silently mouthed to her brother, and they laughed like children once again.

"I guess I should've left them at the office," Nathan said. "But once I found them, I couldn't just leave them there. With the lawsuit and everything, they seemed vulnerable somehow."

"You sound paranoid."

"Have you ever been served? It's strangely invasive. Just handing me that paper felt like he was reaching into my own personal world, violating it or something."

"Sorry you went through that," Courtney said, putting her arm on her brother's shoulder. "I'll help you go through the boxes." Nathan looked at her and smiled. Courtney felt overcome by the need to dig into the notebooks that very moment— how wonderful it would be to get a piece of her father back after all these years. To live with him for another moment, through these notebooks. Courtney took the top off the first box, and gently removed the first notebook. It was dated 1970. Before she was born. She had always felt so close to her father, always felt like the favorite, but now, here it was. A way to get to know her father before he was even her father.

"Dinner's in five minutes!" Addy called out from the kitchen, this time louder, and more forcefully.

Courtney could hear her nieces stirring upstairs. She had gotten used to these countdowns that Addy did each night before dinner. At first, she found them incredibly annoying. Why announce that there were fifteen minutes until dinner, then ten, then five? Why couldn't she just tell everyone once dinner was actually done?

But then she realized that Addy usually had to say things to the girls once, twice, three times, before they'd do it. Alarms blared in the morning, the snooze button ringing out every seven minutes until, finally, Addy walked in to rouse them. Addy would ask about homework assignments over and over again before the girls would sit down to do them. And the dinner countdown. Did they ignore the ten-minute warning, only to spur to action at the five-minute warning?

How exhausting, Courtney thought, to have to constantly call out countdowns. How exhausting, she thought, to have everyone ignore every third thing that you said. Courtney felt a pull of something—tenderness, was it?—for her sister.

"We should see if Addy needs help in the kitchen," Courtney said. Nathan followed closely on her heels, and Addy's face lit up when she saw them. "I'll set the table."

"The girls can do that," Addy said. "Would you mind checking the rice cooker? If it's done—"

"It's done," Courtney said, before the words were fully out of her sister's mouth. "Let me get it into a serving bowl and onto the table."

"Thank you."

"The green beans are done, too," Nathan said, as he picked up the pot and drained them in a colander.

"Thanks, guys."

"Red or white?" Gary said, coming up from the basement with Diego. Diego pulled the wineglasses down as Gary got out the corkscrew.

"Let's do white," Nathan said. "The tannins give me a head-ache."

"No, they don't," Addy said, laughing.

"Tannins have been proven to give headaches," Diego of-fered helpfully.

"Don't defend your husband," Addy said. "He's lying. I've seen him down an entire pitcher of sangria by himself."

"Sangria doesn't give me a headache," Nathan said.

"Sangria is made from red wine," Addy said, and for a mo-ment, Courtney watched her siblings stare each other down. She so enjoyed seeing them go head-to-head like this.

"I could go for some sangria," Gary said and immediately made his way to the fridge for some fruit.

"I just gave the girls a five-minute warning," Addy said. "We don't have time for sangria."

"There's always time for sangria!" Nathan and Diego said in unison.

Addy, Gary, and Courtney all broke out in laughter. A refer-ence to an old family joke.

"Grandpa Ritchie used to say that anytime we went out for Mexican," Addy explained to Olivia and Emma, who had just breezed into the kitchen and were setting the table. "Do you remember that from when you were little?"

"Every time," Gary added. Banging his hand on the edge of the table with every syllable: "Ev-er-y time!"

"No, that's not why he said it," Diego said. "When we came back from our first trip to Spain, Nathan was trying to show Ritchie how to make a *tinto de verano*. Ritchie loved it, and loved that it was so easy to make. He was going on and on about how they used to love to make sangria, but it took too long. So, then Lizzie said—"

Nathan joined in with his husband, calling out the punch line, as if they'd rehearsed it: "There's always time for sangria!"

"So, it was something Mom used to say?" Addy asked, looking confused. She took the chicken out of the oven and transferred it to a serving platter. "I thought it was Dad's thing."

"You're both wrong," Courtney said. "It was the thing they used to say when they didn't want to go to a party, or if they wanted to be late. Remember that awful annual party the Coopers used to throw? One year, Dad insisted on bringing a massive punch bowl filled with sangria, and we were an hour late. It became our tradition. Don't want to go somewhere? Make a time-intensive hostess gift that gives you the perfect excuse for being late."

"No," Nathan said, shaking his head. "It was like—if we were cooking dinner, and we were about to serve the wine, he'd say, 'Who wants sangria?' Like that."

"Wrong," Courtney said, filling her glass with the red wine.

"You're both wrong," Addy said. "It was a cute thing he used to do with the girls."

"Addy's right," Gary said.

"Of course she is," Nathan said, offering his brother-in-law a sly smile. "Addy's always right."

"Maybe we're all right," Diego said. "Maybe more than one thing can be true at once."

Everyone paused for a moment, considering Diego's words.

Addy was the first to speak: "Well, that's just wrong."

"Let's make a toast," Nathan said. "To Spain."

"To going out for Mexican," Addy countered.

"To that horrible annual barbecue at the Coopers' house. May I never be invited back there again."

"To Grandpa Ritchie," Olivia said.

Emma took the sweet family moment as an opportunity to sneak a glass of wine. Courtney caught her niece out of the corner of her eye, and quietly grabbed the glass, pouring the wine into her own goblet.

"To sangria," Nathan said.

At that, they all clinked glasses. They drank, they ate, and they had a lovely family dinner. They talked about other family jokes, they talked about the family store. They talked about the food; Addy had prepared yet another delicious family meal. No one dared talk about the one thing they needed to discuss: the fate of the ring.

53

Addy

Addy stared at the shoe. Was it a shoe or a boot? It was hard to tell, given the extent of damage. Duke had made the shoe his own, and had chewed it so extensively that it was barely recognizable. All that remained was the hot pink label on the inside of the sole: *Lizzie and Ritchie's.* It had to be Courtney's—both she and her daughters wore a size eight, not a six and a half.

Addy walked over to Duke's dog bed, where she found the shoe's mate. Duke had tucked it underneath the bed, saving it as a treat for later. She picked it up—it was a black bootie, neither shoe nor boot—and patted Duke lightly on the nose with it. "No," she said, and Duke whimpered in response.

Courtney walked into the kitchen, as Addy stood, holding the shoes.

"I'm so sorry about this," Addy said, and her sister merely shrugged. Duke came over to Courtney and lay down at her feet. He looked up at her and whimpered—a doggy apology.

Addy looked at Courtney, waiting for more of a response. "I mean," she said, "we'll pay for new ones."

"That's really not necessary," Courtney said, looking down at her phone. "I'm pretty sure I got them from the store for free."

"Perfect," Addy said. "Then, I'll have Gary bring home a new pair for you today." Addy examined the shoes that Duke had used as a chew toy.

"I'm a six and a half," Courtney said, not looking up from her phone. "But I doubt they're still in the store. I got them when I was here two Christmases ago."

Addy ignored the subtle dig. She knew she hadn't invited Courtney to Christmas last year, but there was nothing she could do about that now. All she could do was move forward. "Well, they sometimes have old stock," Addy said hopefully. "I'll just text a picture to Gary now."

Addy held the shoes up and snapped a photograph to send to her husband. Duke had really done a number on them—they were barely recognizable.

"I really am sorry about this," Addy said. "I'm just so sorry."

Courtney finally looked up at Addy. Addy suddenly felt as if she were about to cry. "It's not a big deal," Courtney said again.

"It was careless," Addy said. "And it's my fault. I mean, it's my dog, right? I take full responsibility." She continued rambling: "Let me fix it. I'll feel much better if I can fix it."

"It's a pair of two-year-old booties," Courtney said. "I don't understand why you're freaking out about it."

Addy paused. Courtney was right—there was no reason to be freaking out over this. She was apologizing for the wrong thing. Addy knew this. But how could she even begin to say sorry for a lifetime of hurt?

Gary texted back: We don't have them in stock. I can bring this season's version.

Addy couldn't bring herself to speak. She simply handed Courtney the phone instead.

"Fine," Courtney said. "Better, actually. Score!"

"I still feel awful about the original pair."

"Why?"

"Because something that belonged to you got destroyed in my house. I feel responsible."

"Well, Gary's fixing it, so don't."

"Okay, good."

Courtney put her head back in her phone. Addy supposed that meant that the conversation was over.

Emma walked into the kitchen. "Oh, no. Duke?"

"Yeah," Courtney said, laughing as she looked up to answer her niece. They giggled in unison, and Addy wondered why she didn't have such an easy relationship with her sister. Or her own daughter, for that matter.

"Daddy's bringing Aunt Courtney a new pair home," Addy said. "Should I have him grab one for you, too?"

"Yes, please!" Emma said. And then, turning to her aunt: "Twinsies!"

"Well, again," Addy said to Courtney, "I really am sorry. I hope you can accept my apology."

Courtney regarded her once again. She squinted her eyes as she said: "Sure. All is forgiven. Are you sure it wasn't you who ate my shoes and not your dog?"

"What?"

"You are apologizing very profusely for something that your dog did."

"I just feel bad about it."

"I can see that."

"I feel bad about a lot of things."

Courtney furrowed her brow. "Well, this one was easily fixed."

"Right," Addy said, and smiled. Warmly, she hoped. Addy wanted to say more. Wanted to apologize more. There was a lifetime of things Addy wanted to say to her sister. But Courtney's head was already down in her phone again.

54

Courtney

SY: Are you free for dinner this Saturday?

COURTNEY: i'm actually still in ny.

SY: Is that an invitation?

COURTNEY: i don't think i can do this anymore. i shouldn't have done it in the first place. i'm sorry.

Her cell phone rang. Courtney didn't even know what the sound was at first—no one ever called her. All of her friends just texted.

"There's nothing to be sorry for. I enjoyed your company." Of course it was Sy on the phone.

Courtney leaned back onto the couch and looked out the window with a glass of leftover sangria from the night before. "Yes, but I took all of that money from you. It was wrong. I'll pay you back." Ever since she'd found out about Holly, Courtney couldn't stop thinking about secrets. How destructive they could be. How they always seemed to pop up at the most inopportune times.

"There was nothing wrong with what we did. I wanted to spend the night with a beautiful woman, and I did. I was more than happy to pay for that pleasure."

"That's not what dating should be."

Sy laughed. "Oh, Courtney, make no mistake. I did not consider that to be a date, in the conventional sense of the word. I know a young woman like you would never go out with an old man like me."

"Are you kidding? That's half the couples in LA."

Sy laughed again, this time deeper. Courtney couldn't help it—hearing his deep, throaty laughter made her smile. She had forgotten how good it felt to make someone laugh.

"I wanted something easy, something straightforward. You have no idea what dating is like for a man like me. Everyone wants something from you. Every woman who dates you is counting your money, redecorating your house on the first date. You know, in some ways, what we did almost felt more honest."

"That actually makes me feel better. Thank you."

"You shouldn't feel badly in the first place. I was having lunch with a friend when he showed me the site. He'd been doing it for fun, for a lark. He showed me the app and let me scroll through. Then I saw your photograph. You looked so much like my wife when I first met her, that I signed up for the site right then and there and contacted you."

Courtney didn't know what to say. She finished off the glass of sangria and then padded over to the fridge for another. She filled her glass and then settled back onto the couch.

Sy continued. "I hope you aren't offended. I just wanted one more night with my wife. Does that sound funny?"

"No," Courtney said. She wanted something like that, too. A love so strong that even when the other person died, you still looked for them. Something like what her parents had had. Or at least, what she used to think her parents had. If it was true that her father had a long-standing affair with Maggie, then all the stories, everything she'd believed her whole life, wasn't true. "Tell me about her."

"Oh, well, where to begin? When we met, I had all but given up on love. I'd been engaged to a woman I later found out had been cheating on me with my best friend. I wasn't looking for love. I'd resigned myself to the fact that love wouldn't work out for a person like me, a workaholic, but then, there I was, at the rehearsal for my cousin's wedding, when they pair me up with the most beautiful woman you'd ever laid eyes on. I swear, when we walked down the aisle, I felt like that was it. Like one day we'd walk down the aisle at our own wedding together. And we did, just eighteen months later."

"That's so romantic." Courtney was surprised that even with the veracity of her parents' love story now in question, she could still be a sucker for a perfect meet-cute.

"It is. Or, it was, I should say. We had a wonderful life together, and I miss her dearly every day. I miss the way she used to greet me at the door when I came home from work each night. I miss the way she held my hand when we walked. I miss the way she would close her eyes when she was concentrating very hard on something. I just miss…well, I miss her. So, I don't really have much interest in dating. I already had the love of my life. Seems greedy to think I could have it twice."

"Right."

"So, why don't I come to New York for dinner this weekend? I've got some meetings I can set up for Friday, and it sounds like you could use some cheering up. Why so down?"

Courtney didn't know where to begin—the massive debt she'd accrued, losing the apartment her parents had bought for her, burning down her brother's apartment, or now being stuck at her big sister's house with no plans to leave. Or was it the fact that she now appeared to have a secret half sister? A fourth person with whom she'd have to share the proceeds of the sale of the ring. If she could convince her brother and sister to even sell it once the DNA results came back, that is.

Courtney settled on a simple truth: "My life doesn't seem to be working out quite the way I meant it to."

"Whose is? Text my assistant the address, and I'll have a car pick you up on Saturday at seven."

55

Nathan

Nathan pulled out the notebook dated 1978. The year his mother met his father for the second time.

> *My love,*
>   *Seeing you again has ~~turned~~ lit my world on fire.*
>   *My every thought, every waking hour, is ~~filled~~ consumed with thoughts of you. Your ~~soft~~ silky hair, your full lips, the soft skin at the small of your back.*
>   *Each day, I count the minutes until we can see each other again. I long to taste the sweetness of your mouth, feel the touch of your fingertips, ~~touch~~ graze the insides of your soft thighs.*

*MAKE MORE ROMANTIC, STUPID!

Nathan ran his finger along the page, as if the very act of touching it might make it spring to life, might make sense of it. "Who did you write this to?" Nathan thought. But he knew. Of course he knew.

For as many love letters that Nathan had read, he'd never actually written one before. He'd tried many times, started many love letters that he abandoned halfway through. It seemed terrifying, he thought, to lay yourself bare on the page like that. You couldn't take it back, you couldn't explain it away. Your soul was right there, for anyone who picked it up to see. Was it brave to put yourself out there like that? Or just stupid?

There were love letters that Nathan had seen before, that his mother had given him to read. Nathan knew every word of those letters by heart, especially the early ones. He'd heard the story countless times afterward. Lizzie had kept Ritchie's love letters in an old hatbox, and Nathan had taken to reading them so often that, eventually, he just moved the hatbox into his room. He read the letters at night, carefully committing them to memory, like a prayer.

But he'd never seen this letter. Well, he had. His lawyer had emailed a photograph of it to him earlier in the week. It was Holly's proof of the affair between Maggie and Ritchie.

And now he was staring at a first draft of that letter. The pieces added up—he'd seen all the early love letters Ritchie had written to his mother. Sure, he'd never read a draft of one in Ritchie's notebooks like he was doing now. His mother only had the final versions, the completed love letters. Lovingly written in careful handwriting on fine paper. A delicate present for his mother, written with care.

So, why hadn't he seen this one? Clearly because this letter hadn't been written to his mother. This was a draft, and the final version ended up in Maggie's hands. Nathan couldn't bring himself to believe the truth—this letter had been written for Maggie.

But if his father had had an affair, what did that mean? Sure, it meant that he had a half sister that he hadn't known about, but what did it mean for the larger picture? The love story he'd believed his entire life was a lie. What other parts of his life were a lie?

Is that why he married a man who would betray him, as well?

His mother should have left. Should have made the separation final. She should never have taken Ritchie back. How different his life would have been if his mother hadn't reconciled with his father. He refused to think about the most obvious, that there would be no Courtney, and focused on the deception instead.

Nathan knew what he needed to do. He needed to leave Diego.

56

Addy

Addy sat back on the fainting couch in her bedroom. She almost never lay down in the middle of the day like this in her bedroom—it felt indulgent. When they'd bought this particular piece of furniture, Addy had envisioned lazy afternoons spent with a book, evenings cuddled up with Gary. But they never seemed to have time to relax like that. There were always things to do, places they had to be. Meals that had to be cooked. Meetings that had to be attended, plans that had to be honored.

But this was her priority now. Everything else faded away. The claim on the ring had seemingly taken everything over, had made everything else pale in comparison. There would be no fighting over the ring with Nathan and Courtney—first order of business was to make sure that they didn't lose their rights to the ring entirely.

Banding together against a common enemy was better than what they'd been doing before, Addy thought. She hated fighting with Nathan. Hated disagreeing with him. Usually they so easily compromised, spoke to each other as if through ESP. She didn't like disagreeing with Courtney, either. Sure, she'd spent a huge part of her life ignoring her little sister completely, but now things were different. She would be different.

The fainting chaise seemed the appropriate spot to crack open her father's private notebooks from 1969. She'd heard the stories of his scandalous youth, so she thought it prudent to prepare herself in case anything in these pages did, in fact, cause her to faint.

Addy smiled as she saw her father's familiar scrawl. She loved his notes about what fights he'd gamble on, the funny way he had of keeping a diary, just one or two sentences each day. She thought about how she would sum up each day of hers with just a sentence. What would that look like?

Monday: brought blueberry muffins and the good coffee to the office. Gary and Nathan did not care.

Tuesday: spent two hours preparing a beautiful roast chicken dinner, with sautéed broccoli and wild rice on the side. Olivia and Emma did not care.

Wednesday: spent one hour in a meeting at school to go over the schedule for the girls next year. No one cared.

Addy put her head down into the notebook:

6/23/69, MSG, Frazier vs. Quarry
Vegas favors Frazier 9-5
F 2-1 favorite
Frasier 203.5 lbs
Quarry 198.5 lbs
Q lost to Ellis 15 months ago
Referee: Arthur Mercante

Maggie, 516-555-3569

Seeing her Aunt Maggie's phone number was jarring. This was proof that he had pursued Maggie. Of course, she knew the story: when her parents first met, her mother was only sixteen years old, a kid in her father's eyes, and he'd dated her older sister instead. So, this didn't prove anything she didn't already know. Or did it?

Addy considered the facts: Maggie dated her father in 1969. But once Lizzie saw Ritchie again in 1978, they had dated exclusively. How did this fit what Maggie's daughter was claiming, that Maggie had also dated her father in 1978, and that he had never stopped seeing her?

Proof. Addy needed to see proof. As she read countless drafts of love letters, she realized: Why only one? If Maggie did, in fact, carry on a lifetime affair with her father, wouldn't there be more love letters?

Addy emailed the family lawyer from her phone:

Is this all there is? One love letter does not an affair make. I'm going through eight banker's boxes worth of notes and drafts of letters. If they did, in fact, have an affair, where are the rest of the letters? Where's the proof?

Rudy Katz responded immediately:

You should've been a lawyer. I was thinking precisely the same thing. I've already made a request that the other side produce all other letters that they have.

Addy smiled to herself as she read the email. She loved getting praise like this—she'd done a good job. Of course she had. Addy loved being proactive. Doing something always made Addy feel better, helped her to feel calm. Taking action on a problem, to Addy, was like taking a Xanax. The world was out of control, but there was something she could do. It was a fact: if Ritchie had been having an affair with Maggie, there would been have more letters.

Addy silently praised herself for her cleverness. Maggie's daughter wouldn't be able to produce more letters. Addy was sure of it. She was sure there was no affair, and this would just be one more piece of proof, along with the DNA test which would eventually come back, that Holly Morgan was not her half sibling. That she had no claim on the ring, or the family business, or any part of her life.

The next day, the lawyer wrote back to Addy. Addy prepared herself to be showered with still more praise—*You've cracked the case! Congrats!*—but this was not that email.

There was an attachment so large that it was almost filtered out by Addy's spam filter. What the lawyer sent over, cc'ing Nathan and Courtney, was a file containing dozens of love letters, *allegedly* (his word) from Ritchie to Maggie, covering the time period of 1969–2015.

Seeing all of this made Addy feel slightly faint.

57

Ritchie, 1999

Ritchie needed a plan. He'd gambled away and won back hundreds of thousands of dollars through the years, and he'd realized something: the wins didn't really mean a thing. They just evened out the losses. Ritchie figured that despite all the winning streaks he'd been on, he'd never actually won anything gambling. He'd only broken even.

Ritchie needed a real job. Stable income. None of the get-rich-quick schemes he'd tried with Ace over the years had worked out. There was the compact disc company, belly-up inside of six months; the direct-to-consumer makeup company, closed down by the FDA before they'd made any money off it; and who could forget the infomercials they'd done for the vacuums that were supposed to revolutionize the way people cleaned their homes? There were one or two lawsuits still pending because of that one.

There was the job dealing cars through a friend of Lefty's. Ritchie was the sort of man who could convince anyone of anything, so the job seemed like a good fit. But there was an unwritten hierarchy at the car lot, one which Ritchie couldn't crack with his charm. He wasn't one of the guys who got to sell the expensive cars—anytime he got a whale on the hook, his manager swooped in to take the commission away from him— and selling the inexpensive cars was barely worth the hours he'd put in. Barely worth the effort.

After the separation in 1992, Ritchie knew he needed something better. He'd gotten a job at a brokerage house where Ace had an in. A friend of his second cousin. And Ritchie did well for a while, just like he thought he would. Until he didn't. Ritchie lost his shirt in '93, but he was able to recover. Just a few smart investments, and he was back in the black.

Ritchie had been making easy money, riding high, and getting friends and family to invest with him. Everyone was making money, everyone was happy. Until October '97. The mini-crash of the stock market. Ritchie lost big. Only this time, it wasn't just *his* money. He'd been able to brush it off in '93 when it was his own money he was losing. But now, he wasn't the only one who went down—all his friends and family were losing their shirts right along with him. And it was his fault. They had gambled on Ritchie and lost. He could barely look at himself in the mirror.

"It's not your fault," Ace assured him. "It's just the market. You know when you bet on the stock market, you could lose. Everyone knows the risks."

Ritchie needed something new, a fresh start. And he found it, while walking through town one night.

It didn't look like much from the outside, just a little shop on the main drag of Central Avenue, the heart of their Long Island town. He must've passed by it dozens of times, but it never registered. But looking at the *For Sale* sign in the window, Ritchie could picture himself inside. Minding the store, selling whatever it was that they sold there. It could be a place for him to rebuild himself. A place he could go straight.

Ritchie wrote down the telephone number in his notebook. Later that night, he called and was surprised to find that the person who answered was someone he knew—Charlie Newton, the grandfather of Nathan's classmate. Charlie was a fixture in their small Long Island town. Well-liked and well-respected, he'd even won the Small Businessman of the Year Award a few times, through the Chamber of Commerce. Ritchie liked the idea of everything Charlie represented.

All his life, Ritchie had been underestimated. He'd been called a *degenerate*, a *deadbeat*, a *loser*. The only thing he'd ever done right in his life was to marry Lizzie. And seven years ago, he'd almost ruined that, too. With this store, he would show Lizzie that all along she'd backed the right horse.

The men made a deal. Charlie was eager to retire and move out to Arizona, so he sold the store, and all its merchandise, to Ritchie for a song.

Two weeks later, Ritchie was in business. He knew nothing about retail, but he was eager to learn. And Charlie was just a phone call away, he reminded Ritchie every time they spoke. The only thing Ritchie did know was how to run numbers—years of calculating statistics of various bets in the casinos while under the influence of a few gin and tonics had taught Ritchie how to do math in his head. And retail seemed to be all about the numbers. Items of clothing in, items of clothing out. Electric bills, gas bills, phone bills. Price paid to the wholesaler, profit made from selling to the customer.

First order of business: rename the store. That was simple. He called the store Lizzie and Ritchie's, in a romantic gesture, and decided to throw a big grand opening party to mark the occasion. He would keep the whole thing a secret from Lizzie, and surprise her with it at the celebration. Ritchie was careful to keep the marquee outside the store wrapped in fabric, so that no one could see the new name of the store until the big unveiling.

It was a whirlwind month as he readied the store for the big party: food, drinks, invitations… There was no detail too small for Ritchie to handle. Ritchie wanted to open the store with a big splash and announce to the world that this was it. This time, he was going straight. This time, everything would change.

58

Ritchie, 1999–2000

Lizzie screamed out loud with delight when Ritchie pulled the cloth down from the marquee, revealing the name of his new store: Lizzie and Ritchie's. She fell into his arms, and they kissed, oblivious to the crowd of people, waiting for the grand-opening party to begin.

"Gross," six-year-old Courtney said, and Ritchie couldn't help but laugh.

"Let the party begin!" he announced to the crowd, as they all filed into the store.

The store was filled with friends and their kids. Ritchie had hired a local band to play music near the fitting rooms, and the tables in the middle of the store, which usually held clothing, were commandeered by the caterer, who set out platters of chicken, steak, and two different types of potatoes. Waiters walked around with fancy hors d'oeuvres—caviar on blinis, sushi, and steak tartare—and glasses of champagne with a tiny raspberry at the bottom. Ritchie saw Addy and Nathan sneaking more than their fair share of bubbles, but they were teenagers and it was a party, so Ritchie turned a blind eye to it. Courtney and her friends orchestrated a huge game of hide-and-go-seek, so as the teenagers shopped, they would giggle as they'd find a six-year-old crouching down beneath the racks.

Feeling Lizzie's pride in him filled Ritchie up. He felt happier than he had in years, just knowing that he'd done right by her. After all these years, he was no longer a degenerate. He was a small business owner, and worthy of the woman he loved.

The energy of the party was just right—friends eating, making toasts; women and their daughters trying on the clothes, buying tons; and owners of the neighboring stores introducing themselves, telling Ritchie how impressed they were with how seamlessly he'd taken over. Even Ritchie's stuffy in-laws seemed impressed, which made him feel good in a way that made him embarrassed. (Later that night, when Lizzie would mention it, Ritchie would pretend that he hadn't noticed.) By the time the cake came out at 11 p.m., Ritchie barely knew where the night had gone. But no one seemed in a rush for the night to end, so after the cake was served, the guests all stayed and danced along to the band for another two hours.

Ritchie couldn't remember a party as fun. But once the party was over, real life set in. With nothing more to look forward to, the days stretched on endlessly.

The busy work of retail took hours each day. Phone calls to suppliers, meetings with the building manager, fixing the little things that needed attention each day—a light bulb here, a table there. After dealing with customers all day, he'd handle the books after the store closed at 5 p.m., coming home just in time for dinner to be on the table at 7:15 p.m. It gave Ritchie less free time with which to get into trouble. But it was a grind.

Day in, day out, so much of the same. The drudgery of bills, the simple things it took to keep the store running. It was just so boring. And it took so much time to get it all done. Ritchie longed for something exciting to happen, anything to happen, really, to take him out of his routine. But nothing ever happened.

Six months in, Ritchie could barely tell which day of the week it was. Every day seemed to be exactly the same as the one before. Every morning, he'd open up the store. Every afternoon, teenagers would come in to browse. Every night, like clockwork, he'd lock the front doors of the store. He'd head back to his office for two hours to do administrative things—answer phone calls, pay bills.

One year in, Ritchie sat down at his desk, dreading the tasks at hand. He grabbed the first envelope off the pile: his insurance bill. He studied the bill for a long time. Longer than was necessary. How could they charge so much for a place so small? The amount it cost for Ritchie to keep the store up and running never ceased to amaze him. He wondered when he would ever make enough money that he could stop sweating every bill. When he could pay bills without first furiously checking the bank balance, trying to figure out which checks would clear, and which he'd have to hold back for a week or two.

It felt like he was paying more in insurance than the place was even worth. Then it hit him: the store was worth more dead than alive. The fire insurance on this thing would ensure a huge payday, and then Ritchie wouldn't have to work his fingers to the bone. He'd have time to see Lizzie. Time to see the kids.

As if on cue, Addy called from college. She gushed on and on about her digital marketing class, and all but begged Ritchie to let her work at the store for the summer. *An internship*, she called it. She said he didn't have to pay her; she could earn three credits in the hours she'd work. Ritchie did the math—three college credits were not cheap. Not cheap at all. And it would make Addy so happy. Who knows? Maybe she'd even help, make the business more profitable so that he could hire some staff to do the things he hated doing himself.

"Sure." Ritchie shrugged, even though his daughter couldn't see him. After all, he could set the place on fire and collect the insurance in September just as easily as he could in May.

59

Addy

"I can't believe we're going to lose the store." Nathan slumped his head into his hands over his coffee. Addy stood at the stove, making eggs for breakfast, and Gary put his arm around his brother-in-law's shoulders.

"It's going to be okay," Gary said. "We'll figure this all out."

"Gary's right," Addy said, spinning around to the kitchen island, doling out the eggs onto Nathan's and Gary's plates. "We are not going to lose our store."

"*Our* store," Nathan muttered under his breath, toward Gary.

They were always making subtle digs like this, and Addy usually ignored them. It was the sly glance at each other, when Addy brought coffee to work, or a shared inside joke over the dinner table. Did they think she didn't know? She knew. She heard. She saw. Addy usually let it slide. But sitting at her kitchen counter, waiting to be served breakfast, as if they were her children, Addy couldn't let this one go.

"Must you always do that?" Addy tried to hide how much her brother's words angered her, but her voice betrayed her. The sound came out loud, louder than she'd intended, and she could feel her jaw hardening as she spoke. Nathan and Gary continued to eat their eggs, drink their coffee, seemingly oblivious to what was bubbling up inside Addy's chest.

Nathan laughed. With his mouth still full: "No, it's just funny."

"Yeah, I know. 'Addy invented the internet,'" Addy said, tossing the used pan into the sink to soak. It sounded out, like a gong. "I've heard the joke. Do you really think that's funny?"

As her husband said: "Of course we don't," Nathan said, at the same exact time: "Well, kind of."

"Oh, really? Look who's found his voice," Addy said, looking around the kitchen, as if searching for an audience. "You can't stand up to anyone else in your life, but now this is how you speak to me? The person who has always stood by you? Always fought your battles for you?"

"Takes all the credit for me," Nathan said.

Normally, he would have made a comment like this under his breath. Addy was taken aback at how Nathan said it so firmly, so unabashedly.

"Do you really think I haven't contributed anything to this store?" Addy said.

Gary: "Of course you do." Nathan, at the same time: "Twenty years ago. More. *We* run the store now."

"You think I don't do anything for the store?" Addy was no longer trying to modulate her voice. The time for being reasonable, it seemed, had passed. Addy picked up the coffee maker and brought it to the kitchen island. It landed on the hard counter surface with a slam. "Do you honestly think I don't contribute anything?"

Gary: "Of course you do. We appreciate everything you do." Nathan, at the same time: "*We* run the store, Addy! It's our store now. You don't work there anymore."

"Every major decision is passed through me. When you refinanced five years ago, who spoke to the banker? When they tried to raise your insurance premiums last year, who talked it out with you? Who told you what to say? You two couldn't take a shit without asking me first."

Gary: "Of course we can't." Nathan, at the same time: "Are you kidding me right now? Do you hear yourself? Do you actually hear the words coming out of your mouth?"

"And now you have *my* girls modeling for you for free. For free!"

Gary: "And we appreciate that so much, honey." Nathan, at the same time: "The girls *want* to model for us."

"Because I let them."

"Do you fucking hear yourself right now?" Nathan said. Addy took a step backward, as if Nathan's words had hit her, physically. She cleared her throat and straightened her back. Nathan continued, this time louder: "What are they? Your property? Are you just loaning them out, like you do your card table when your friends want to play canasta?"

"Do *not* make it sound like I'm one of those moms who sits around all day and does nothing, dammit. Neither of you have any respect for how much I do all day."

"You're so right, honey," Gary said with a wide smile. "We are so sorry."

"Don't think you can get out of this just by being cute," she said, turning toward her husband. "I'm mad at you, too." Gary held his hands up, a surrender.

"This is just like Theta Alpha Nu all over again," Nathan said.

"You're right," Addy said. "Yet another thing I have to take care of for you, without any credit."

"No," Nathan said. "I mean, you're being a bully."

"I'm a bully?"

"Don't you think that everything you say—all the credit you take for the store—diminishes my accomplishments? Don't you think that I want to be proud of what I've done? Do I get any credit for taking the store and growing it? For being there every day and putting in the work?"

"I'm not trying to diminish your accomplishments, Nathan. But two things can be true at once. We can both be responsible for the success of the store. It can belong to both of us."

"It belongs to our family," Gary said, throwing his arms out to envelop both Addy and Nathan into a group hug. Addy was perched uncomfortably over the island, but she didn't want to ruin the moment. "It belongs to all of us," Gary continued. "Nathan, I literally could not have asked for a better partner all these years. I love coming to work because I get to hang out with you. And, Addy, my Adelaide, you are the heart and soul of the store. We know that you built it from the ground up. So what if we like to tease you every once in a while about it? And yes, we talk every problem and decision out with you. Because you're smart and have a great perspective, and we love you. So, let's not fight about this. We need to band together and make sure that Maggie's daughter does not take the store away from us. Or, hell, if she really is your half sibling, then we'll welcome her in. But we'll make all the decisions together, like we always do. Like a family."

"Oh my God," Nathan said to Addy, as Gary released them from the group hug. He pointed at Gary as he spoke to Addy. "You married our father. The peacemaker, the snake charmer. Gary, you're good. Maybe you should've been a used car salesman."

"Selling cars, selling clothes," Gary said, shrugging. "Same difference."

"Oh my God," Nathan said again. "Did *I* marry our father? Was our father a cheating bastard and then I mistakenly married a cheating bastard?"

"Diego's not cheating on you," Addy said, pouring herself a cup of coffee. She sighed. How many times would she have to have the same conversation with her brother? "Diego would never cheat on you. There's got to be some other explanation for everything. Do you want me to talk to him?"

"He's not up yet." Nathan raised his eyes to the ceiling, to where Diego was still fast asleep in Addy's guest room.

"Addy is *not* talking to your husband for you," Gary said. "Just no. You will go to Diego tonight and talk it out. Like an adult. Which you are."

"Right," Nathan said, nodding. "I know."

"And anyway, you didn't marry a cheating bastard," Gary said, "because there's no proof that Ritchie cheated. Just like there's no proof that Diego cheated."

"You didn't marry Dad," Addy said to her brother, grabbing his hand. "You married our mother, who was kind and loving and wonderful. And why you insist on fucking it all up for no reason, I'll never know."

60

Addy

"Another three bottles are gone." Addy was downstairs, picking out a wine for dinner when she'd noticed it. Three more wine bottles, missing. Vanished. As if they'd never been there before. Addy had been noticing that she couldn't find the specific bottles she wanted each night, bottles she knew (thought?) were downstairs, and now this confirmed it. She *knew* that there were three bottles of the Wölffer Summer in a Bottle next to the cedar closet. She'd had an entire discussion with Gary about it—whether or not to buy them, even though they only drank rosé in the summer. Addy knew exactly where she'd left them, and she knew for a fact that they hadn't opened any of them yet.

"What's that?" Courtney replied. Addy had momentarily forgotten that she'd come downstairs with her sister, and she became acutely aware that she was doing that thing Gary hated—talking to herself.

"The wine," Addy said, still distracted by her thoughts. It had been happening almost every night—wine going missing. A half a bottle left in the fridge, no longer there the next day. Bottles here and there that Addy could have sworn were downstairs, now nowhere to be found. "Some of it's missing. I know for a fact that I had three bottles of this rosé that I really wanted to open tonight. Do you think that the girls are drinking?"

"No."

"You've been spending so much time with them lately. Did they say anything about that party last weekend? Do you think they snuck the wine out?"

"I'm sure it just got misplaced," Courtney said, examining her fingernails. "Or you forgot that you drank it."

"No, that's the thing. Gary and I had a whole conversation about this wine. I know exactly where I left it, and I know that we definitely did not drink it. Gary hates drinking rosé when it's cold out."

"You can't possibly know every bottle you have down here. There are so many." Courtney fanned her arms out to demonstrate.

"I'm going to have a talk with the girls."

"Don't do that." Courtney's voice wavered. Addy took an audible sigh. It wasn't her sister's fault, she didn't understand the gravity of this. She didn't have kids, how could she know?

"Court, this could be serious. If they're bringing wine to parties every weekend, someone could get hurt. Someone could drink too much or, God forbid, drive drunk. I know it doesn't seem like a big deal, but it's a really big deal."

Addy spun and walked up the steps, taking them two at a time. When she got to the kitchen, Courtney grabbed her arm. "Wait."

"I think I should talk to the girls on my own first. I mean, they'll definitely want to talk to you about it later—I'm sure they love having someone to complain about me to—but I want to talk to them alone first. You understand, right?"

"Yes. No. I mean, stop. The girls didn't drink the wine."

"So, they *did* tell you about it?" Addy's voice caught in her throat. Of course her girls would have talked to Courtney about it, not her. Courtney was the cool aunt, the beautiful aunt who took perfect pictures for Instagram. What was she? Just a dowdy housewife who didn't even work. "Then, it's settled. They're grounded."

"They didn't tell me about it."

Addy sighed again. "You don't have to cover for them. Even if they brought it to the party and didn't drink it, I still need to have a talk with them. They can't take alcohol from the house and then let minors drink it."

"They didn't take it. I did."

"Courtney, I'm happy you're getting so close to the girls, really I am, but you don't need to cover for them. They need to learn a lesson."

"I'm not covering for them. I drank it."

"I don't understand."

"It's nothing, really," Courtney said. "After dinner, I like to have wine. What can I say? You've got great taste in rosé."

Courtney laughed, but Addy stayed straight-faced. "There were three bottles."

Courtney made a cute face and scrunched up her shoulders. "Oops!"

"Oops?"

"I'm sorry," Courtney said. "I didn't think it was that big of a deal. You just have so many bottles down there. So. Many. Are you preparing for a second Prohibition or something?" Courtney laughed at her own joke.

"Do you have a drinking problem?" As the words spilled from her mouth, Addy recognized the gravity of them. What she was saying, what she was accusing her sister of. She should have said it differently, of course she should have. But it was too late now—the words were out there. Like toothpaste out of the tube, impossible to put back.

"Of course I don't have a drinking problem," Courtney said, laughter in her voice. She said the words *drinking problem* as if they were dirty. "Things have been a bit tense around here, if you haven't noticed."

"That's a lot for one person to drink, Courtney."

"Says the person with a two hundred bottle collection who watches it so obsessively she notices when a few bottles go missing."

"If you're struggling, we can help you. I can help."

"What do you know about anything?" Courtney said, her eyes turning dark. "You barely even know me."

"I know," Addy said, reaching out for her sister's arm. "I know that. I was hoping that maybe we could change that."

Courtney bristled from her sister's touch. She covered her arm protectively in the spot that Addy had tried to touch. "Just because you buy me new shoes and deign to bring me downstairs to pick out wine with dinner doesn't mean anything's changed."

"Listen," Addy said, softening her voice. "Dad had an addictive personality. We have to be careful."

"I'm fine."

"I never have more than a glass or two of wine at a time. I'm really mindful of everything I drink," Addy said. Seeing that her words had no effect, she tried another angle. The truth: "Once, in college, I drank so much I had a blackout."

"Sounds to me like *you're* the one with the problem."

Her sister's words landed like a punch to the stomach. Addy took a deep breath in, and continued. "What I'm trying to say is, we need to remember where we came from. Every day."

"Again, I'm not the one with a basement filled with alcohol. That's you."

"Right." Addy looked at her sister and realized that she barely even knew her. And that was her fault. But how to fix a lifetime of resentment? "I'm only trying to help."

"I don't need your help." Courtney's voice was strong, defiant. But Addy could see her eyes softening. "I went my whole life without it."

"I'm sorry about that."

"Are you?"

Addy took a moment to think about it. She'd flat-out ig-nored her sister for her entire life. Who was she to say that she now wanted a relationship with her? Maybe it was too late for that. Addy always told her girls: *you've made your bed, and now you have to lie in it*. Maybe it was Addy's turn to lie in the bed that she'd made for herself.

"I *am* sorry," Addy said. "And I'd like to try to find a way forward. Everything I'm saying to you now isn't coming from a place of judgment. It's coming from a place of love. I'm trying to help you. I'd like to help you, if you'd let me."

"I don't need your help," Courtney said again, and walked out of the kitchen. Addy followed her into the mudroom. "Never have."

"Where are you going?" Addy asked, as Courtney grabbed a set of car keys. "Dinner's in fifteen minutes."

"Out. Can I take your car?"

Addy didn't respond. She stood in the mudroom staring dumbly at her sister. But it didn't really matter. After all, it wasn't really a question.

61

Nathan

"Are you cheating on me?" Nathan took a deep inhale and held his breath. But this was something, wasn't it? The fight with Addy had fortified him—he could stick up for himself, fight for himself, and he didn't need her help. He didn't have to hide away in the back office doing paperwork. He could have a confrontation and get things out in the open and advocate for himself, and everything would be okay. Nathan exhaled and looked at his husband across the loft.

Diego laughed out loud. He bent over at the waist, that's how hard he was laughing, but Nathan didn't see what was funny.

They stood in their destroyed apartment, waiting for a meeting with the contractor. It looked move-in ready, but only if you didn't look up. Once you looked up, you saw the real problem. You could see straight up from the place where their ceiling should have been to the roof of the building, which was patched up with a temporary fix. It looked bad, but their contractor promised them that it could be fixed, and would be even better than new, once he was done.

"I'm serious," Nathan said. He furrowed his brow. What was

funny about this? There was nothing funny about what he was asking. Again: "Are you having an affair?"

"Of course I'm not," Diego said. Now it was Diego's turn to have a befuddled look on his face. Diego rubbed his eyes as if answering the question was exhausting him. "Why would you even ask me that?"

Nathan opened his mouth to respond, but Diego continued, "And knowing my father's history, I think it's in pretty bad taste that you would even say that to me."

Nathan hadn't thought of that. The many nights they'd stayed up talking about how Diego's father's affairs had changed him, had colored the way he saw his father. It impacted their relationship, especially in the beginning, when they were still figuring out what it meant if they agreed to be a couple. If they agreed to be monogamous. Nathan couldn't believe he'd been so callous, so myopic, not to consider that.

"I'm sorry. I didn't mean to—"

"Didn't mean to what?" Diego asked, his face twisting into a pained expression. "Accuse me of doing the thing that almost tore my family apart? You know how my father's affairs have affected my life."

"I think my father had an affair with Maggie," Nathan said, almost before the words were fully out of Diego's mouth. "I think it's true."

"So, we're back to you, then?"

"What's that supposed to mean?"

"Everything is always about you, Nathan," Diego said, standing up and walking to the kitchen. It was amazing how completely the contractor had put the kitchen back together, as if there had been no fire at all. He pointed at Nathan. "*You* have to work late, *you* have to take care of the family business, *you* are never around."

Nathan didn't respond. He considered Diego's words carefully. Was everything in their relationship always about him?

Diego blurted out: "Are we getting divorced? Is this—starting a fight, accusing me of doing something you know I'd never do—your way of getting out?"

"No. I thought *you* were cheating on *me*," Nathan said, standing up from the couch and walking over to where Diego stood. "*You're* getting in shape, *you're* getting all these new clothes. I assumed it was for another man. Then, the receipt from the theater. And the text."

"What text?"

"Apparently Frank can't wait to see you again."

"Frank is a woman," Diego said.

"You're cheating on me with a woman?"

"No," Diego said, shaking his head. He took his phone from his pocket and held it out for Nathan to see. "These texts are from my friend Frank. Her maiden name is Franklin, so everyone calls her Frank. We're taking a theater boot camp class together. At an off-Broadway theater. Voice, dance, and scene work. I wasn't ready to tell you yet, so I paid for the class in cash. I think I want to give acting one more try."

"Why didn't you think you could tell me?"

"The same reason I've been working out, dressing better, trying to make our lives better, everything perfect," Diego said quietly. He looked up at Nathan, and their eyes met. They stood, face to face, in their destroyed apartment. Nathan took a deep breath and could smell the outside air, fresh and brisk, making its way in through the hole in the ceiling.

Diego took Nathan's hands in his own and spoke: "It's for you. It's all for you. How could you not know that? I live my entire life for you. Can't you see that?"

"I don't know what to say."

Diego gave Nathan's hands a gentle shake. "Nathan, I love you. I just want you to notice me. I want things to be the way they were before. Something's lost lately, I'm just trying to get it back. Why do you think I do all these things for you? The fitness classes, the cooking, the party..."

"I don't want the party," Nathan said. And then, without thinking: "And knowing *my* father's history, I think it's in pretty bad taste that you would even plan a party with a gambling theme for me."

"Right," Diego said, and looked up toward the ceiling. Or where the ceiling should have been. His arms fell to his sides. "I get that, and I'm sorry. But you and your sister are named after characters from *Guys and Dolls*. I thought we were all in on the joke together."

"I don't find that particular joke funny," Nathan said quietly. He walked back over to the couch and sat down. Diego didn't follow. "I don't want the party. Never did."

"Why didn't you say so?"

"I didn't know how."

"And now you want a divorce, but you don't know how to say it?"

Nathan couldn't respond. Did he want a divorce? Or had Addy been right all along? He was making something out of nothing. This was just a lull in their relationship. No long-term relationship could be on fire at all times. It wasn't realistic. Should he listen to his sister? Was he just fucking it all up for no reason?

Diego regarded Nathan, waiting for Nathan to speak. When he didn't, Diego said, "Oh. That's it, then."

"No, that's not it. I'm just trying to think." Nathan looked up at his husband, ready to walk back over to the kitchen and give him a kiss. Ready for this silly argument to be over. Nathan had misjudged everything, had been wrong about everything, and it was time to kiss and make up. Maybe that was the problem between them all along? Not enough kissing.

"If you want a trial separation, I can stay in the city. You can stay out at Addy's," Diego said, sitting down at the kitchen island.

"There's no roof," Nathan said, pointing up at the ceiling.

"I can stay at my parents' place. Or better yet, I'll go with my parents to set up the Vegas residency. Spend some time out there. I'd been thinking about doing that, anyway."

It was what Nathan had wanted, or thought he had wanted. Only he didn't want it anymore. "I don't want you to go."

"I'm not sure you want me to stay." Diego ran a hand through his hair, his body pointed toward the door. "And my mother could use some company in Vegas."

"Don't leave." Nathan stood up, and walked over to the kitchen, but by the time he was next to Diego, he could feel it. It was too late.

"Maybe you're right. Maybe we could use a little time apart," Diego said. "I don't think we need to wait for the contractor. I'll text and tell him that everything looks like it's coming along. Can I tell him you'll check back again in a week or two?"

Hours later, even as Diego packed up the car and headed to the airport, Nathan wasn't really sure what had happened.

Maybe it was a self-fulfilling prophecy. Nathan was turning forty, and he couldn't stop thinking about his mother. What had it been like for his mother to turn forty, having been separated from the man she loved? How had she felt?

Nathan was about to find out.

62

Courtney

"And now my sister thinks I have a drinking problem," Courtney said. "Could you believe that?"

Sy looked at her from across the table, clear-eyed and open. "Do you?"

"Of course I don't." Courtney set her wineglass down. It seemed odd to be talking about the fact that she didn't have a drinking problem while she was, in fact, drinking. She'd already had two glasses of wine, and they hadn't even ordered appetizers yet.

Sy had met Courtney in Manhattan, like they'd arranged, and Courtney felt her shoulders softening the more time she spent in Sy's company. Even though she hadn't seen him in person since that one night in LA, being with Sy was just so easy, so comfortable, like a warm hug. She was able to forget about her problems when she was on the phone with Sy. It had become part of her nightly ritual—relax with a glass of wine, talk on the phone with Sy.

Sy had his driver pick Courtney up on Long Island, and then take her into Manhattan for their quiet dinner. It was the first time she'd been out of her sister's house since finding the ring, since the fire, since the lawsuit, and Courtney welcomed Sy's company. It was nice to be around someone she wasn't related to. It was nice to be around someone to just talk, without expectations attached. Without any subtext. Without any skin in the game. Sy was lonely and wanted Courtney's company. Courtney wanted company, too.

Her friend, Lindsay, had texted her earlier in the week:

LINDSAY: sooooo?

COURTNEY: in ny w fam. taking some time off fr la

LINDSAY: u missed audition for the new keanu reeves thing. thought maybe you were off on an island with your sugar daddy

COURTNEY: actually seeing him again this weekend. just as friends

LINDSAY: $$$$$$$

COURTNEY: srsly. just as friends.

LINDSAY: east coast making u soft. get whut u deserve. never ever ever see one of these guys without getting paid

Courtney had thought about that for a while—what she deserved. She'd thought that what she deserved was to keep living the life she'd always lived. The security of two loving parents, the luxury of trips to exotic locations, and a successful future sprawled out ahead of her, endless possibilities. She'd taken it for granted that she'd go out to LA and do well. Get jobs, be able to support herself. It had been a defeat when her parents bought the apartment for her. She'd thought she would be mak-

ing enough money to support herself and buy her own place inside of six months. But that never happened. Life in LA was so
much harder than she'd anticipated, and it felt like a gut punch
every day, waking up to that reality.

Why should anything have to change? How could she have
predicted that she'd be an orphan by age twenty-nine, with not
even a dollar to her name? She didn't even have the apartment
her parents had so generously bought for her anymore. She was
a loser. A failure. Even Sy wouldn't want anything to do with
her if she hadn't resembled his first wife.

Courtney looked across the table at Sy, and he smiled gently
at her. "There's nothing wrong with it if you do have a problem," he said, pointing to the wineglass. "It's just something you
have to watch, a thing to be managed, like I do with my choles-
terol. Addiction is biological. It's nothing to be embarrassed—"

"I can stop drinking anytime," Courtney said, before the
words were even fully out of Sy's mouth.

Sy regarded her. "Can you?"

"Why are you doing this to me?" Courtney said, her voice
almost a whisper.

"I thought we were becoming friends," Sy said. "Didn't we
agree to that? A friendship? Friends help each other. And I think
you're lovely. I want to help you, if you need it."

"I don't need your help," Courtney said. "And I don't need
hers."

"Understood. But I'm a phone call away anytime you need
me. I have a little experience with this, myself. My granddaughter is in recovery. I think it's an act of bravery to admit that you
need help."

Courtney didn't know how to respond.

Sy filled the silence: "Now, shall we order?"

Courtney forced a smile and then checked the menu. Being
with Sy reminded Courtney of being with her father. He ordered a round of appetizers for them to share, which she knew

was something her friends hated—men ordering for them—but she loved. It made her feel taken care of in a way that she hadn't felt since her father had died.

"So, things haven't gotten better at your sister's house, I take it?" Sy's voice was gentle, his face open and warm.

"I thought they were getting better, but then she accused me of being an alcoholic." Courtney laughed nervously, and then quickly drew her napkin to her mouth, as if to stifle it.

"Sibling relationships can be difficult," Sy said, pausing to take a sip of his wine. "But they're valuable. Maybe at some point in the future, you'll come to see this time spent at your sister's house as a gift."

"Maybe," Courtney said, as her mind drifted off. Was it just because Sy was old that she felt all his words were infused with wisdom? When he offered advice, Courtney felt compelled to consider it. Now that they'd agreed they were both coming from a place where neither one wanted anything from the other, his words felt neutral. Maybe she did have a problem. Maybe you didn't have to hit rock bottom to see that your relationship with alcohol wasn't healthy. Maybe she could check out a meeting, just to see.

And then another thought, this one harder to admit to herself: maybe Addy really did care about her. Maybe Addy had been right.

63

Courtney

This felt like an invasion, of sorts. Courtney was having trouble bringing herself to open the first notebook. These were words he'd never intended his youngest child see—should she be reading them?

Courtney wondered: Did death take away your rights to privacy? Now that he was gone, shouldn't she rely on her father's memory alone? Was it fair to read his innermost thoughts, the things he assumed no one would ever see?

But she'd seen him reading to her mother from the notebooks. He'd even written a poem or two for her when she was a child, she recalled, so maybe it was okay? Maybe Ritchie would welcome the idea of his children reading his private notebooks. A way to keep himself alive long after he was gone. He lived on, in her memory through his stories, so maybe this was the same as that? She could easily conjure his image when she thought about how he would tell her a story.

Courtney could remember where she was the first time she heard each tale; could practically smell the seawater from the Atlantic City boardwalk as he told her about how he lost big on the Frazier vs. Quarry fight; could practically taste the fresh pineapple they'd eaten on a beach in Puerto Rico as he regaled her with the time he and his Brooklyn friends snuck into a fancy members-only Long Island beach club; and could practically hear the din of the Vegas strip, as he recounted, for an entire craps table, how he lost his spleen in a fist fight over a stickball game.

Courtney had the box from 1992, the year before she was born. She opened the first notebook.

My love,
You ~~told me~~ asked me to tell you something that was true.
~~What can I say?~~ I know only this—I love you. ~~I love you so~~ ~~much~~. Let me say it again: I love you. Only you. ~~I know I gam=~~ ~~ble~~. You say that I love the cards and the chips more than you, but that's not the truth. It's you. It's always been you. It will always be you.
Ours was not ~~some regular~~ an ordinary love, ours was ~~beauti=~~ ~~ful~~ a mad, furious love. A love that was stronger than either of us could even know at the time, an all-consuming thing. ~~Bigger than~~ The kind they write novels and love songs about, musicals and operas. Our love is ~~grand~~ monumental, epic, extraordinary. Our love is the stuff of legends.

Love,
Ritchie
1992

Courtney studied it. The cross-outs, the edits—this was the first draft of a love letter. She smiled deeply as she thought of her father, the way the lines on his forehead would become more pronounced when he was really concentrating on something. She could almost hear his pen as it hit the paper. She always noticed that—how when he scribbled in his notebook, he always pressed down on the paper so hard, it would make a sound. Sometimes, at school, she'd try to take notes in her notebook in that same way, produce the same sound. But she never could.

She loved this idea of her father crafting a love letter, bit by bit. Doing it over and over again until he got it right. Making notes to himself to make it better. That's what she remembered about her father. That's the man he was. Flawed, yes, but always trying to get better. Always trying to improve.

Courtney kept reading. She couldn't get over it, this feeling that her father was with her again. She'd missed him so deeply over the past seven years, and tears fell from her eyes before she even realized what was happening.

Courtney loved the way her father always wrote in script. She loved the way he looped the letters *t* and *d* so dramatically, the key to forging his signature on school forms, tests, and bad report cards. She'd learned early how to expertly copy her father's handwriting—first, by tracing it on old school tests she'd saved. By the time she was in high school, she could sign her father's name as naturally as she could sign her own. Courtney lazily ran the tip of her finger over the entry in the notebook, tracing the letters.

Then, all at once, she realized. Courtney took out her phone and pulled up the scans of the letters that the lawyer had sent over as proof of her father's affair. The first letter in the stack, that one had all the hallmarks of his handwriting, could be matched perfectly with what she'd seen in her father's notebooks. The *t*s and the *d*s were perfect matches for her father's own. But the rest of the love notes? Those other notes were written in another hand. It was difficult to tell at first; great care had been taken with each one. They were pretty good fakes, Courtney thought, but not as good as she could have done.

These other letters, the so-called "proof" of an affair, were not written by her father. Which left only one conclusion: the rest of the letters had been written by someone else.

64

The ring, 2008

What Addy thinks happened in 2008: the ring was stolen.

What really happened in 2008: the ring was stolen.

It should have been the perfect night. Thirty years of marriage. A lifetime. A milestone to be celebrated. Their marriage hadn't been an easy one. But whose is?

Traditionally, the thirtieth anniversary is called the pearl. But more modern interpretations consider it the diamond. Since we're talking about Lizzie and Ritchie here, let's stick with the diamond, shall we?

The store was making good money, had been for a while, so Ritchie had proposed they celebrate their thirtieth anniversary with a big, splashy party in the city, and then stay at a hotel overnight. It would be like the grand opening of the store but even bigger. Lizzie couldn't think of anything more perfect.

Ritchie let Lizzie take the lead. She spent six months planning it. She'd fallen in love with the hotel a friend recommended, and when she saw the rooftop pool, she immediately asked if she could host a hundred people there for dinner and dancing. Lizzie had a vision for the party: candles floating in the pool as they danced the night away. An elegant dinner, pretty cocktails in frosted glasses. She would run into the city any spare moment she could, choosing flowers, lighting, a band, the menu.

Lizzie and Ritchie had so much to celebrate. Initially, they'd been upset when Addy accidentally got pregnant at age twenty-five, and then doubled down by marrying Gary and having the twins. But how many couples get to say they celebrated their thirtieth wedding anniversary with their happily married daughter and son-in-law, along with their two-year-old grand-daughters?

Nathan was still struggling with his acting career, but he had a lovely group of friends and had recently met a very nice man. Even though he hadn't found the thing that would bring him fulfillment professionally, they knew Nathan's new beau was something special and thought he'd be around for a while. Things were still new, but Lizzie and Ritchie were hoping Nathan would see fit to bring Diego to the party.

Courtney, their baby, was fifteen years old and so much more focused than Lizzie had been at that age. Courtney got straight As in school and never got into trouble. Ritchie liked to joke that, with Courtney, they'd finally gotten things right.

Hard to believe that Lizzie had met Ritchie at age sixteen, just one year older than Courtney was now. Courtney hardly seemed old enough to meet the man she would marry. But Lizzie supposed she hadn't been, either. After all, it wasn't until nine years later that they had found each other again.

When Lizzie had thrown Ritchie out of the house after he admitted that he'd lost it gambling, they'd both thought it was over for good.

Ritchie had spent the time apart thinking of Lizzie, plotting ways to get her back. He gave her one month to cool off, but by month two, he was back to writing love letters. He mailed the first one to her tiny rental house, and it came back marked *return to sender*. He delivered the next one by hand. But Lizzie refused to accept it. She pressed it back into his palm, unread. It wasn't until six months later that she would even look him in the eye.

Lizzie spent the time apart trying to forget about Ritchie. But being away from him had been the worst nine months of her life. It was as if he was a part of her, and when he was gone, she'd felt his absence every day. She thought about him every moment, saw his crooked smile in Nathan's beautiful face, felt his nervous energy always building in Addy. When they got back together it felt like a foregone conclusion, even though she'd doubted her decision over and over in those first days. It was only when she'd found out she was pregnant with Court-ney that she'd decided, once and for all, to stay.

Staying wasn't easy. Not at first, when the anger over Ritchie's gambling simmered over the surface of everything, and not even in years later, when Lizzie felt she had to look over her shoulder, for fear of being blindsided again, resentments building. Some-times, when she woke up in the middle of the night, she'd qui-etly sneak his notebook into the bathroom, where she'd read it in the light of that tiny night-light by the sink. Ritchie had recorded his thoughts and secrets in his notebooks, but when Lizzie read them, all she ever found was shopping lists, inven-tory numbers, and silly love poems. First drafts of love letters he'd later give to her, carefully written on beautiful stationery.

Through it all, there was one thing that couldn't be denied: theirs was true love.

A week before the party, the weather forecasts predicted rain. Still, Lizzie gasped when she woke up and opened the blinds on the morning of the party. Ritchie kept wishing the rain away, but it was like a bad joke: every time he thought about the rain stopping, thunder would bellow out. As long as the skies clear by 5 p.m., Ritchie thought, repeating those words over and over again in his mind, like a prayer.

They drove into Manhattan in the early afternoon, and the rain was so strong, Ritchie had to slow the car down so they could make it to the hotel safely. Even as they got ready for the party in their hotel room, rain beat down tirelessly on their windows.

But then, when they walked up to the rooftop, they found that the weather had cleared. The sky showed off, in stunning shades of gold, crimson, and apricot, and the air felt cool and crisp.

"It's perfect," Lizzie said, rushing across the rooftop to gaze at the sky.

Ritchie followed and spun her around for a kiss. As their lips touched, they could hear the delicate click of the photographer's camera, capturing the moment.

Ace's family was the first to arrive.

"I knew that Ritchie would order the skies to clear up by five," Ace said, as he walked into the party with wife number four, Sue.

"I never had any doubt," Lizzie said, greeting her friends.

Waiters came by with the signature cocktail of the night: a mix of champagne, St. Germain, and grapefruit juice, along with elegant small bites: caviar on potato chips, seared scallops served inside small shells, and tuna tartare on wasabi crackers. The band played a mixture of late '70s hits and Lizzie's favorite songs from the '80s. Flower arrangements filled with tuberose, lily of the valley, and lilacs perfumed the air. Gary took long stems of the lily of the valley and fashioned them into floral crowns for Olivia and Emma to wear.

Lizzie and Ritchie danced with their friends. They danced with their kids. They danced with their grandkids. Instead of sitting down for dinner, they strolled around the party, greeting each guest. And a team of three photographers were there to catch every minute.

Addy and Gary left the party, at 10 p.m. on the dot, the girls fast asleep in their arms, and made their way down to their hotel room. The rest of the guests shuffled out shortly after that.

Lizzie slipped off her high heels as they made their way down to their hotel room. Ritchie had gone all out, booking rooms for the whole family, and a large suite at the end of the hall for him and Lizzie. It gave Lizzie a lovely peace of mind, knowing that each of her children would be down the hall. With Addy and Nathan out of the house, she never got that feeling anymore—the sense of calm that comes late at night, when a mother is certain all her children are safe and sound, happily sleeping in their beds.

Lizzie undressed and brushed her teeth.

"I'm not ready for the night to be over," Lizzie said, as she walked out of the bathroom and saw Ritchie in bed.

Ritchie pulled the covers back. He was exhausted from the party, but never one to turn down what Lizzie seemed to be suggesting. "Me, neither," he said, his voice low, patting Lizzie's side of the bed. "Let's not let the night end."

But that wasn't what Lizzie had meant. She was already changing out of her nightgown, back into the dress she'd worn to the party. "Let's go for a late swim."

"The pool closes at ten," he replied, looking at her sideways. "Remember, you said it would be perfect for the party. It would end early so that Addy could get the twins to bed. It's probably locked."

"You're right," Lizzie said. "'You don't seem like a jump the fence kind of girl.'"

Ritchie regarded her and, a few seconds later, remembered. It was what he had said to her when they saw each other again at a party nine years after they'd first met. Ritchie had wanted to go to the beach, but Lizzie had said it was closed. They'd settled on a restaurant on the bay for dancing instead.

"'You have no idea what kind of girl I am,'" Ritchie said back, reciting Lizzie's line.

They rushed out the door and back upstairs to the pool. Lizzie dove in headfirst, and Ritchie joined soon after. They splashed, they laughed. He kissed her, pressed against the edge of the deep end.

"I love you, Lizzie Morgan."

"I love you, too, Ritchie Schneider. You are exactly the person my mother warned me about."

"After all these years," he said, "I am still drowning in you."

When they came back to the room, dripping wet, their hotel room door was wide open.

"The ring," Lizzie said, as she entered the room. "My ring!"

65

The ring, 2008

"You put the ring into the safe when we got ready for bed, before we decided to go swimming." Ritchie squinted—his tell—and Lizzie knew that he was just as uncertain of the fate of the ring as she was. "It's still in the safe."

Lizzie screamed, as she saw the hotel room safe, door opened wide.

Ritchie took a deep breath. "I'm sure it's here somewhere. Let's just look around."

Lizzie pointed at the open safe and yelled: "It's been stolen!"

Ritchie quietly closed the door, and insisted on searching the room for another half hour, not yet ready to admit what they both knew was the truth: the ring had been stolen.

Lizzie threw herself onto the bed. She covered her face with a pillow and screamed. Her body heaved with sobs.

Ritchie joined her, rubbing little circles onto her back. "It's okay, don't cry."

"I lost the ring!"

"You didn't *lose* the ring. It was stolen."

"But it was my fault!" Lizzie cried. "I should never have taken if off. That ring was a symbol of our love."

"Our love is a symbol of our love," Ritchie said, and Lizzie could see that imperceptible squint—Ritchie's tell. He was lying. "We don't need a ring to prove it."

"I loved that ring." Lizzie's voice was soft, defeated.

"I know you did," Ritchie said. He took a deep breath and exhaled. "Which is why I never told you about what happened two years ago."

Lizzie's nerves felt on high alert as she turned to face her husband.

"You shouldn't cry about the ring being stolen," Ritchie said.

"Because we have insurance?" Lizzie asked, her words coming out slowly, tentatively.

"No," Ritchie said, rubbing his eyes, "because that one was a fake."

Lizzie felt her heart drop into her stomach. "The ring I was wearing? It wasn't real?"

Ritchie could barely stand to answer his wife. With tears in his eyes: "I'm so sorry. I mess everything up. I'm so sorry, Lizzie."

"Was it ever real?" Lizzie couldn't help herself. Tears streamed down her face, faster than she could wipe them away with her hand. Her breath caught in her throat, and she concentrated on taking a deep breath in.

"Yes, of course it was," Ritchie said, gathering Lizzie into a hug. She pulled away from him, and sat herself up straight. She tried to take deep, measured breaths, but found it difficult to breathe at all.

Ritchie got off the bed, and kneeled down before his wife. Bowing down before he made his confession. Ritchie took a deep breath, exhaled slowly. "It was real, but then, six months later, I had to sell the diamond for some cash for the down payment on our house, so I had Pete the Jeweler replace the stone with a cubic zirconia."

Lizzie couldn't process what she was hearing. The champagne and late-night swim had gone to her head. And now this. She closed her eyes and put the heels of her hands against her eye-lids. It was too much to take. If the ring wasn't real, what was?

"I bought back the real stone—the original stone—four years ago, but then I lost the whole ring in a card game two years ago."

Screaming: "You gambled with my ring?"

Ritchie continued as if he'd had this speech stored up in his mind, ready to go. "Luckily, Ace convinced the Captain to sell it to Pete the Jeweler for some fast cash. Pete held onto the ring for all this time, just waiting for me to have enough funds on hand to replace it."

"So, when did you replace it?"

"I haven't replaced it. Yet. But I will. For a while, I kept thinking that maybe the ring was safer in Pete's hands, you know?"

"Okay," Lizzie said, quietly. It was a lot to process. She could feel the champagne sloshing around in her belly, threatening to come up. But she'd dealt with worse in her thirty-year marriage to Ritchie—once your husband comes home and tells you that he gambled your house away, there's no challenge you can't get past.

"And that's the truth. The whole truth. Cards on the table."

"Oh, that's it?" Lizzie asked, and laughed, despite the headache starting to take form behind her eyes.

The next morning, after a quick stop at the bank, they got to Pete the Jeweler's storefront at 10 a.m. on the dot. The diamond anniversary, after all.

"So, I guess it's a good thing the Captain won that game, huh?" Pete the Jeweler said to Ritchie.

"Excuse me, are you trying to say it's a good thing that my husband gambled away my ring?"

"When you put it like that, it sounds bad," Pete said, his brow furrowed as he considered Lizzie's point. "But think of it this way—if he hadn't lost the ring to the Captain, the Captain would never have sold it to me. I've had the ring—diamond, setting, the whole shebang—this whole time. If I hadn't, it would have been stolen last night, right?"

"In that case, thank you for keeping it safe for me," Lizzie said.

Pete the Jeweler disappeared into the back of the store.

"You know," Ritchie said, "Elizabeth Taylor used to say that you could never truly own a piece of jewelry."

"I think I'm about to own that ring," Lizzie said. "Again."

"She said we were the mere custodians of jewelry, keeping it safe for the next generation."

"That's a lovely sentiment," Lizzie said. "But once he puts that beauty back on my finger, I'm never taking it off again."

66

Addy

"You were right," Addy said.

"What was that?" Courtney straightened herself up from where she was lounging on the window seat in Olivia's room, curled toward the sun like a cat.

"I said you were right." Addy couldn't help but smile when Courtney's eyes registered what she was saying, and then bulged out ever so slightly as she processed it.

"One more time."

"You. Were. Right." Addy had to laugh—her sister had a point. Addy was used to being the one who was right. Courtney had earned this victory. She'd discovered something Addy and Nathan had missed. Addy got down on her knees and held her hands out. "All hail Courtney! The one Schneider sibling who was smart enough to read between the lines."

"The lines themselves?"

"Or would it be, *the way the lines were written*?"

"Shame on you for not being a disciple of the handwriting of Ritchie Schneider."

Both women laughed. Addy couldn't remember the last time

she'd had this with her sister—an alone moment, an unguarded moment. A time where they could laugh together, appreciate each other, enjoy one another's company. Their relationship was mostly a series of Addy feeling resentful, acting unsympathetically, and bossing her sister around. Tossing her crumbs. But this? It was nice. Addy wanted more of it.

"The DNA test came back," Addy said, getting up from the floor and sitting down in a nearby chair. "You were right. There was no affair. She's not our half sibling. She's our cousin."

"She dodged a bullet. This isn't an easy family to be born into."

Addy tossed a pillow in her sister's direction. Courtney caught it, and drew it close to her chest. She lay back on the window seat.

"I'm sorry," Addy said.

"For what?"

"Nothing. Everything. Our whole lives."

"Oh, just that?"

"I'm serious. I hate that we've spent our whole lives hating each other, not knowing each other."

"I never hated you."

"I know. Thus, the 'I'm sorry' part. I was horrible to you, and I'm so sorry. I was wrong. And I'll tell you that as many times as you need to hear it."

Courtney didn't respond. She held her hand out and motioned with her fingers: *again.*

"I'm sorry. I was wrong."

"One more time?"

"I'm sorry. I was wrong."

"Okay, I accept your apology."

"I know it's not as easy as that. But just know that things will be different now. I'm going to do better. I'm going to be better. Maybe you could even stay out here a little longer?"

Courtney looked at her phone. "Maybe. Hey, isn't it ten minutes until dinner?"

"Oh, yeah, I completely forgot. Let me go get dinner started, and I'll call up when it's almost ready."

"I was kidding," Courtney said. "Just poking a little fun at your ten-minute warnings."

"Oh," Addy said, feeling the sides of her face heat up. "That. You know, I just like everyone to know what's coming up, what's expected of them. It's something I've been doing since the girls were little. They used to say that you have to define parameters with kids."

"A lot is expected of *you*," Courtney said, her head back in her phone.

"I'm not complaining," Addy said. "I certainly didn't mean to complain."

"Pizza's coming in thirty minutes."

"What?"

"You've been cooking three meals a day for five adults and two teenagers for almost a month now."

"Well, the girls are sleeping at their friend's house tonight, and Diego's...well, Diego's not here...so it's just the four of us."

"I ordered pizza. You still like veggie, right?"

"Right." How funny that Courtney would remember how Addy liked her pizza. Did Addy know how Courtney liked hers? Addy's eyes began to tear up.

"It's just pizza."

"I know that," Addy said, jumping up and running her hands down her sides to smooth her shirt. "Remind me how you like yours?"

"I like plain," Courtney said. "Classic."

"Right," Addy said. "I'm sorry I never knew that."

"Again, it's just pizza."

"Of course," Addy said. "Right. It's just pizza. I'll go pick out a wine."

Courtney nodded.

"Actually, let's skip the wine tonight," Addy said.

"You don't have to skip it on my behalf," Courtney said. "But I *have* been thinking about what you said."

"I didn't mean to hurt you," Addy said. "I was trying to help."

"I understand that now." Courtney stood up and gave Addy a hug.

Thirty minutes later, Addy, Courtney, Gary, and Nathan assembled at the kitchen table for pizza—one plain, one veggie. The conversation was light, effortless. Enjoyable. As if their shared history didn't include countless slights and constant bitterness. They savored each other's company fully, in a way they never had before. Addy could not stop smiling. She missed having Diego there, but when she reached across the table to touch Courtney's arm, her little sister didn't shy away.

They talked about the food, they talked about the lawsuit, and how happy they were that it had been withdrawn. No one mentioned the thing that hovered in the periphery, the one thing they really needed to discuss: who would get the ring.

But that question would have to wait. Addy's phone rang out, interrupting their dinner. She glanced at the screen and didn't recognize the number. Usually, she'd let a call like that go directly to voice mail, so she put her phone back down onto the table, facedown.

"Aren't you going to get that?" Nathan asked, his mouth full of food.

"I wasn't planning to." Addy gave her brother a look—*what, you answer your phone?*—and he gave one right back—*yes, I actually do.* Addy rolled her eyes at Nathan and begrudgingly answered.

"Hello, I'm looking for an Addy Schneider."

"Who's calling?" Addy carefully asked. She threw a dirty look in Nathan's direction. He shrugged.

"Security at the Golden Nugget."

"The what?" Addy's thoughts were a jumble: *Would they finally figure out who got ownership of the ring only to discover they'd have to sell it, anyway, because of an old gambling debt of their father? Would her father's complicated legacy haunt her for the rest of her life? When would she be out from under his past?*

Addy put the phone on speaker so that everyone could hear. "Ma'am, I'm calling from the Golden Nugget Hotel and Casino in Atlantic City."

Gary looked at her. "What's going on?"

"This is Addy Schneider. Is this regarding my father? Because he's been dead for—"

"Mrs. Schneider," the voice on the phone said, cutting Addy off, "we have detained two young women for illegally gambling in our casino."

67

Addy

"Everyone in the car," Gary said, as soon as Addy hung up the phone.

"I'll just—" Courtney began.

"Leave the dishes," Gary said. "We need to go."

Courtney and Nathan went to the mudroom to grab their coats, but Addy wandered into the living room.

"Add?" Gary said. "We've got to go." Courtney and Nathan stood behind him, Nathan holding out Addy's coat for her to take.

"I just need my armor," Addy said, under her breath, kneeling down in front of the safe. "I need to put it on."

Her family watched as she pulled out her diamond earrings and put them on, one by one. Then, the diamond solitaire necklace that had belonged to Lizzie. Addy froze, and then turned around to her husband and siblings. "The ring."

"I don't think you need to wear an eleven-carat ring to go to Atlantic City," Nathan said.

"No, the ring," Addy said. "It was right here in the safe. Right behind the earrings."

"Fine," Gary said. "Then, just grab it, and let's go."

"I can't," Addy said. "It's gone!"

PART FOUR: CARAT WEIGHT

68

Nathan

"We will deal with the ring once we've got the girls," Gary said, as everyone piled into the car.

"Easy for you to say," Nathan said, buckling his seat belt roughly. "You don't care about the ring."

"I care about it," Gary said, as he put the address for the Golden Nugget into his car's navigational system. "But I care more about my girls."

"I care more about my nieces, too," Nathan said. He wasn't used to disagreeing with his brother-in-law. Speaking up for himself was new for Nathan, and it gave him a rush of adrenaline. Maybe this was why Addy did it so often? "But I also care about the ring."

"People are what's important," Gary said, pulling out of the driveway. "Not things."

"I think we're all really upset right now," Courtney said, grabbing Nathan's hand. "Let's try to calm down until we figure out what happened."

"You're just happy that it's been stolen," Nathan said, pulling his hand away. "Now we can make an insurance claim, and you can get your precious cash."

Addy gasped. "I didn't get the ring insured."

"If I hear one more goddamn word about that ring," Gary said, "I am throwing you all out of the car. My girls are missing. Who cares about the fucking ring?"

"I mean, they're not *missing*," Nathan muttered. "We know exactly where they are."

Gary swerved the car to the curb. "Get out."

Nathan laughed. "Are you serious right now?"

"I mean it," Gary said. "Get out of my car."

Nathan unbuckled his seat belt and got out, slamming the door behind him. He stood on the side of the road, grateful that they'd barely made it out of the driveway and it was only a one-minute walk back to Addy's house.

"Stop it!" Addy said, yelling out the car window. "Nathan, get back in the car." Then, to Gary: "You're acting like a child."

"You're all acting like children!" Courtney said. "I wish we'd never found the ring in the first place."

"Do you really mean that?" Addy asked, tilting the mirror so that she could look at her sister.

"Yes," Courtney said. "Everything was just fine before that stupid ring came into our lives."

"Was it?" Addy asked.

Courtney looked down into her lap, and Nathan felt a surge of sadness for his younger sister. He got back into the car, and then reached over to Courtney and grabbed her hand.

"I'm actually kind of happy this whole mess brought you back into our lives," Nathan said softly.

"Me too," Addy said.

Gary pulled the car away from the curb and continued driving.

"I guess I'm glad that I'm back, too," Courtney said. "So, I'm grateful to the ring for that. But it made me into an ugly person. I mean, at first. At one point, I thought about just taking the ring, catching a red-eye to LA, and selling it without you knowing."

"But you didn't do that," Nathan said. "Things are different now, right?"

"Right," Courtney said.

"We told Dad we would always look out for you, and we didn't do that," Nathan said. "I'm sorry."

"I don't need looking after," Courtney said. "I'm not a child."

"Family looks out for each other," Addy said. "And we're a family. Even if we didn't always act like it."

"Well, I'm living rent-free in your house now," Courtney said. "So, maybe we can call it even."

"It's not even," Addy said. "Not by a long shot. But I'm grateful to have a second chance with you."

"Me too," Nathan said, still holding Courtney's hand.

"Me too," Courtney said. She gave Nathan's hand a squeeze.

69

Addy

This room seemed familiar. Too familiar. It was the room that had featured in many of her nightmares, anxiety dreams that took her back to the most shameful period of her life.

Not this exact room, of course it wasn't this exact room. But the idea was the same—it was the place where security detained you for breaking casino rules. It wasn't the police, and you weren't necessarily being arrested, but they put you there to scare you. And it worked. It worked every time. Each time Addy found herself in a room like this, she'd been scared. Terrified. And now her girls were here for illegally gambling, underage.

Addy had a secret. Something that no one in the family knew. Not even Nathan. Certainly not Gary. And definitely not her girls. Never her girls.

Addy was a gambler. (Addy *used to* be a gambler, she would hasten to correct. Gambling was in the past.) She didn't have a problem, don't *call it a problem*, but she'd enjoyed gambling. She'd enjoyed it very much.

Maybe she'd enjoyed it a little too much.

But could anyone blame her? With her father, how was she

supposed to not gamble? To not feel perfectly at home in a casino, or at a racetrack, or at a card game? Gambling was in her blood. It was her birthright.

It had begun innocently enough, as these things always do. Some friends were driving out from UCLA to Vegas for the night, and did Addy want to come? (Of course she wanted to come.) She didn't think she'd gamble much. After all, they were freshmen in college and didn't have a lot of expendable cash. But it would be fun, she thought. She would bond with her friends, she thought. They stepped foot into the newly built Bellagio, and it hit her. That instant feeling—you could smell it in the air, too, couldn't you?—the high she got from the air in a casino. She heard the relentless buzz of the slot machines, calling to her like a siren.

"Quick game before getting settled into our rooms?" Her friends fanned off to various quarter slot machines, but Addy made herself at home in Pit 9. Blackjack. She loved the frenetic pace of the game, how she'd run the numbers in her head as they played. Addy paid close attention to the cards—her father had taught her the game, taught her to keep an eye out for the picture cards being dealt, the little beauties that could turn your fifteen into a twenty-five in the blink of an eye, losing you your hand.

It became a thing they did more often, driving to Vegas for the weekend, and like everything else Addy did, she wanted to be the best. A friend told her there was a better system of keeping track of the face cards, and gave her a book about counting cards. This was what Addy was looking for—a way to be even better at what she was already good at, a way to beat the house.

It wasn't cheating. That's the thing Addy always got stuck on. It was not illegal to count cards. It was merely frowned upon by the casinos. Of course it was—it gave players an advantage. It helped them win. And she was a real gambler, not a dabbler like her girlfriends, who spent maybe thirty bucks, tops, over the course of a weekend at the slot machines. Addy gambled real money. Shouldn't she have a real shot at winning? But, of course, the house always wins.

The first time she was picked up was at the Bellagio. When she thinks back to that night, it fills her belly, makes her hands go cold. The pit boss took her by the arm and asked her to go speak privately. He had handled her roughly, but Addy still dumbly assumed they were taking her to an office to talk about getting her rooms comped for the night, or a free dinner for her and her friends. But they didn't go to an office. They went back through a door marked *Private* and walked down a concrete corridor where she was left in a concrete room, alone, for what seemed like hours. They let her off with a warning and told her that as long as she stopped counting cards, she would be welcome to come back at the Bellagio.

But Addy couldn't stop. The very next day, she did it again. Asking her to stop was like asking her to stop her heart from beating. She simply could not. This time, she was told she could never return. They took her photograph and sent her off.

The next time they went to Vegas, Addy insisted they stay at Caesars. *Old school*, she told her friends. And they all went along with it. Once she'd been thrown out of Caesars, her friends didn't want to switch hotels again. They wanted to be regulars at a casino, like the Rat Pack. But then Mandalay Bay became the hot new place to stay, and her friends had already forgotten what they even liked about Caesars in the first place. By senior year, Addy was banned from Mandalay Bay, the Luxor, MGM, and the Venetian.

Still, she couldn't stop. Addy no longer needed the pretext of a girls' night out or a girls' weekend. She drove the four hours to Vegas by herself on days she didn't have class. And on some days she *did* have class. Addy was winning so much money, it would have been *irresponsible* to stop, she told herself. After all, she would never end up like her father—losing so much money that he lost their childhood home. Every time her winnings went over ten thousand dollars, Addy would deposit them directly into a CD at the bank, or her savings account, or, even one time, a safe-deposit box that could barely fit all the cash. Addy would save nest egg after nest egg, her security policy.

She probably would be sneaking off to casinos still, if Ace hadn't caught her being carted away by security one night at Binion's in downtown Vegas. He sweet-talked the head of security into letting Addy go, in his care, and that's when he put the fear of God into her.

"Please don't tell my father," Addy pled, as they took a cab back to the Treasure Island Hotel on the strip, where her friends were staying.

"Kid, this is not what your father wanted for you." Ace rubbed his eyes roughly and let out a deep exhale.

"I know."

Turning to face Addy: "He doesn't want his daughter to be a degenerate like him."

"He's not a degenerate."

"Depends on who you ask."

"Please don't tell him." Addy tried to keep the tears at bay.

"Let's make a deal—I won't tell him this time. And you are going to call me if you ever get into trouble like this, ever again."

"I promise."

"But you are never going to get into trouble like this again."

"Okay."

"I'm serious," Ace said, looking at Addy, straight-faced. "I don't care what you need to do. Go to Gamblers Anonymous, get yourself into therapy, do something. But not this. You cannot do this."

"I can stop."

"Sure, kid. Sure you can."

Addy got herself into therapy the following Monday. She never stepped foot in Vegas again. There had been other things she felt her addictive personality getting attached to in the years that followed—she was particularly careful around alcohol, only drinking a glass or two of wine at any one time. And she watched her sugar, because the less she drank alcohol, the more she craved sugar. There were things that she was addicted to that worked out well for her—she was utterly, completely addicted to Gary, and she didn't think that would ever go away—but for the most part, weekly therapy was good for Addy.

Being in Atlantic City now was like getting a visit from an old friend. That specific smell of a casino, the way the sounds of the slot machine drew her in, the cheers from the craps table. And now, the room.

"What are you going to say to the girls when you see them?" Gary asked Addy. The chairs in the room hadn't been updated since the 1970s. They were aluminum, not exactly designed for comfort. Gary leaned back in his, and looked at her.

That part was easy. Addy knew exactly what she would do when she saw her girls. First, Addy would hug them. A big giant bear hug, one arm for each girl. She'd tell them how much she loved them. Then she'd tell them how worried they'd been, and how they must never sneak off again. Then, the lecturing would begin.

The door opened, and a security guard led Olivia and Emma into the room. Addy jumped up from her chair, and gathered her daughters in her arms.

Addy was about to tell her girls how much she loved them, how worried they'd been. But then Addy noticed something on Emma's finger.

"You are wearing my mother's ring," Addy said.

"For armor," Emma said.

"For luck?" Olivia said, her voice high and uncertain.

"For God's sake," Gary said, enveloping all three of his girls in a hug, "who cares?"

70

Courtney

Courtney had started helping Addy cook each night since bringing the twins home from Atlantic City. Things in the house had been tense—Courtney knew Addy had been talking to the girls, doling out punishments, giving lectures on a seemingly everyday basis. There was only one time when things calmed down, and that was when Addy cooked dinner.

Her sister knew quite a lot about cooking, Courtney was surprised to learn, and she loved the gentle rhythms of the kitchen. Courtney found it so soothing, preparing a meal and then watching people enjoy it, and she'd begun leafing through Addy's cookbooks in the afternoons, excited about planning the menus for the day. She was also enjoying her sister's company.

On the menu that night: Courtney was making meatballs. She'd gone with Addy to the butcher that morning, and had her ingredients laid out in front of her, like on a cooking show. They'd bought three pounds of meat and, looking at the work set out before her, Courtney felt a little overwhelmed. But as she began rolling the meatballs, she found herself relaxing, her shoulders releasing. As she continued the simple motion over and over again, she let her mind wander. About her family. About Sy. About how far she'd come in just a few short weeks.

Courtney thought about Holly. Maybe it was unfair how they'd banded together against her as a common enemy. Maybe the right course of action would have been to figure it out as a family. Even now, knowing that she wasn't their half sister, she was still their cousin. And that meant something, didn't it?

Courtney heard the door to the mudroom open, shaking her from her reverie. She had found it odd the way Addy always left it unlocked. Yet another mystery of suburban life Courtney would never quite understand. Anyway, it was probably Gary and Nathan, home for dinner. Courtney gently placed the meat-balls into the large pot of sauce—Addy's special recipe—and walked toward the mudroom. "Ten minutes until dinner," she called out, channeling her sister.

But it was not her brother or her brother-in-law who she saw. Standing in the mudroom was a man, a gigantic man, who addressed her by name.

"Courtney?"

She meant to say something along the lines of *Who's asking?* or, more to the point, *Who the fuck are you?* but instead, when Courtney opened her mouth, a high-pitched scream escaped her lips. She wasn't sure where it came from—surely with the stress of the money she owed, and the lawsuit and the possible half sister, she was due for a good cry, or maybe what she really needed was this: to scream at the top of her lungs.

She instantly knew who the man was and why he'd tracked her down to Addy's house—this was her bookie's muscle, and he was coming to collect. Duke came running into the mud-room. He barked so loudly that the man fell back a step, and backed into the door.

Addy appeared by her side, as if from thin air. "What the fuck is this?" Duke continued barking madly, and Addy rubbed the space between his ears to calm him down.

"Hey, Addy," the man said. Courtney wasn't sure what to process first—the fact that this enormous and very scary man knew her sister by name, or that Addy had grabbed a softball bat that had been sitting in the corner of the mudroom and had it poised and ready to swing. "Can't we do this nice, Add?"

"No, Reggie," Addy said, her face a stone, "we cannot do this nice. You just let yourself into my house, unwelcome. Unwanted. You need to leave."

"The door was open," Reggie said. "You really should lock it."

Duke arranged himself between the women and the man, ready to pounce, if need be.

"Get out," Addy said, tightening her grip on the softball bat.

"Your sister owes our mutual friend money."

Addy turned to Courtney: "Is this why you want to sell the ring?"

Courtney looked down, unable to answer her sister.

"Fine, my sister owes some money. But isn't this a bit over-kill?"

"Lefty asked me to send a message."

"How about you send one back—Lefty forgives her debt and I don't turn him in to the authorities."

"You know he's not gonna forgive her debt."

"He did it for me, now he does it for her."

It took Courtney a second to process what her sister was saying. *He did it for me.* What had Lefty done for her? Was Addy saying that she used to gamble, too? That seemed impossible. Her perfect sister Addy used her father's bookie, too? She tried to articulate a thought, but instead choked out: "What?"

"That was twenty years ago, Add," Reggie said. "And if I recall correctly, you lost two grand at a poker game that turned out to be fixed. These are hardly the same things."

"*You* fixed the game," Addy said. "That was *you*. That's how you hooked up with Lefty in the first place. So, now go fix this for me."

"Your girl's in the hole for two hundred and fifty K," Reggie said, speaking directly to Addy. "You know Lefty cannot let that go."

Addy took a second before responding. Courtney could see it in her sister's eyes—the shock over the amount, the disappointment. But Addy immediately righted herself and got her game face back on. "Let's leave her out of this," Addy said, taking a deep breath, keeping the bat up in the air, ready to fly. "It's between Lefty and me now."

"He's not gonna like this, Add."

"I don't care what he does and does not like," Addy said. "He should never have taken action from my baby sister. Never. Knowing our family history, how dare he?"

"Add, he just tells me where to go."

"How fucking dare he?" Addy said, her voice louder, more forceful. "You tell Lefty to give me a call, and we'll handle this together."

The man put his hands up, as if in surrender, and walked out of the house. "You'll be getting a call from the man."

"I'd expect nothing less." The door closed behind him, with a slam.

"Holy shit," Courtney said. "You're a boss."

"I'll call Lefty," Addy said softly, putting the softball bat back where it belonged. "Let's call some brokers in LA and get your apartment sold so that we can pay him off and be done with this."

Courtney didn't respond. She couldn't respond. Things had taken a turn with Addy. Things were better now. They were establishing a relationship, finally, after all these years. How could she tell her the truth? How could she tell her that the apartment was gone? That she'd already sold it to cover a past debt with Lefty?

Addy searched her face. When Courtney didn't speak, Addy said, "Oh."

"I'm so sorry, Addy. I can explain—"

"You don't have to explain. I get it. I'll take care of things with Lefty. I have a few nest eggs I can tap."

"I can't let you pay my debts."

"I'm your sister. You can let me help." Addy put her hand on her shoulder, and Courtney had to fight to keep the tears at bay.

"This is my mess. I'm sorry they came here, and I'm sorry I put our family in danger, but I can't let you do that."

Addy considered this. "Okay, understood. How about this— I front you the money, just to get Lefty off your case. Stop the juice from running. Then you work off your debt at the store?"

"I think I should head back to LA and handle this on my own."

"I think you should accept my help," Addy said. "I think you should stay."

71

Nathan

"Please come home."

"Hey," Diego said, but he seemed distracted. Nathan should never have let him leave without a fight. What was he thinking, letting Diego run off to Vegas without him? "I'm backstage, can I call you back?"

Nathan knew he should let Diego get back to work. Backstage meant he was at the venue where Diego's father would be performing for the next six months. Two shows a night, 7:30 p.m. and 10 p.m. It was a fifty-two-hundred seat stadium at the MGM Grand, and they had only two weeks to completely renovate the stage and get it ready for his father's upcoming residency.

Diego's father knew exactly what he wanted or, to put it more accurately, what his fans would want. It needed to be intimate, it needed to be epic. It needed to be the exact same show he'd been doing for his whole fifty-year career, but completely different. To open the show, he would come out and sit on a stool, holding his red guitar, like he used to. Then, they'd segue into some big, dramatic song-and-dance numbers featuring his music from the '80s, highlighted by pyrotechnics and strobe lighting.

A team of twenty backup dancers. Toward the end of the show, he'd have an intimate moment—Diego's mother would come out onto the stage for a slow dance, which was a hallmark of his '90s concerts. And then the final number, his famous song, "Beautiful Woman," which he'd begin acoustically by himself. But since this was Vegas, that part of the show would get an over-the-top upgrade, worthy of the extravagant venue. Halfway through the song, a curtain at the back of the stage would drop to reveal a full forty-nine-piece orchestra, which would help him finish the song with a bang.

"I miss you," Nathan said. He sat down on his father's old couch, in his office. "Do you miss me?"

"Of course I do," Diego said quietly. "But I should get back to work."

Nathan couldn't let him get off the phone. What would his father do here? Well, that was easy: he'd write a love letter. But there was no time for that, and anyway, Nathan couldn't think of anything romantic to say.

"Please don't."

"I'll call you later," Diego said. "I'm needed here."

"You're needed *here*," Nathan said. "I love you. I miss you."

"I miss you, too."

"Then, come home."

"I can't," Diego said. "You know that. I'm working."

"Well, then, finish up, and then come home."

"Things are happening here," Diego said carefully.

"Things?"

Diego explained: the night before, the singer in the tiny cabaret off the casino had gotten sick, and Diego's father suggested to the casino manager that instead of closing the cabaret for the night, perhaps they let Diego fill in. The manager loved it—Pedro Garcia Flores' son doing a small, intimate set, which would surely drive business to his father's upcoming residency. Diego had two hours to prepare, but he didn't care. He got to sing for the first time in years. Not to audition, not to prove anything. He got to sing simply because he loved it.

Diego had improvised an entire forty-five minute show for the eleven people in the audience (he'd counted). He sang a few songs, told some funny stories, and then, in an echo of the famous moment from his father's '90s shows, when he'd bring Diego's mother up to the stage to dance, Diego invited an audience member up from the crowd to dance. The show had been a success, but more important, Diego felt good about himself. For the first time in a very long time, Diego felt happy and at peace. He felt like himself again, a version that had been long lost.

"That's amazing! Do you think they're going to give you a show?" Nathan asked.

"I don't think that's the point," Diego said. "I had fun doing it. And I would love to do it again, if there's another opening. But I'm also loving being one of the producers on my dad's show. This has been really good for me."

"When we met, you were so happy to stop working for your dad. You wanted to get out of his shadow. Why now?"

"I spent so long running away from my father's legacy, his help, and it defined me for too long," Diego said. His words poured out in a jumble. "Because that's the thing, your family does define you. If you have nothing to do with your family, like your aunt, then that defines you. If you choose another man as your family like your mother did, that defines you, too. So, now I'm going to take my father's help, just like you did. Because family defines you no matter what. If your father is the biggest superstar in the world, or the biggest gambler in the world, that's who your dad is. No use running away from it."

"So, when are you coming home?" Nathan asked. When Diego didn't answer, Nathan clarified: "*Are* you coming home?"

Diego let out a deep breath. "Look, I'm just taking things day by day, minute by minute. I'm done with worrying all the time. Worrying if I'm good enough for you, worrying if I look good enough, if I made our life good enough. Vegas is full of opportunities, and I'm going to chase them. From now on, I'm going to focus on what *I* need. Try to remember who I used to be. Can you understand that?"

"Understood," Nathan said, and hung up the phone. He closed his eyes for a moment, to process what had just happened. Diego wasn't coming home right away. Maybe he wouldn't be coming home at all.

Nathan got up from his father's couch, sat down at his desk, and began to write.

72

The ring, 2015

Lizzie dressed carefully for the funeral. It seemed so surreal, this. Dressing to bury the love of your life.

But today was Ritchie's funeral, and she would dress up, look nice, and honor the man she loved. Forty-six years of marriage. They'd almost made it to fifty, to half a century. Making it to the golden anniversary. Sounded like the sort of thing Ritchie would bet on with Ace. But Ace had died suddenly, just a few weeks prior, in a car accident. No, that wasn't right. Ace hadn't died, had he? Lizzie searched her mind for an answer.

The doctors said Ritchie died of a heart attack. Addy and Nathan said he died of a broken heart, because watching the love of his life deteriorate on a daily basis was too much for him to bear. But Lizzie couldn't understand that logic. After all, she was still there. She was alive.

Lizzie put on the clothes she had laid out the day before—a simple black sheath, nothing too flashy, and a pair of pointy-toed flats. She put her hair back in a bun (what would people say if she appeared too vain on the day of Ritchie's funeral?), and tucked an embroidered handkerchief into her purse. Today would be a day filled with tears.

Nathan and Diego picked her up to drive her to the funeral home. Lizzie never failed to appreciate how her son-in-law, Diego, was the consummate gentleman. Always opened the door for her, always extended his arm for her to take. Lizzie would tell Diego that even though she'd been in love with his father's music for as long as she could remember, it was Diego who was the special one. The one she loved now.

The funeral director seemed to drone on forever as he explained how the service would go. Thank goodness she had Addy to take care of the details. Addy sat at the head of the table, the typical firstborn. She even had a pad and a pen at the ready, nodding along as the funeral director noted the order in which the children would give their eulogies. Lizzie looked down at her hand. At the ring. Even in the funeral home's cheap fluorescent lighting, the ring still sparkled beautifully. It caught the light so that it glittered, no matter how she moved her hand. The ring mesmerized her, as it always had. As Ritchie always had.

Ritchie used to say that the ring was the perfect symbol of their love: beautiful and complicated. Hopeful. Enormous.

As the funeral director wrapped up his talk, he told them that they would each have time alone with Ritchie. A few moments to say their final goodbyes. Addy went in with Gary, and Nathan went in with Diego. When it was Courtney's turn, Lizzie couldn't help but feel sad that she'd have to go in alone.

"Should I come with you?" Lizzie asked.

"I'm okay," Courtney said, though it was clear that tears were building up behind her beautiful blue eyes.

Then it was Lizzie's turn. She sat next to the coffin, unsure of what to do, unsure of what to say. She looked in and could hardly recognize the man inside. His face was bloated, not handsome the way it'd always been. And they'd done his hair wrong, all wrong. Lizzie used her fingers to smooth it back into place, the way Ritchie had always worn it. As she reached down to hold her beloved's hand, one last time, she noticed that her children had placed things inside the casket.

Addy had put in old photographs. So they would know that Ritchie was loved, she would later tell Lizzie. Nathan had put in one of his prized possessions: a love letter that Ritchie had written to Lizzie decades ago. Courtney put in a few chips from the Golden Nugget, won with Ritchie on her twenty-first birthday. All beautiful remembrances. But Lizzie hadn't thought to bring anything with her.

Suddenly, a memory bubbled to the surface. Something about passing through the gates of the underworld. How funny to be remembering a lesson she'd learned in seventh-grade English class when most days she struggled to recall what she had eaten for breakfast. But she remembered it so vividly now, sitting in Mr. Perez's class, studying Greek mythology for months on end. The story of Charon, the ferryman who brought souls from the world of the living to the world of the dead. You needed to give Charon a coin, or something of value, for the passage. If you couldn't pay, you were destined to wander the banks of the River Styx for all of eternity.

Lizzie couldn't allow the love of her life to wander for all of eternity. She opened her purse to find a coin to leave in Ritchie's casket—those chips from the Golden Nugget might not be of value in the underworld. But she hadn't carried coins for years, not since she used to leave change for parking meters in the glove box of her car. Lizzie didn't even drive anymore. The only thing of value that she had in her purse was a very expensive lipstick Addy had bought for her one day on a shopping trip in Manhattan. But she couldn't very well put that into Ritchie's casket.

She looked down at her hand and had her answer. Lizzie slipped her diamond ring off, the ring that had symbolized so much in their married life, and placed it in the coffin.

No, no that wasn't it. That's not how it happened. Lizzie

struggled to recall how it had actually happened as she walked out of the room, but she found that she could not remember. Her children were waiting for her as she walked out of the room; Addy put her arm around her shoulder, and Nathan handed her a tissue. She hadn't even realized that she'd been crying. She blotted the tears away just as Courtney enveloped her in an enormous hug. The tears started again. She walked out into the chapel with her children, all holding hands. All united.

As she took her seat for the service, the pastor began his speech. He told family anecdotes, and Lizzie got confused— had she told this man these personal stories? But she looked to her children's faces, a mix of sadness and recognition, and realized that she must have shared these moments with the pastor. He told the story about Ritchie losing the house as if it were a funny anecdote, as if it hadn't devastated their family, and she supposed that that's what it was now—just a story. They'd survived it, they'd moved past it. It was just a part of their long and complicated history now. Then, he told the story of how they came back together, the story of how the Liz Taylor Ring came to be a part of their family mythology, and Lizzie felt Nathan grab her hand and give it a squeeze. As he released her hand, Lizzie felt that something was not quite right.

She looked down at her hand, and the ring was no longer there.

73

Nathan

"But why do I need Excel when I can just run all of these numbers in my head?" Courtney took her index finger and tapped it to her temple, as if to show Nathan where the figures would be stored.

"My God, you sound exactly like Dad," Nathan said, laughing, as he leaned over the desk to tap the keyboard and show Courtney how he organized the various spreadsheets. Nathan had never considered it before—how much Courtney was like their father. His whole life, he'd seen her as a separate entity: there was Addy and Nathan, and then there was Courtney. But he was slowly learning who his little sister was, how she fit into the whole of their family, and he discovered something new about her every day. "You can feel free to memorize all of the numbers, like Dad used to do, but we still need records of everything for the accountants."

"Right," Courtney said, biting her lower lip. Nathan examined his sister again. Ritchie used to bite his lower lip when he was balancing the books, too.

"Ready to go over QuickBooks?"

Addy waltzed into Nathan's office without knocking. Now that she'd be working in the store alongside Courtney in a more permanent position, a more defined role, Nathan would need to get her an office. Even though he'd be gone for the next two weeks, there was no way he was letting Courtney and Addy share his office with him. "I got the good coffee and muffins from that place we like." She set two cardboard carrying trays on the edge of the table.

Nathan was going out to Vegas to save his marriage. He'd followed his father's advice, advice from a long time ago, which was to write Diego a love letter. Nathan poured his heart out into a handwritten letter asking Diego if they could start over. Diego had responded with a love letter of his own. It was so beautifully written that Nathan had suggested Diego might have a career as a songwriter ahead of him. After reading Diego's letter, Nathan immediately booked a ticket to Vegas.

"Break?" Courtney asked. "I think I need some coffee before tackling QuickBooks, anyway."

"Sure," Nathan said, and picked up the coffee cup marked with his initials. Addy always got everyone's coffee orders correct.

Olivia and Emma walked into his office next, each carrying a box filled with muffins. The sweet smell of fresh-baked goods filled the room.

"How's it going in here?" Gary said, also entering Nathan's office without knocking. Seeing his daughters, he enveloped them both in a bear hug at the same time, making them giggle and yell out: "You're squishing us!" Gary released Olivia and Emma, grabbed his coffee and a chocolate chip muffin, and then settled himself in his usual spot on Ritchie's old couch.

"She's a natural," Nathan said, and wondered why that statement made him feel annoyed. Surely, he should be glad that his little sister was picking everything up so quickly. If it weren't for her, he couldn't go to Vegas for two weeks to be with Diego.

And anyway, they'd brought Addy, Olivia, and Emma in to help, too. He tried to focus on this: it would take four people to do his job. He had the power of four regular humans! "She can do it all in her head, just like my dad used to."

"That's great," Gary said. "Because I can't do it in my head, and I can't work QuickBooks, either."

Nathan laughed. "This is why we're perfect business partners. I like doing all of the stuff you don't like, and vice versa."

"Lemme get in there," Olivia said, trading spaces with her uncle. "I used to play with this after school all the time."

"You can show me later," Emma said, grabbing a blueberry muffin, and sitting next to Gary on the couch. "Mom, are you gonna give Nathan the speech about our shared history of addiction? Are you going to tell him that if he ever gambles again, you will kill him?"

"I think I can take her," Nathan joked, winking at his niece.

"I would have you on the floor inside of a minute," Addy replied.

"Girls, who would win in a fight?"

Addy spoke before her girls could pipe in. "Fine, but if you get detained like I used to do, or like my daughters just did, stay cool. Call me, or if I'm not around, the ghost of Uncle Ace will appear. Either one of us will be there right away to put the fear of God into you."

"Great speech," Nathan said.

"She's right," Courtney said. "Don't gamble. Or if you do, you can come with me to some meetings. They're not as bad as they look."

Nathan put his hand on his little sister's shoulder. He knew that she was just joining in on the joking around, but he didn't want to miss the opportunity to tell her how he felt about what she was doing. "I'm proud of you for going."

"Thanks," Courtney said. "Sy's granddaughter has been showing me the ropes. And Addy's going to come next week, too, right?"

"I am."

"I'm glad," Nathan said. "But it's weird that you're now friends with an octogenarian who once paid you to go out with him? We can get that out in the air, right?"

"It's weird," Olivia said, shaking her head in agreement, as Emma said at the exact same time: "It's sweet!"

"Don't take Courtney's inventory," Addy said. "See, I'm ready for the meeting! I remember a lot from my Gamblers Anonymous meetings!"

"I think you're using that phrase incorrectly," Nathan said.

"Now you're taking *her* inventory," Courtney said, unsuccessfully stifling her laughter.

"Did I somehow become the butt of the jokes here?" Nathan asked. "I like it better when Addy is the butt of the jokes."

"Well, I *did* invent the internet," Addy said, smiling as she took a sip of her coffee.

"Exactly," Nathan said. "See, I told you that joke was funny."

"Do you guys do any work here?" Olivia asked. "Or do you just make fun of each other all day long?"

"I vote for making fun of each other all day long," Courtney said. "After all, Nathan's job is so easy, I can do it all in my head."

Nathan couldn't help but laugh again. It was nice, having his family all gathered together, all invested in the family business, but still having fun. He wished Diego were here, too. His family was not complete without Diego. And he would spend the next two weeks in Vegas reminding his husband of that. They were a family—he was part of the Flores clan just as Diego was part of the Schneider clan—and they would be together and support each other in every way that they could. Without work to do for the next two weeks, Nathan would have time to focus on his marriage, focus on his husband. And he couldn't wait to get started on this new chapter. But not before one last dig at his little sister and brother-in-law alike: "Court, you could probably do Gary's job very easily as well," Nathan said. "It's just a lot of dinners and drinks dates with buyers and salespeople. Most of them are pretty old. So, you'll do great!"

"Old people are awesome," Courtney said. "I mean, you should know. You *are* one, after all."

"Ha!" Addy cried out.

"What are you laughing at?" Nathan said. "You're a year older than me!"

"Eleven months," Addy corrected. "Eleven months!"

"Does eleven months really matter once you're forty?" Olivia asked.

"Olivia's right. You're *all* old!" Emma said.

Gary grabbed Olivia and Emma and squeezed them both tight. "Could an old man do this?"

"Oh my goodness, that's exactly what an old man would do," Addy said. Then, turning to Nathan: "Are we old?"

"Don't look at me," Nathan said. "I'm not even forty yet."

"True," Courtney said. "What will we be doing to celebrate?"

Nathan thought about it for a moment. When Courtney had first blown into town, this question was fraught with danger. But now, things were different. He was different. And his relationship with Diego? Definitely different. "I don't know," Nathan said. And he really didn't. There was so much he didn't know, going forward. So much he needed to work on, so many things he wanted to change. "Maybe something smaller? And there's definitely someone new we'd have to invite."

"Oh, I'd love to bring Sy," Courtney said. "That's really thoughtful of you."

"Not Sy," Nathan said. "I mean, of course you can bring him, if you'd like. We should invite his granddaughter, too. But, that's not who I meant. There's someone else we need to include."

74

Addy

Don't say lawsuit. *Whatever you do,* Addy thought, *just don't mention the lawsuit.*

"Oh, hi," Holly said, answering the door in a pair of sweatpants and an old T-shirt. She looked around as if searching for some explanation. Addy and her daughters, showing up on her doorstep without notice. Without warning.

"We're so sorry to drop in unexpectedly like this," Addy said, but she was lying. She wasn't sorry about it. What they were doing was purposeful. They'd planned it this way. Addy was afraid that if she'd called first, Holly would have refused to see her. So, she and her girls had gone to Holly's place without announcing themselves. Rude, yes. But hopefully, effective. "Do you mind if we come in?"

"We brought coffee!" Olivia said, holding up a container that held four cappuccinos. She smiled brightly, and Addy smiled, too.

"And the good muffins," Emma said, offering up the box that held a dozen muffins. Assorted flavors, since they didn't know what type she'd like. Emma didn't smile quite as brightly as her sister had, even though Addy had reminded them over and over in the car that they were to smile as if their lives depended on it. Addy bumped her hip into Emma's, and instead of smiling more widely, she threw a hurt look in her mother's direction.

"I don't think this is a good idea," Holly said, looking behind herself. She slowly began to close the door. "I'm sorry."

"Wait!" Addy said, holding her hand out to stop the door. "Please just give us another chance."

Holly paused, as if considering Addy's words. She furrowed her brow.

"We would have called, but we just didn't think you'd agree to see us, with the lawsuit and everything—" Addy hadn't meant to mention the lawsuit. But it was like the elephant in the room—don't say *lawsuit*. Don't say *lawsuit*!

Holly didn't answer, yet again, so Addy filled the air with her nervous energy. She rambled on: "Okay, well, so, I'm sorry about the lawsuit and the ring and everything. I'm sorry about the DNA test. I'm sorry about how things played out."

"You mean having your lawyer inundate me with discovery requests?" Holly took a step backward and held the door open.

Addy tried to stay positive—it was an attack, sure, but at least, now they were speaking. And she'd taken a step, holding the door open. Addy looked at her daughters who stood perfectly still. She motioned to Olivia, who handed over the coffees.

"Thank you," Holly said, opening the door a bit wider so they could all come in. She led them to the living room.

Addy tried to be gentle as she and her daughters arranged themselves on the couch. "Well, we needed to retain counsel since you were suing us. But look, just because you're not our half sister doesn't mean we can't still have a relationship. We want to get to know you. You're our cousin."

"So what?" Holly took a sip of the coffee.

Addy answered: "So, it means we're family."

"Just because we're family doesn't mean we have to get to

know each other. I should never have come to your house for dinner. It was a mistake."

"I know," Addy said. "And I'm sorry about that. My lawyer told me not to invite you over."

"At least he was good for one thing." The edges of Holly's mouth began to curl up.

Addy laughed. Laughing at a shared joke was a way to bond, she'd read somewhere. She elbowed Emma so that she'd laugh along, too. Then Emma elbowed Olivia, and soon, all three were laughing along, really loud, to a joke that wasn't particularly funny in the first place.

But it worked. Holly's expression softened. "I'm sorry about the lawsuit. It was stupid."

"We're sorry, too," Addy said. "We never really knew your mother, but maybe you could tell us about her?"

"Maybe that's not the best place to start," Holly said, and reached for a muffin. Emma held out a napkin for her.

"I could tell you about *my* mother," Addy said. "Or my father?"

"I'm not sure that's the best place to start, either," Holly said, looking down.

Holly rubbed her temples and stared out the window, as if she was lost in thought. It took all of Addy's energy not to fill the empty space with nervous words, but she could tell Holly wasn't done speaking. She looked to her daughters, and they smiled back at her. It was as if they were all thinking the same thing. They slowly sipped their cappuccinos, waiting for their cousin to find the right words. "So, I guess my mother made up all of those letters. My lawyer had them analyzed with a handwriting expert. It turns out my mother wrote all of them. Well, except for that first one, but he said something about notebooks that your brother found? I guess that proved that the one *real* letter was actually written to *your* mother, after all."

"Right," Addy said, her voice soft.

"Toward the end of her life," Holly explained, "she suffered from Alzheimer's. One of her nurses suggested she try writing as a way to remember, a way to try to recover some of her past."

"I'm so sorry to hear that," Addy said. "Our mother had it, too."

"Oh," Holly said. "I'm sorry."

"Thank you."

"You know, I guess I always knew the truth," Holly said. "My whole life, growing up in Texas, there were whispers. People talked. They said I was the product of an affair between my mother and the lawyer she worked for. That she had followed him out to Texas and got pregnant. Some people say she knew he was married with children, some people say she was duped."

"That must have been so difficult for you."

"It was. And I think that's part of the reason I wanted to move here, away from where I grew up. But I loved my mother with all my heart. I don't want you to misunderstand me."

"I think it's possible to love someone deeply but not always like them," Addy said. She couldn't help but think of her own father. The lying, the toll it took on their lives. He'd been gone for seven years already, and it still hovered over her life, like a film.

"I grew up feeling completely alone. I never really knew who I could trust."

"You're not alone anymore. You have us now." Addy looked Holly directly in the eye as she said the words.

Holly gave a small smile. "Before she died, I found a drawer full of these letters. I think I knew the truth, deep down. I guess I always knew what they really were. But it was like a revelation. It gave me answers. It gave me closure. It made it so that she wasn't the villain of her own story. It was like I needed it to be true. So I started researching you. Your family. And I couldn't stop."

"I would have done the same thing," Addy said, getting up from the couch and sitting down next to her cousin. "The exact same thing."

"You seem like this perfect family. My family was far from perfect. Well, my mom, I should say. It was just us. And now, it's just me."

Addy nodded and could see a tear forming in the corner of Holly's eye. She passed her a napkin.

"Thanks," Holly said, dabbing at her eye.

"Now you've got family." Addy put her hand on Holly's shoulder, and Holly leaned into it.

"And anyway, we're not perfect," Emma said. Addy turned to her daughter, surprised to hear the sound of her voice. She and Holly had been having a moment, hadn't they? Emma didn't seem to notice. She continued: "Far from it. My mom had a massive gambling problem when she was younger. Crippling, really. She can't even step foot inside a casino. Well, the ones she's not banned from. And my Aunt Courtney went out with an old guy for money, actually she's really good friends with him now, but anyway. Oh, and she just started AA."

"And we were recently detained in Atlantic City for underage gambling," Olivia said, eager to pipe in. "So, we're just about as messed up as your average family."

It took Addy a moment to realize her mouth had dropped to the floor.

"Then, I suppose we'll get along just fine," Holly said with a laugh.

75

Nathan

Nathan had forgotten how much he loved Diego's voice. It was different from his father's famous voice, more delicate somehow, and it had a silky quality to it that Nathan found unbelievably sexy.

The crowd did, too. Diego was filling in for the cabaret show for the sixth night in a row, and instead of getting a routine down pat, he'd been improvising a new one each night. Because of this, the audience members from the night before kept coming back, and word of mouth was spreading. Each of the cabaret's forty seats were filled that evening. Before curtain, Nathan had given up his front-row table so that two more people could attend. Nathan watched from the side of the stage, and he held up his camera phone, recording clips for Diego's Instagram. Nathan had started Diego's page on his first night in Vegas, and thanks to a shout-out on his father's IG page, four days later, Diego had four hundred and fifty thousand followers.

Nathan stopped the live video at the end of the song and posted it to Diego's stories. He'd been FaceTiming his nieces constantly throughout the week to get tips for Instagram.

"People love it when you go live," Emma said.

"When you finish a live video," Olivia instructed, "make sure you save it. Then, you can post it later as a Reel, and it will appear in the feed."

"And that's good?"

"Bet," Olivia said. "It helps with the algorithm."

"Diego knows all this stuff," Emma said. "He's the one who taught us a lot of this."

"Diego's busy," Nathan said. "So, what else do I need to know?"

He was sure to save the live video, just like Emma had said. Nathan silently patted himself on the back as he saw the video appear in Diego's photo library. He turned the camera back on to get a candid shot of Diego, but as he did so, he heard his husband talking about him.

"My husband is just like a lot of your kids," Diego quipped. "Here I am, trying to talk to him, but he's on his phone."

"I was posting to your Instagram!" Nathan called out.

"But you missed me inviting you on stage for the last number," Diego said. How could the show be ending so soon? Nathan couldn't get enough of Diego. The audience couldn't, either. "Let's try this again. Ladies and gentlemen, usually for my last number, I call an audience member up on stage for a dance. And tonight, that lucky audience member is my husband."

Nathan realized what had happened a moment too late. As the crowd applauded for him, and Diego stood with his arms opened wide, Nathan waved his hands furiously. "I can't!" Nathan yelled. "Ask an audience member."

Diego walked toward him, mic still in hand. "Ladies and gentlemen, could you believe that my husband has been in Vegas with me for four days and he still has not danced with me?"

The crowd erupted in cheer. "No, seriously, I can't," Nathan whispered to Diego. "I haven't been onstage in, like, twenty years."

"You can and you will," Diego said, and he put his hand out. Nathan grabbed it, and they danced their way back to the main spotlight.

Dancing with Diego felt like the most natural thing in the world. With his head on his husband's strong shoulder, Nathan could almost forget the crowd that was watching them. It was him and Diego, the way it had always been. He could feel the rest of it slipping away, the unfounded fear that Diego had been having an affair, the family drama with the ring, the lawsuit, and it was just the two of them.

Nathan looked up at Diego: "We're going to be okay, right?"

Diego whispered back: "Yeah, I think we are."

76

Addy

Once she started, she just couldn't stop. True to her personality type, Addy was now harboring a new obsession: reading her father's notebooks. There was no reason to keep reading them. The lawsuit had been withdrawn, she'd made a good first contact with Holly, but still, Addy couldn't stop.

She loved sitting in her bedroom, on her previously unused fainting chaise, and flipping through the pages. There was something meditative about the sound of the paper as she turned each page. Here was her father, her complicated father who she loved deeply, despite his flaws, with his soul bared. Addy loved reading the stories he'd told over and over, his whole life, and she loved reading the ones she hadn't heard before, too. Reading his words made her feel like she was with him again, still getting to know him. Still loving him, even when he was at his most unlovable.

"Hey, Mom, we made dinner." Addy had hardly noticed when Emma came into her bedroom. She was so immersed in what she was reading—a story about a nurse making fun of her name right after her mother had given birth—that she hadn't heard the door open.

Addy startled. "You scared me," she said, laughing. "I never hear you coming."

"That's what they say about me," Emma said, a sly smile playing on her lips. Addy considered her daughter—when she smiled like that, she was a dead ringer for Ritchie.

"When you do that little smile, you look just like your Grandpa Ritchie, right before he laid out some ridiculous plan."

"Well, this evening, my plan is to make you dinner."

"*You* made dinner? I guess I lost track of the time."

"It was Aunt Courtney's idea," Emma said. "She said you do all the cooking around here, so Olivia and I helped her cook dinner. Well, I mean, they cooked, but I helped."

"I'm impressed."

"Don't be. I'm pretty sure we're all going to die from salmonella."

"I'm sure it's great."

"We can always order in a pizza if it's not."

It was great. They'd taken her chicken piccata recipe and made a few tweaks. It had more of a lemon flavor, and it was tender and sweet. Courtney made a big show of *plating it* (her words) over linguine, cooked al dente. There was no vegetable on the side, but Addy didn't mention it.

Gary made a batch of homemade iced tea, instead of serving wine that night. He sliced a lemon and put one on each glass. It complemented the food well. Addy was impressed, but wondered for a moment what they needed her for, if they now knew how to cook.

"This is incredible," Addy said, savoring the perfect bite of chicken and pasta. "So flavorful."

"We tweaked your recipe a little bit," Courtney said. "I hope you don't mind."

"Mind? I love it. After dinner, do me a favor and write down what you did, so that I can make it this way next time."

"I, for one," Emma said, "think the most impressive part is

that Courtney made a delicious dinner for us, and she didn't even burn down our kitchen."

Nathan and Diego both laughed. Loudly. Back from Vegas for two days, they couldn't resist coming to Addy's for Sunday night dinner.

"Do I smell garlic bread?" Gary asked.

Just then, Olivia jumped up from the table and rushed to the oven. She pulled out a tray of garlic bread, browned almost to the point of burning, but not quite.

"It's not burned!" she called out, as she set the tray on the kitchen island and found a serving platter to transfer the garlic bread onto.

"Attempting to burn down the house," Gary said. "A family trait, inherited from the Schneider side."

"Holly couldn't make it?" Nathan asked Addy.

"No," Addy said. "She said she had something tonight, but maybe she'll be free the next time you come home?" She tried not to sound sad when she talked about Nathan and Diego's new arrangement—they planned to stay in Vegas for the remainder of Diego's father's tour. Addy knew it was good for Diego, and good for Nathan and Diego's marriage, but she couldn't help but feel sad. She liked being able to see her brother and brother-in-law anytime she wanted.

"We'll be back in three weeks, right?" Nathan asked Diego.

"Yes," Diego said. "We'll be in for four days. I have some good news—I have meetings set up with some New York producers about the possibility of making my show a more permanent thing."

"That's incredible!" Addy said and immediately felt guilty. Was she happy Diego was making his dreams come true? Or just that her brother and Diego would be back in New York? She told herself that two things could be true at once, and brushed the guilt away.

"Is that why you came in this weekend?" Olivia asked.

"What, your uncles can't fly home to surprise you?" Nathan asked. Addy smiled at the mention of home as New York, not Vegas.

"Tell the truth," Diego said. "We came home because Nathan wanted to pick up more of Ritchie's notebooks to read. Could you believe he's still reading them?"

"Of course I can," Courtney said, her mouth full of garlic bread. "I'm still reading them, too."

"You are?" Diego said. "Okay, Addy, back me up. It's weird, right? It's like—the lawsuit has been withdrawn. Stop invading the man's privacy!"

"I was literally reading them before I came down for dinner," Addy said.

"Remind me to never tell you where my diaries are," Diego said.

"You keep a diary?" Nathan asked.

"I think it's sweet," Gary said. "They miss Ritchie. I miss him, too."

"There is one weird thing," Addy said. "I'm in 1993 and basically... Well, I don't know how to say this, but... The ring is fake. So I guess all that fighting was over nothing. The ring isn't even real, after all."

Nathan replied, "I'm in 2004, and the stone was just replaced from a fake, back to the real one."

"What?" Addy said. "So, the ring is real? Court, what year are you in?"

"I'm in 2008, and the ring was just stolen. So, I'm not even sure how the ring comes back into play anymore."

"Okay, everyone needs to grab a year and start reading," Addy said. "Before dessert, I'm getting more boxes out."

"Or," Gary pointed out, "we could just get the ring appraised."

77

Ritchie, 2013

Ritchie wanted to unhear everything he had just heard. That couldn't be right. There had to be another explanation.

But there wasn't. He had heard the doctor, as clear as day.

"I think we'll go for a second opinion," Ritchie said, not unkindly, and got up from his seat without even shaking the doctor's hand.

"I don't think that we need one," Lizzie said, her voice barely a whisper. Ritchie hadn't even realized she wasn't following him out of the room. She stayed planted in her chair, across from the doctor. "Alzheimer's explains so much."

Ritchie shook his head. No. It couldn't be right. Alzheimer's was the sort of thing you wished on your worst enemy, not something you ever thought the love of your life would be diagnosed with.

"Yes," Lizzie said. "Why don't you sit back down so that we can talk about treatment options?"

But Ritchie couldn't sit back down. He couldn't go back into that office with that doctor. Sitting back down, across the desk from that man, would be like admitting it was true. And there was no way it could be true. There had to be another explanation for the recent falls Lizzie had suffered, for the small memory lapses she'd been experiencing. One day, she'd forgotten where she'd left her car keys. The next, she'd forgotten how to get to her hair salon.

Ritchie walked down the hallway, certain that Lizzie would eventually follow him out. When she didn't, he asked one of the receptionists to use the phone. He called Ace.

"One of your kids is a doctor, right?" Ritchie asked him, in lieu of hello.

"Yeah," Ace said. "Donnie's a podiatrist. You got a problem? He'll get you in right now."

"Lizzie," Ritchie said, barely able to choke the words out.

"You had that appointment today?"

"I'm still here."

"Then, why the hell are you on the phone with me?" Ace said. "Get off the phone and go to Lizzie. We'll sort everything out later."

"I can't go back there," Ritchie said, rubbing the sweat off his forehead with the sleeve of his shirt. "If I go back in there, then, it's…its…"

"Then, it's what?"

"Then, it's true."

Ace sighed audibly. "Buddy, listen to me. If you had that much control over the universe, Quarry would have beat Frazier. Every time you played roulette like a jackass, your number would have hit. We both could have been rich off the horses. But you don't control the universe. No one does. So, get back in there. Hold Lizzie's hand. And play the cards you're dealt. There's no other way."

"Right," Ritchie said, a tear falling from his eye. "But you and I both know, the house always wins."

"Listen to me, I love that woman like a sister. We're going to take care of her, and everything will be all right."

Ritchie chanted Ace's words—*everything will be all right*—like a prayer as he walked back down the hallway to the doctor's office.

When they got home, Lizzie went to lie down for a bit. Nothing like a diagnosis of Alzheimer's to make you want to get under the covers and hide from the world.

Ritchie made his way to the closet and opened the wall safe. His hands knew every piece of jewelry, knew the exact amount of cash in every envelope. He grabbed the large black ring box at the back.

The Liz Taylor Ring, they'd called it. Every time he looked at the ring, it took his breath away. It was big, that was for sure, but it was more than that. It was so bright, so clear, that he swore that if you stared at it long enough, it could tell you the secrets of the world. The Asscher cut was so complicated, with so many steps down into its depth. Like a house of mirrors. You could gaze into it for hours and still not find the bottom. He put it onto his pinky finger, where it barely fit, and moved it from side to side, watched it catch the light.

It was real, and then it was fake, and then it was real, and then fake again. It was real in 1992, when Ritchie presented it to Lizzie as a promise. A symbol. Six months later, he sold the diamond. It took him twelve years to earn the money to get it back, only for it to be lost again.

The real one had been lost in a card game in 2006, but luckily, Ace convinced the Captain to sell it to Pete the Jeweler for some fast cash. Pete held onto the ring, knowing that when Ritchie had the money, he'd be there to buy it back. Ritchie began setting aside money once again, and Pete made Ritchie a fake, so that Lizzie wouldn't know what had happened. The fake one had gotten stolen in 2008, which forced Ritchie to tell Lizzie the truth, lay all his cards on the table. They went together to Pete's store to buy back the ring that was rightly Lizzie's. That had belonged to her all along, even when she didn't have it.

This ring wasn't just a ring. It was a symbol of a life spent together, a family they'd fought to keep together. This ring traced their history, from the first day they met until the day they broke up, to when they got back together again, that time for keeps.

But two months ago, Lizzie had left it in the freezer. At the time they'd laughed—after two glasses of wine at dinner, she'd mistaken the freezer for their wall safe. Then, last month, he'd found the ring under their bed. He reasoned that Lizzie must have taken it off before going to sleep, and it had fallen off her bedside table. She must have been too tired to put it back in the wall safe in their closet. Luckily, he'd found it when he was looking for his reading glasses, which had fallen off his own beside table. He'd explained the incident away, once again, and put the ring back where it belonged. But then last week, he'd found it at the bottom of a jar of peanut butter.

Ritchie needed to save the ring.

He called Ace and they met for dinner. "Where can I park the ring to keep it safe?"

"Sell it back to Pete the Jeweler," Ace said. "Worked last time. Have Lizzie wear a fake, while the real one stays safe. Simple."

Ritchie considered this. He texted Pete the Jeweler: How soon could you get a fake made up for Lizzie's ring?

Pete the Jeweler: About a week.

Ritchie: Great. Call me when it's ready.

"Pete's getting a fake made up," Ritchie said.

"Problem solved," Ace said. The waitress came to the table and set down their drinks.

The problem was not solved. Not entirely, anyway. "What if I need to keep the ring safe from myself, as well?"

Ace looked at Ritchie. Ritchie looked at Ace.

"I can't gamble it away again," Ritchie said. "If it's in Manhattan, I could get it on my way up to AC. Needs to be further away. Harder to get."

Ace took a sip of his beer. "Sue and I are going to the Caymans next month," Ace said. "Three and a half hour flight to Grand Cayman, then we grab a puddle jumper to Cayman Brac. That far enough?"

"It's the right thing to do," Ace said, and put his arm around his friend. They stood inside the cold walls of the bank vault in Cayman Brac, where they put Lizzie's ring, the Liz Taylor Ring, into the safe-deposit box. Lizzie and Ace's fourth wife, Sue, were at the spa, relaxing, giving Ritchie and Ace a few hours to duck out, undetected.

Ritchie turned toward his friend and tried to respond, but the tears wouldn't stop coming.

"I've got you, buddy," Ace said, and patted his back. "It's going to be okay."

"Yeah," Ritchie said, wiping his eyes with the back of his hand. "I know."

At some point in the night, when they were at the tables, on the precipice of being happily buzzed and full on drunk, Ritchie told Ace, "I'm going to have you take care of the extra key. I can't bear to put another burden on Addy right now. And with all the stress, I don't want her reverting to old habits." (Ace had told his best friend the truth about Addy in Vegas. Of course he had.)

"No problem," Ace said. "The ring is safe here. It will not be gambled away again. By you *or* Addy. I promise."

"If anything happens to me, you make sure the kids are able to get the ring from the Caymans," Ritchie said.

"Sure, boss." Ace said. "Anything you need."

One flaw in Ritchie's plan: Ace would have to outlive Ritchie.

EPILOGUE

The ring

The ring was real. Of course it was. (You knew it was.)

The love their parents shared was real, therefore the ring was real. Or vice versa? Either way, Addy couldn't wait to wear the ring at Nathan's fortieth birthday party that night.

The party would be a small affair, light bites and cocktails at Nathan and Diego's loft. There would be no theme. There would only be love. And music. And family. And friends.

The appraisal came in just as the siblings had agreed what they would do with it—it would be shared, among Addy, Nathan, and Courtney. Eventually it would be passed down to Olivia and Emma and whatever future kids Nathan and Courtney would have. (Nathan and Diego, later that year, would find themselves adopting a beautiful baby girl, and Courtney would take two and a half years before she'd get married and another year and a half after that before getting pregnant. But she'd meet the man she'd marry that night at Nathan and Diego's party.) Emma would eventually wear the ring down the aisle on her wedding day. Olivia wouldn't find much use for it, and only try it on occasionally, to humor her sister and mother, at family parties and holidays. Joy, Nathan and Diego's daughter, would proudly wear it on her wedding day, too, and Courtney would have two sons, both of whom married women who had absolutely no interest in jewelry, and certainly not a ring so large and vulgar.

The ring was real, not a fake. That was the important thing, wasn't it? But what they hadn't expected: the diamond had an inclusion, strong blue fluorescence, and small dots of black carbon. While you can't see these faults with the naked eye, they were there, and they made the diamond worth less than they had originally thought it would be worth. This surprised each of the siblings, and there was a feeling of disappointment that the ring was worth less than they'd previously thought. (Hoped.)

"What's a diamond, anyway?" Nathan said, in a cavalier way that fooled exactly no one. "It's just a mineral from the ground. Why are we fighting over a rock?"

"It didn't symbolize their love," Courtney said. "It symbolized all the ways that love can go wrong. It was real, then it was not, it was stolen, it was retrieved. Maybe the ring is bad luck."

"Well, he did win it through gambling," Addy said.

Yes, the ring had originally been won through gambling. On a bet. But so what? Things have been gotten in worse ways. And anyway, all of life is a gamble. Who you marry, who you love. Whether you live or die. Get on a plane, get into a car. You could drop dead any day, at any time. The love of your life could die, your best friend who held the extra key to your safe-deposit box. Everything you thought about your parents could be wrong. Or it could be right. More than one thing can be true at once.

"I call dibs on wearing it to Nathan's birthday party," Addy said.

The ring wasn't good luck or bad luck. It wasn't a symbol of their parents' love, or the nature of love in general. It was, as Nathan pointed out, only a rock. And its only value was whatever someone was willing to put on it.

No one said that the ring was a symbol of their family, even though it was—flawed, but ultimately lovable. Difficult to wear or even figure out, but still theirs. Beautiful and messy and imperfect and deeper than it first appeared.

Addy was holding her hand in a funny way as they walked into the party. Courtney couldn't stop making fun of her on the drive into the city, but Addy couldn't act natural with such a large diamond on her finger. She felt like she was playing dress-up, like she was playing the part of Lizzie that evening.

Nathan and Diego greeted them at the door. "The place looks gorgeous," Gary said, looking around. And it did—there were tiny votives everywhere, and delicate little lights strewn across the newly repaired ceiling. Everything glowed as if from within, especially Nathan and Diego themselves.

Also, the ring. Because of the diamond's strong blue fluorescence, it glowed under ultraviolet light. The black light the DJ was using made the diamond gleam brilliantly, and even though this was one of the faults that brought down the diamond's value, the Schneider siblings couldn't help but think it was one of the things that made the ring special.

"Thank you," Diego said, looking around at the loft, as if through his brother-in-law's eyes. "Turns out, we didn't really need a theme."

"The theme is *there is no theme*," Nathan said, with a little chuckle.

"It's fab," Emma said, and brushed past her parents and uncles to make a beeline toward the bar. She took out her phone as she walked, snapping pictures all the way.

"She's underage," Gary called out across the loft to the bartender. "This one, too," he added, pointing at Olivia. The bartender nodded, and Olivia swatted her father's shoulder.

"You didn't have to forgo the gambling theme just because of me," Addy said, as a waiter came by with a tray filled with glasses of champagne and sparkling cider.

"Or me," Courtney said, grabbing a glass of cider.

"I didn't think we needed it," Diego said.

"After being in Vegas for four months, I've come to realize that less is more," Nathan said.

"You know you love Vegas," Diego said, his lips curling at the edges. They'd had this conversation before.

The guests filed in: Sy was there, of course, with his grand-daughter, who Courtney had grown quite close to through their weekly AA meetings. He brought with him another surprise: his grandson. Holly came with a date, who Olivia and Emma both approved of wholeheartedly. The producer for Diego's new cabaret show came, too, and Addy grilled him on whether the show would definitely be in New York, or if it could potentially move to another city. (It would definitely be in New York, in a tiny theater downtown.) Most of the folks from Diego's boot camp theater class were there, including Frank, who brought her husband and two preteen sons. Diego's parents flew in and tried to keep a low profile, even though their appearance in Soho meant that photographers were stationed outside the building for the entire night. A few neighbors stopped by. And friends. So many friends.

Diego caught Nathan's eye through the crowd. He tapped his lips twice with his index finger—sending a kiss telepathically from across the room—and Nathan sent one back.

Diego took the mic at around ten, and sang a delicate version of "Happy Birthday" to his husband. Next, he asked his dad to come up, and together, they sang a duet of "Beautiful Woman" while Nathan and Diego's mother danced along to the music.

The Schneider siblings danced happily well past midnight, a stronger family than they had been before. And a larger one, too. Holly. Sy. Sy's grandchildren. They all took turns wearing the ring that had defined such a large part of their family his-tory, the ring that signified a new beginning. Addy passed it to Nathan, who put it on his pinky. Nathan passed it to Courtney, who watched it glow in the light, over and over again. Then, Courtney watched carefully as each of her nieces had their turn.

Olivia got nervous when it was her turn. "Take it back, Mom. I don't want anything to happen to it."

"Nothing's going to happen to it," Addy said, and she meant it. The ring was real, the ring was fake. The ring was a symbol for everything, the ring was just a ring. All of these stories are true. None of these stories are true. More than one thing can be true at once.

The ring was back in play.

★ ★ ★ ★ ★

FINDING ELIZABETH TAYLOR
IN *THE LIZ TAYLOR RING*

The life of Elizabeth Taylor is an endless source of inspiration. Like my character Lizzie Morgan, I have long been fascinated with the star—her beauty, her talent, her love life, her philanthropy, and of course, her vast jewelry collection. There's so much richness in the life of this one incredible woman.

While *The Liz Taylor Ring* is a story about a fictional family, I took inspiration from every part of Elizabeth Taylor's remarkable life. There's a lot about Elizabeth Taylor mentioned in the text itself, but there are also some more subtle references that you might have missed. I hope you'll enjoy this list of a few such references.

CHAPTER 1
The family name Schneider is our first homage to Elizabeth Taylor. *Schneider* is German for the word *tailor*.

CHAPTER 2
When Lizzie's mother calls the 33.19-carat Krupp Diamond (now known as the Elizabeth Taylor Diamond) *vulgar*, this references

when Princess Margaret said the same thing to Elizabeth Taylor at a dinner party. Elizabeth invited Princess Margaret to try it on, and when the princess admired the ring on her own finger, Elizabeth remarked that the princess didn't seem to think the diamond was quite so vulgar when *she* was wearing it.

Lizzie's sister, Maggie, takes her name from one of Elizabeth Taylor's defining roles: Maggie the Cat in *Cat on a Hot Tin Roof*. If there is anything sexier than Elizabeth Taylor in that white slip, then I haven't seen it. (Except for Elizabeth Taylor in the white bathing suit from *Suddenly, Last Summer*, which is referenced in Chapter 40.)

Lizzie's mother, Katharine, takes her name from Katharine Hepburn, who played Elizabeth Taylor's controlling and manipulative aunt in *Suddenly, Last Summer*.

CHAPTER 3

Addy's business acumen reflects that of Elizabeth Taylor. Taylor was the first woman to negotiate and receive one million dollars for a film, for her role in *Cleopatra*. When she launched her first fragrance in 1987, it was the start of a billion-dollar perfume business.

CHAPTER 4

Elizabeth Taylor had a number of close relationships with gay men throughout her life. Montgomery Clift was one of her best friends, and her friendship with Rock Hudson inspired her AIDS activism, including a founding role in the American Foundation for AIDS Research (amFAR) and the establishment of The Elizabeth Taylor AIDS Foundation.

The love letters that Nathan reads like a good luck charm reference the love letters Richard Burton used to write to Elizabeth Taylor. (Swoon!)

CHAPTER 5

Elizabeth Taylor knew her fair share of gamblers: her first husband, Conrad "Nicky" Hilton, was known for his gambling, and her third husband, Mike Todd, was known to be a gambler as well. Additionally, Elizabeth Taylor's film *The Only Game in Town* was about a Vegas showgirl who has an affair with a compulsive gambler, played by Warren Beatty.

CHAPTER 8

Sy offers Courtney use of his private jet. Elizabeth Taylor's third husband, Mike Todd, died when his private plane, the *Liz*, tragically crashed. Elizabeth would have been on the plane, too, but had stayed home because she was sick.

CHAPTER 11

Lizzie and Ritchie dance to Fleetwood Mac, recalling the relationship between Stevie Nicks and Lindsey Buckingham, which was often compared to that of Elizabeth Taylor and Richard Burton.

CHAPTER 12

When Addy objects to *sexually suggestive photographs* of her children, it reminds us that Elizabeth Taylor was a child star, whose first role was at age ten. In her iconic *Life* magazine photo shoot at age seventeen, the images are undeniably sexual.

CHAPTER 13

Nathan and Diego met when they were both trying to make it on Broadway. Elizabeth Taylor was no stranger to the Broadway stage—she made her Broadway debut in "The Little Foxes" in 1981, and starred opposite Richard Burton in "Private Lives" in 1983. Richard Burton's Broadway experience was far more extensive, and he was a highly respected stage actor before making his mark on the silver screen.

Diego's father, Pedro Garcia Flores, was born in Mexico. Elizabeth Taylor and Richard Burton lived in Mexico when Burton filmed *The Night of the Iguana*. They loved it there so much that

Burton purchased their Puerto Vallarta home, Casa Kimberley, as a birthday present for Taylor.

CHAPTER 16

Maggie's abusive marriage refers to Elizabeth Taylor's marriage to Nicky Hilton.

The mention of Maggie riding is a reference to *National Velvet*, one of Elizabeth Taylor's earliest roles.

Lizzie's gold halter dress at the club is meant to evoke the stunning gold ensemble Elizabeth Taylor wears on her entrance to Rome in *Cleopatra*. (Google *Elizabeth Taylor entrance to Rome* to watch this iconic scene.)

CHAPTER 17

The pool party scene references the first time Richard Burton saw Elizabeth Taylor. According to Burton's diaries, he saw her from across the pool, at a party, while she was still married to her second husband, Michael Wilding. She put down her book, lowered her sunglasses, and looked at him. (Elizabeth would recall their first meeting a bit differently, instead taking place at her and Wilding's home.)

When Ritchie says "Can't you see that I'm drowning in you?" this is a reference to how Richard Burton called Elizabeth Taylor *Ocean* because he felt he was drowning in her.

CHAPTER 24

Addy's dog, Duke, reminds us of two of Elizabeth Taylor's earliest roles, *Lassie Come Home* and *Courage of Lassie*. Elizabeth Taylor was a lifelong animal lover and always surrounded herself with pets.

CHAPTER 25

"When they kissed, Lizzie never wanted it to end." Elizabeth Taylor and Richard Burton famously continued kissing long after director Joe Mankiewicz called *Cut!* at the end of love scenes on the set of *Cleopatra*.

CHAPTER 26

Pulchritudinous was one of the words that Richard Burton used to describe Elizabeth Taylor. (Dreamy, right?)

CHAPTER 34

Elizabeth Taylor and Richard Burton bought a yacht in 1967, which they called *Kalizma*, named after their children Kate, Liza, and Maria. They lived on the *Kalizma* for years, with their family, a full staff, and a menagerie of pets.

Ritchie remarks that everyone at the wedding on the yacht is staring at them, talking about them. During the filming of *Cleopatra*, studio publicists tried to downplay the affair between Elizabeth Taylor and Richard Burton. But everywhere the couple went, tons of photographers followed. Federico Fellini, who was in Rome at the time, called the reporters, who buzzed around endlessly, *paparazzo*, meaning *buzzing insect*. With that, the term *paparazzi* was invented.

When Lizzie asks Ritchie "Who do you love?" this references the famous moment when Richard Burton asked Elizabeth Taylor the same thing. At a dinner in Rome, during the filming of *Cleopatra*, Burton drunkenly asked Taylor, "Who do you love?" right in front of her husband, Eddie Fisher. She replied: "You." This moment is immortalized in the Lindsay Lohan made-for-TV movie, *Liz & Dick*. (You should immediately Google *Liz and Dick who do you love* and go watch that clip. I'll wait.)

CHAPTER 37

When Nathan says all humans have scars, it brings to mind the emergency tracheotomy Elizabeth Taylor had, while filming *Cleopatra*. She was self-conscious about her scar, and turned the 69.42-carat Cartier Diamond (a pear shaped stone later known as the Taylor-Burton Diamond) that Richard Burton bought for her into a necklace to hide it. (Fans of *The Grace Kelly Dress*: the first time Elizabeth wore this necklace was at Princess Grace's fortieth birthday party, the Scorpio Ball. Rude to try to upstage the birthday girl, or impossible to upstage your friend who is a literal princess? Discuss amongst yourselves.)

CHAPTER 38
Maggie's walk-by-them-in-a-swimsuit trick is reminiscent of the beach scene in *Suddenly, Last Summer*. (Please note that no actual cousins were cannibalized in the writing of this chapter.)

CHAPTER 39
Maggie's daughter, Holly, takes her name from Elizabeth Taylor's *Suddenly, Last Summer* character, Catherine Holly.

CHAPTER 46
Courtney's friend, Rebecca, insists on VIP treatment for Addy. Elizabeth Taylor and Richard Burton starred in *The V.I.P.s* in 1963, a film that capitalized on the public's desire to see Taylor and Burton together. They would make a total of eleven films together: *Cleopatra, The V.I.P.s, The Sandpiper, Who's Afraid of Virginia Woolf?, The Taming of the Shrew, Doctor Faustus, The Comedians, Boom!, Under Milk Wood, Hammersmith Is Out*, and *Divorce His—Divorce Hers* (made-for-TV movie). Elizabeth Taylor also did an uncredited cameo in Richard Burton's *Anne of the Thousand Days*.

CHAPTER 49
The style of Ritchie's diaries is an homage to the style of the Richard Burton diaries, in which he would often only use a sentence or two to describe each day.

CHAPTER 62
Elizabeth Taylor was the first celebrity to openly check herself

into the Betty Ford Center for treatment for addiction. Betty Ford, herself, served as Elizabeth's sponsor.

CHAPTER 65

Lizzie throws herself onto the bed when she discovers the Liz Taylor Ring is gone. When Elizabeth Taylor temporarily lost La Peregrina, a 55.95 carat pearl once owned by Spanish royalty, she went into the bedroom of her hotel suite, threw herself onto the bed, and screamed into a pillow.

When Ritchie gets up off the bed, and kneels down before Lizzie, this references the famous scene from *Cleopatra* where Cleopatra tells Antony: "You will kneel!" (Google *Cleopatra you will kneel*. Go watch that sexy scene and hurry back. I'll wait.)

CHAPTER 69

It was at a hotel suite at Caesars in Las Vegas that Elizabeth Taylor famously lost La Peregrina, though it was later found in her puppy's mouth.

CHAPTER 72

The line "She was alive" references two of my favorite Elizabeth Taylor moments. Of course, it's a reference to the famous Maggie the Cat line in *Cat on a Hot Tin Roof*: "Maggie the Cat is alive! I'm alive!" (Google *Maggie the Cat is alive*. Go watch this brief clip now. Warning: watching this scene may cause you to want to watch the entire movie immediately.)

But also, in an interview with Hedda Hopper, Elizabeth Taylor would defend her affair with Eddie Fisher, while she was still grieving the tragic death of her third husband, Mike Todd. She famously said: "Mike is dead and I'm alive." (Oh, dear.)

When Lizzie puts the ring in Ritchie's casket, this references the rumor that Elizabeth Taylor supposedly left a $100,000 diamond ring in Mike Todd's casket before he was buried. Thieves later dug up his grave and desecrated his corpse, reportedly looking for the diamond.

CHAPTER 74

Maggie running off to Texas is an homage to the setting of the film *Giant*, which Elizabeth Taylor starred in with Rock Hudson and James Dean.

EPILOGUE

(Fans of *The Grace Kelly Dress*: not only did Grace Kelly attend Elizabeth Taylor's fortieth birthday party... Princess Grace led the conga line!)

AUTHOR'S NOTE

There's just something about jewelry. The sparkle, the glamour, the way it makes you feel when you put it on. A piece of jewelry can make you feel beautiful. It can make you feel loved. It can remind you of the person who gave it to you—make you feel like they are with you, even if they are long gone.

For every piece of jewelry that I own, I can tell you who gave it to me, what occasion it marked, and where I was in my life when I got it: the delicate diamond studs, gifted to me by my husband, to mark the occasion of my first son's birth; the double strand of pearls, a twenty-first birthday gift from my parents; and the gold ring with a star, given to me by my Grandma Dorothy, after I told her it was the piece of her jewelry that I most loved. She took it off her finger and handed it to me, saying that I shouldn't have to wait for her to die to wear it. She wanted to watch me enjoy it while she was still alive.

Heirlooms, in particular, are so incredibly important to me—I wear the gold ring with the star from Grandma Dorothy all the time, and I love having a piece of her with me as I go through my day-to-day life. I also have two other rings that belonged to my grandmother that I treasure. On important days when I need to feel her spirit with me, I wear all three at once. I've worn Grandma Dorothy's rings to family bar mitzvahs (I wouldn't want her to miss a fabulous party), and I've worn them to important meetings (her spirit fortifying me to do well). I've worn them on trips to the supermarket, and I've worn them to big, fancy weddings. When I wear them, friends and strangers alike ask me about them, and I get the chance to talk about her. When I wear them, my kids ask me about her, the woman who gave them their blue eyes.

Thinking about heirloom jewelry gave me the idea for *The Liz Taylor Ring*—what if a ring that was thought to be long lost were to be found again? As with *The Grace Kelly Dress*, I wanted to tie an heirloom item to a famous actress, channeling my other obsession: old Hollywood. Once I decided to write about jewelry, there's no other Hollywood star that comes to mind but Elizabeth Taylor.

Elizabeth Taylor's jewelry collection is legendary, but for me, it was always about the Krupp Diamond, which is now known as—what else?!—the Elizabeth Taylor Diamond. I love that Richard Burton gifted it to Elizabeth Taylor for no reason at all. I love that it belonged to Vera Krupp, of the German munitions family who supplied arms to the Nazis, and Elizabeth Taylor often quipped that it was perfect for a "nice Jewish girl" like herself to own it. I love that Elizabeth Taylor wore it every day of her life.

My seventh novel, *The Liz Taylor Ring*, pays homage to the rings passed down to me by my grandmother, as it traces a priceless family heirloom—a long-lost diamond ring inspired by the famous Krupp Diamond—that reappears, leaving three siblings to determine its fate. Just as millions of fans have been swept away by the stories of Elizabeth Taylor's astonishing life, I hope that you, too, will be swept away by this story of sibling rivalry, an all-consuming love affair, and an eleven-carat diamond.

ADDITIONAL READING

Researching this book was a joy. I relied on so many sources to create *The Liz Taylor Ring*. A few of these are listed below.

ON ELIZABETH TAYLOR AND RICHARD BURTON:

Books:
Furious Love by Sam Kashner and Nancy Schoenberger

The Richard Burton Diaries edited by Chris Williams

Elizabeth Taylor: My Love Affair with Jewelry by Elizabeth Taylor

How to Be a Movie Star: Elizabeth Taylor in Hollywood by William J. Mann

A Passion for Life: The Biography of Elizabeth Taylor by Donald Spoto

Film/Television:
Elizabeth Taylor: Auction of a Lifetime

Liz: The Elizabeth Taylor Story, based on the novel by C. David Heynmann

Liz & Dick

The Unauthorized Biography of Elizabeth Taylor

Here's Lucy, Season 3, Episode 1

Burton and Taylor

Unauthorized Biographies with Peter Graves, Episode 3

ON GAMBLING ADDICTION:
Born to Lose by Bill Lee

Hats and Eyeglasses by Martha Frankel

All Bets Are Off by Arnie and Sheila Wexler

Molly's Game by Molly Bloom (book and film adaptation)

ON ALCOHOL ADDICTION:
Blackout: Remembering the Things I Drank to Forget by Sarah Hepola

Drinking: A Love Story by Caroline Knapp

Quitter: A memoir of drinking, relapse, and recovery by Erica C. Barnett

ACKNOWLEDGMENTS

Thank you to my amazing agent, Jess Regel, who always believed in me, even when I didn't fully believe in myself.

Thank you to my incredible editor, Melanie Fried, who saw the potential in this book, even when it wasn't fully on the page.

Thank you to the fabulous HarperCollins sales team. Thank you to my phenomenal publicity and marketing team: Heather Connor, Justine Sha, Leah Morse, Pamela Osti, and Randy Chan. Special thanks go to Loriana Sacilotto, Margaret Marbury, Susan Swinwood, Rachel Bressler, and Heather Foy. Thank you to Lindsey Reeder, Katie Didow, Hodan Ismail, and Abi Sivanesan for the wonderful digital media support. And for that cover art that truly took my breath away, thank you to Quinn Banting.

Thank you to Rich Green and the incredible team at The Gotham Group.

I've been so lucky to work with some brilliant editors for my personal essays over the past few years. Thank you to Dan Jones of the *New York Times* Modern Love; Libby Sile, Rory Evans, and Liz Vaccariello of *Real Simple* magazine; Hannah Swirling and Lorraine Candy of the *Sunday Times Style*; and Amy Joyce of the *Washington Post*.

Thank you to Jillian Cantor, whose own writing humbles me, and whose edits, advice, and encouragement helped me through.

Thank you to my dear friends who have been reading first drafts of my work since forever: Shawn Morris, Danielle Schmelkin, and JP Habib.

Thank you to Michelle Gable for the support and encouragement when I needed it.

Thank you to Randi Janowitz Shinske, of Red Velvet Luxe of Ridgewood, New Jersey, for the research on diamonds. Thank you to Jeff Kaplan for the research on private jets. Thank you to Nicole Eisenberg and Tandy O'Donoghue for the research on estate law. All mistakes are my own.

My last novel, *The Grace Kelly Dress*, came out at the dawn of the 2020 pandemic. There were a whole host of marvelous friends who rushed in to help promote my novel in a new publishing landscape that they were figuring out as they went along: Andrea Peskind Katz, Zibby Owens, Courtney Marzilli, Ashley Spivey, Renee Weingarten, Robin Kall, Jackie Ranaldo at the Syosset Library, Julie Buxbaum, and the team at A Mighty Blaze, led by Caroline Leavitt and Jenna Blum. Thank you to Liz Fenton, Lisa Steinke, and Kristin Harmel for putting my book on air. Thank you to Kristy Barrett, Cindy Burnett, Suzy Leopold, Lauren Margolin, Carilyn Platt, Jamie Rosenblit, and Linda Zagon for the constant support. Thank you to my dear friend Adrianne Roth, who said, "We're not canceling." Thank you to the team at Grace Influential, who welcomed me as graciously as her Serene Highness would have. Publishing a novel takes a village—to anyone I surely missed, please know that I do appreciate you more than you know.

Thank you to my mom and dad, who inspired my love of reading and writing from a young age.

Thank you to Ben and Davey, my endless sources of inspiration.

Thank you to Doug, my husband and my best friend. I'm lucky to have a man who understands that a woman needs big love and big jewelry.

The
LIZ
TAYLOR
RING

BRENDA JANOWITZ

Reader's Guide

GRAYDON
HOUSE

1. Family stories are an important part of *The Liz Taylor Ring*. Which family stories morphed or changed as we saw them through the eyes of different characters? Which family stories turned out to be true or false? Do you have any family stories that have changed over time? Stories that different relatives remember differently?

2. Each sibling wants the ring for a different reason. Do you have heirlooms in your family? How were they distributed? Why did each family member want the item?

3. Addy tells Emma that wearing jewelry feels like wearing armor. Do you agree or disagree with this statement? Do you have a favorite piece of jewelry?

4. Who was your favorite Schneider sibling? Why? Who did you relate to most?

5. If you have siblings, what is your relationship like with them? How do you think you would have reacted differently or similarly to the Schneider siblings in the same situation?

6. Did you understand Lizzie's decision to choose Ritchie over her family?

7. How do you think the Schneider siblings' own love stories will influence their own children?

8. The characters often remark that "two things could be true at once." Do you believe this sentiment to be true?

9. What's your favorite Elizabeth Taylor movie?

10. What's your favorite piece of Elizabeth Taylor's jewelry?